Acclaim For the Work
of ROGER ZELAZNY!

"Genuinely moving."
— *The New York Times*

"Tricky and brilliant and heartfelt and dangerous."
— *Neil Gaiman*

"Superior."
— *Washington Post Book World*

"Genius…The characters are intriguing, the events cosmic and dazzling…A masterpiece."
— *Salisbury (N.C.) Post*

"A poet with an immense and instinctive gift for language."
— *Greg Bear*

"A rousing good tale."
— *The Village Voice*

"A unique blend of…rich poetic vision…fast-paced action and singing imagery."
— *The Magazine of Fantasy and Science Fiction*

"[A] master of prose technique [and] paragon of the storytelling art."
— *Robert Silverberg*

Bruno winked. "Yes, Maria was to have been here tonight," he said. "But she telephoned earlier to say that she was not feeling well. I told her to stay in bed. It is a pity. She was looking forward to this opening." He traced a half-salute and left. I watched him plow his way through the throng.

I headed for the front door then, wondering why she had not answered the telephone when I'd called.

The cab deposited me before her building, and I located her name and apartment number on a mailbox in the hall. Mounting to the third floor, I found her door and knocked. There was a line of light at the door's lower edge, but no sounds came from within.

I knocked again, then tried the door. It was locked.

It wasn't much of a lock though, so I fetched the picks from my wallet and opened it.

She was inside, lying in a sprawly position, one leg on the sofa and the other hanging over its edge. Her blue skirt was hitched up above her knees and her head was twisted at an unusual angle. There were red stains on her face, her throat, her blouse.

Quietly, I entered, locking the door behind me...

The Dead Man's
BROTHER

by **Roger Zelazny**

A HARD CASE CRIME NOVEL

A HARD CASE CRIME BOOK

(HCC-052)

First Hard Case Crime edition: February 2009

Published by

Titan Books
A division of Titan Publishing Group Ltd
144 Southwark Street
London
SE1 0UP

in collaboration with Winterfall LLC

This book is a work of fiction. Names, characters, places, and incidents either are the products of the author's imagination or are used fictitiously, and any resemblance to actual events or persons, living or dead, is entirely coincidental.

ISBN 978-0-85768-363-2

Cover design by Cooley Design Lab
Design direction by Max Phillips
www.maxphillips.net

Typeset by Swordsmith Productions

The name "Hard Case Crime" and the Hard Case Crime logo are trademarks of Winterfall LLC. Hard Case Crime books are selected and edited by Charles Ardai.

Printed in the United States of America

Visit us on the web at www.HardCaseCrime.com

THE DEAD MAN'S BROTHER

I.

I decided to let him lie there, since he was not likely to bother anyone, and I went to the kitchen and made coffee. As the stuff gurgled, I lit a cigarette. The police had to be notified, of course. But since very few people know when my alarm goes off, I figured he could be allowed to get a bit stiffer. I sat there in my old blue robe, stared out at the gray morning, nursed my hangover.

It had been a very pleasant party, and I was certain that he had not been present.

It was a long knife—Gurkha—that had been hanging on the wall. Now it was in his chest.

I smoked and thought about it.

Carl Bernini. That was his name. I don't really know where he came from. We had worked together once, years ago. Had a falling out. Hadn't seen him in ages. It was puzzling to me, our coming together again this way. I hadn't done it, though, and I sought after ways to uncomplicate matters as quickly as possible.

I poured a cup of coffee, sipped it, thought, then went and knocked on the door to the back room.

After some coughing and kicking around, Bill Mailer opened it. He and a varying number of guys and gals lived in the back. I put them up, fed them. In return, he and his crew kept the place clean and waited on customers when I was out of town. He was well over six feet in height, dwarfing me, built like a stack of steel-belted radials, and his harem changed by the week. He was ruddy, and he presented a bullet-like appearance because of his cleanly shaved head. I'd never seen him without a white shirt or failed to smell pot when he was around. He occasionally cracked his knuckles, and he was much more intelligent than his blank, blue-eyed expression seemed to indicate. Also, he tended to be completely honest with me.

"What is it?" he asked, buttoning his cuffs.

"Come have coffee with me."

He rubbed an eye, followed me. I poured him a cup, set the sugar bowl before him. He sugared, stirred and sipped.

After a time, he repeated his question.

"Okay," I said. "Come and look."

He rose. He was barefoot, the same as me. We walked into the side room, the one where I keep two Picassos.

"Christ!" he announced, moving to Carl's side.

"Dead, all right," I said.

"What happened?" he asked, dropping the stiffening wrist he had raised.

"I don't know. Thought you might."

"Uh-uh," he said. "If I'd done this, I'd be gone, long and far."

"One of your people maybe?"

He shook his head.

"No, I'd know. One of them would run, too—and they're all there."

"Do you know him?"

"No."

"I do."

"Oh?"

"I met him years ago, in Europe, when I was a student. We worked together for a time, had an argument, parted on less than friendly terms. If someone were to look far enough for a connection, they'd find one."

"Are you going to buzz the uniforms—or…?"

I nodded at the first part. He cracked his knuckles.

"Take your people and clear out," I said. "Call me in a month or so, and if I'm still here I'll let you know whether it's safe to come back."

"Anything I can do to help you?"

"No. Thanks. Don't get involved."

"Okay. Give us half an hour?"

"Take it. He'll stay where he is."

He left the kitchen and I went up, showered, shaved and got dressed. There was fog hanging all over the other side of the window. A light drizzle made noises somewhere overhead.

I waited a while longer before I phoned the cops.

I was shunted about for a time, till I said I had a corpse in my gallery. Then the guy on the other end got interested and told me not to go away, a car would be there shortly.

I went and put up a sign saying CLOSED FOR THE DAY, then stepped outside and wondered: what. I stood there under the awning. I blew smoke back at the fog. I wondered what the hell Carl Bernini was doing in New York. Damned fool. He deserved to be dead. A good man when it came to the Renaissance, though.

Not much of a place, I guess, but it cost me my whole wad. Called Taurus Gallery, after my birth sign. Used to be an old warehouse. I cleaned it up, called it home. Have some nice stuff. Mostly on a commission basis, of course. There's even a Dali back in the vault. He used coded lacquer patterns, and he trusted me with some of the codes. Put a raking light on a Dali canvas and you can see what he did. That is how you can authenticate one, if you know the code. Whatever, I had been quite respectable for years, and now Carl had to show up and get dead.

Together, we had been able to steal a couple of Tinto-rettos, lots of Flemish works, ikons and expensive jewelry.

My parents had sent me to Europe to obtain an education in art history, as well as to put as much distance as possible between us. I was not too popular in our small community. It was in Florence that I met Carl Bernini, who—learning of my background—had suggested an excellent way to supplement my allowance. So it came to pass that when I was not studying art history I was obtaining it.

I quit that sort of thing some time before I came back to the States. Upon my return, the first thing I mentioned to my parents was going into town on the following day, to enlist and serve a hitch in the military. They said they were quite happy to see me back.

I enlisted because I wished to continue my vacation from responsibility, and also because of a certain curiosity as to whether the trail of accidents which had followed me for much of my life would pursue me into a military organization.

That is the story of the Taurus.

I waited.

The rain rained.

Lieutenant McInery said my name slowly, frowning somewhat.

"That's right," I told him.

"Ovid?" he repeated. "Ovid Wiley?"

"Correct."

I spelled the first one for him and he jotted it in his notebook, then, "Never heard a name like Ovid," he said.

"He was an old poet my father liked. I got named after him."

"Was he any good?" he asked.

"I think so."

"Well…what happened here?"

"I don't know."

"What do you mean? Do you know this guy or don't you?—Wait! Don't answer that! We have to take you in, whatever. We can let the guys at headquarters tell you all that crap about your rights. But if you do want to have an attorney with you, you might as well call him from here and have him meet you there. Save time."

"I don't want an attorney. I didn't do it. All I did was find him."

He shrugged, partly to his partner who was standing by the door seeming not to watch me, and partly to me.

"Why don't you make yourself comfortable?" he said. "We have to wait for the homicide crew."

I nodded, moved to a small sofa, seated myself.

"Listen for the radio," he told the other guy, a short, dark man who hadn't even nodded at me; then, "Mind if I look at some of your pictures?" he asked me.

"Not at all."

As the lieutenant moved off, his silent partner seated himself in a chair near the now opened door and watched me.

After being watched for several minutes, I asked him, "Care for a cup of coffee?"

"No," he said.

I had one myself, and as I drank it I considered what my reply would be when I was finally asked whether I knew the dead man. I decided to deny it.

When the crew arrived some of the men set up lights and began taking photos. Others started dusting things. First the knife, of course.

"What time did you find him?" a captain asked me.

"I didn't really look at the clock." I told him, "but it was right before I phoned.

"By the way," I added, "please be careful about the paintings."

He gave me a go-to-hell look and no reply. As he turned

to walk I drew my key ring from my pocket and removed a spare key for the front door.

"Here," I said, "I wish you would take this and lock the place up when you go."

There came a tightening of brows, followed by a faint smile.

"And where do you think you'll be?" he asked.

"Down at headquarters," I said. "Lieutenant McInery told me he was taking me in for questioning as soon as you arrived. He had some sort of message to that effect a little while ago."

He turned and looked at McInery.

"Those were my orders," the man told him.

He shrugged, turned back to me and held out his hand.

"Okay, I'll take the key," he said, "and we'll lock up when we leave. If I don't catch you to give it back downtown, it'll be dropped off here later."

I handed it to him. He turned away then and regarded the late and punctured Carl Bernini.

"Come on," McInery said then. "Let's take the ride."

He escorted me out to the car.

As we moved through traffic I puzzled over the implication that something involved in the situation was not exactly standard procedure. Could it be that something had already turned up concerning my past? It didn't seem too likely. It was too deeply buried and there was no reason to look. But even if something had drifted to the surface, what then? I had never committed a criminal act in the States.

I watched the traffic, the unwashed buildings, the rain, the fading fog, the umbrellaed pedestrians, the occasionally back-lighted, shaded windows. I listened to the sounds of the half-awake city.

My main concern as we drove was that nobody dust fingerprint powder on the Chagall that hung above the body.

We arrived and I was formally informed as to all of my rights. I told them that I was not guilty, that I did not desire an attorney and that I would give them a statement free and clear.

So, "Why did you do it?" inquired a man in uniform to whom I had not been introduced.

"I didn't," I said, and I began the long wait.

After any number of below the belt questions, I said, "Look, I'll be glad to take a lie detector test if you want."

That seemed to soften them somewhat.

"That is neither required or necessary," the first man said. "Just give me a statement as to your knowledge of what happened."

So I did.

"Do you know the man?" he asked then.

"No," I said.

We exchanged a straight-in-the-eye look. Then, "Are you certain?" he said.

"Yes. Why?"

"There was an anonymous phone call earlier, saying that you knew the man when you lived in Europe."

"I give up," I said. "I don't understand what's going on."

"We certainly don't either," he said. "But of course we will have to pursue the acquaintanceship business."

"I don't care," I told him. "Don't you think it odd that I'm the one who turned in the report? If I actually am the one who did it, I mean?"

"I don't know," he said.

McInery and his buddy were called away. My interrogator, a thin, heavily wrinkled man with a jaundiced complexion, had been introduced to me as Del Masters. I was seated across from him in an uncomfortable chair, and the light from the window hit me in the eyes.

"I did not do it," I said. "That's all I can tell you—and it's true. I'm upset."

"Understandable," he said, "considering the circumstances."

"...And I have no way of proving it," I added.

"Did you make any other phone calls than the one to us, or talk to anybody afterwards?"

"No."

"I see. I am afraid we are going to have to hold you for a while."

He got to his feet.

"Wait a minute!" I said. "How long are you going to hold me and what are the charges?"

"Suspected homicide," he said, and he left the room.

I cursed silently. With all the things I had done, it would be rotten to take a fall for something I hadn't.

A couple of guys came in and escorted me to a cell. They took away my matches and my belt and my shoestrings.

"I'm not suicidal," I said.

"Procedure," they answered.

I waited. For three days. I was strangely puzzled when I finally asked to be allowed to phone an attorney and they ignored me. They didn't even question me during that time. It was as if I had been completely forgotten, except at mealtime.

Then the man showed up.

Black suit and plastic briefcase, the latter also black.

He asked me just one question.

"You're Ovid Wiley?"

"Yes," I said.

"We can remove you from this place," he stated.

"Who's 'we', and where to?" I asked.

"I was thinking of McLean, Virginia."

"Great," I said. "What's there?"

"CIA," he said.

"Oh? What's going on?"

"I don't know," he told me. "My Section Chief will have to explain it to you."

"What effect does this have on this homicide business?"

"I couldn't say."

"Could your boss?"

"I suppose."

"Then let's go."

...And that is how the whole, mad vista began its very slow clearance before me.

I was released, and my still-nameless escort nodded to a larger version of himself who was standing beside a car smoking. This man opened the side door and nodded to me. I entered. We were never introduced.

After a time, I cleared my throat and inquired, "Mind my asking where we're headed?"

"I already told you," said the first man, who had taken the wheel and was now studying traffic.

The other sat somewhere out of sight behind me. I guess he wanted it that way.

"I meant," I said, "our immediate destination."

"Exactly," he replied.

"Can't I at least stop at home to clean up, change clothes?"

"No," he said, and he was right.

So I bummed a cigarette from the man in the rear seat, felt scroungy, and watched the taxi drivers pursue their daily duel with everybody. I needed a shave, my clothes were wrinkled, I smelled bad, my muscles ached. I was more puzzled than irritated, however. What could a government agency concerned with security want with a now respectable art dealer, want badly enough to take him away from local homicide people and bring him to their central office? My one connection with their sort of business had been in a small non-war contained by a

damp jungle, some tiny farms, frightened villages, stinking
swamps and slippery, rocky places sometimes called hills.
But there, though, the intelligence people had pulled me
back and given me a job filling out forms and yanking
folders solely because of my performance in the field. I
would get them the information they desired, but I lost
so much in the way of aircraft on my reconnaissance runs
that I began getting the impression that they would rather
have the copters and light planes back than my reports.
So I was considered a poor choice when in the field, and
I did nothing of any interest when not. I did not feel that
the CIA would have any special desire for my skills in the
intelligence area.

What, then?

I pondered this all the way to Kennedy Airport, where
the car was left with the rental service, where no one
noticed the dented fender and cracked taillight from a
small accident on the way over.

All along the line to the ticket counter, I pondered.
Then I said the hell with it and told my escorts I wanted
to go to the men's room and wash up. They agreed, and
on the way there I bought a small throwaway razor and a
tube of shaving cream. When I was finished scraping my
face I saw them watching to see that I did indeed dispose
of the instrument.

I offered to spring for coffee or a beer, since a heavier
than usual mixture of fog and air pollution had delayed the
scheduled departure. They decided that coffee sounded
like a good idea but they paid for their own.

I dislike crowded, busy places, and when a place's busy
crowds are laden with luggage, briefcases, parcels, cam-
eras, bags, hat boxes, umbrellas and God knows what
all, garbed for every clime, babbling, rushing, waiting,
standing, sitting, harassed by children and looking lost,
with half-comprehensible announcements crackling above

their heads, with sonic booms and growling engines somewhere without—all enacted before backdrops of flashing
numbers and symbols and words that most ignore, I
seldom fail to think of Breughel. It disturbs me, too, as
I am rather fond of the mad Dutchman.

We finished our coffee, made our way to our gate and
waited through another delay. Four sleepy sailors, a family
group, perhaps a dozen students and a number of men
with briefcases waited with us. I returned to pondering.

I tuned and focused on the big question again, the one
that had occupied most of my thinking while I was in custody. Why did Carl Bernini die in my gallery? He might
have gone there to steal something. He was a trifle too far
along in years to be learning a new profession. On the
other hand, he might have learned that the place was my
home and have wanted to see me in a hurry. That didn't
wash, though, as there are plenty of other ways of getting
in touch with someone. Whatever, though, he had apparently picked the lock neatly, entered, looked about a bit,
gotten knifed, died where he fell.

I reviewed my knowledge of the man: Carl was, or had
been, somewhere in his middle fifties; height, about five
feet, eight inches; his weight varied within the hundred-
fifties; he wore glasses when he read or worked on locks;
he seldom indulged in other forms of criminal activity than
art theft; he did not drink much other than an occasional
glass of wine; he was a heavy smoker; he never spoke
of any relatives, though he had had a pretty steady girlfriend named Maria Borsini when I had known him; he
was wearing a dark, somewhat shabby suit when I found
him. Simple, basic facts, representing nearly everything I
knew concerning him. And none of it seemed of use to
me now. I felt as if I were trying to seize a fistful of water.

At about this point we were allowed to board. As we
did so, I reflected that I had not thought to ask either of

my escorts for identification. That way, I might at least
have learned their names. I had no doubts as to their
authenticity, but it is nice to know who, specifically, is
spiriting you away.

They gave me the window seat, the larger fellow de-
positing himself beside me, the smaller man on the aisle.
So I fastened my seatbelt, folded my hands and sighed.
Above me, the air jets hissed sympathetically.

May you burn in hell, Carl Bernini! I thought. Then I
chuckled as I recalled how much he had loved Dante.

After a time we taxied, turned, waited, then raced
through fogs along the runway, were airborne, flew.

II

I tried to take a nap and was just about to succeed when we landed at Dulles. Smothering a yawn, I stood with the others and bumped my head on the overhead storage compartment as I always do. I followed my escorts out, and while I dislike Dulles less than many airports I was pleased when we had passed through it and were headed toward a parking lot.

Same seating arrangement, private car, sticker on the windshield.

We drove beneath clear skies, and the air through the open window felt clean and cool. The countryside was not unattractive and traffic was light. There was a pleasant smell to the air and I counted a few squirrels. I wished for a while that I had found something in the country rather than settling in New York. Wishes are always fun for condemned people, old people and accident victims.

I hoped fervently, though, that word of what had occurred in New York had not gotten back to my sister Susan, now a happily married mother of three, who still sends me greeting cards and occasional notes. She would worry. Or my father. He would be mad as hell. Possibly even somewhat concerned. After all, he likes to spend all of his waking hours retranslating Classics, except when he is teaching other people how to do it, and my situation could be distracting. My mother never told me whether he talked in his sleep, but if he did I'll bet it was Greek or Latin. As for my brother Jim, that smug academic, I couldn't care less.

The green persisted, even into Langley township, and we passed several signs directing us toward our destination. Having never seen the place before, I must admit that the sight was only partly what I had anticipated. The place was surrounded by trees and situated on a large piece of real estate. It did not look especially sinister. The architectural style was Mid-Twentieth Century Government, and massive. The first two floors formed a base from which rose five towers that appeared to be connected. They reached five stories higher to attain a circlet of dull glass. The finish was of that white quartz aggregate stuff which is supposed to look spiffy. Would have made a nice hospital.

We passed through the gates and drove to a parking lot, where a reserved place waited. As we walked away from it, heading toward that gleaming pile of concrete and secrets, I wondered idly to which portion of it I was being taken. I never did learn, either. Perhaps if I'd had along a pretty girl and a ball of string...Well.

There were armed guards on the inside, and my escorts presented identification, spoke rapidly and quietly to a guard, then filled out a form. I presume the form concerned me, because they exchanged it for a huge plastic pass they handed to me and told me not to lose. They picked up a couple for themselves and led me away, pausing long enough for me to buy some cigarettes at a concession stand.

As we walked through long, depressing halls, rode higher and walked through more long, depressing halls, occasionally having our passes scrutinized, I noticed signs explaining how to prepare classified wastepaper for destruction and schedules explaining when it would be picked up. I heard the sounds of typewriters and telephones. I felt more and more uneasy, in direct ratio to my escorts' apparent relaxation. They smiled, nodded, even exchanged a few words with some of the people we passed. I was glanced at and dismissed. I felt alien.

We had to pass through several locked doors in order to reach the one opened one, our destination. They gestured me into what proved to be an empty office and I entered.

The room was about forty feet by thirty, its floor completely covered by pale yellow carpeting. Its brown walls were buttressed by five glass-doored bookcases, and several simple etchings were tastefully hung. There was a small conference table, numerous chairs and a wide, shiny desk sporting two telephones, a dictaphone, an intercom unit, an unblotted blotter and a neat arrangement of pens, pads, calendar and bronze baby shoes. The only five windows in the room filled the wall behind it. In the corner to my right were two filing cabinets and a secretarial desk.

I crossed the room partway and seated myself at the end of the conference table closest to the big desk. After a small hesitation, my guides approached and seated themselves, also—the small one directly across from me, the larger to my left.

I drew up an ashtray, opened my cigarettes, offered them around. They shook their heads, so I smoked alone.

Finally, "How long?" I asked.

The man across from me started to shrug, then, "We're a little early," he said. "It shouldn't be too long a wait."

He did not meet my eyes as he spoke, but neither of them had been so inclined for our entire acquaintanceship. They always looked away when I looked directly at them, though I had felt their gazes upon me often and caught them scrutinizing me several occasions.

I heard footsteps and voices, glanced out the door at two men who were approaching. When they entered the room my companions stood. I didn't.

Both men appeared to be in their fifties. The one who

headed toward the desk had gray hair about a shiny bald spot, wore very thick glasses, had a heavily lined face and was smiling. His companion was quite obese and very ruddy. He wore a dark suit complete with vest, chain and Phi Beta Kappa key. He gave me a fishy stare.

The other man—as if it were an afterthought—turned toward me suddenly, stuck out his hand and said, "My name is Paul Collins. This is Doctor Berwick."

So I rose and shook hands. Then Collins turned toward my escorts and said, "Thank you. You may go."

They closed the door behind themselves and Collins told me to sit down. We all did, and then proceeded to scrutinize one another for several moments. While I did not recognize either man, the name "Berwick" served to mesh rusty gear-teeth somewhere in the back of my mind. Still, the memory machine failed to turn over and crank out an answer. I only knew that I had once known something concerning the man.

"You seem to have left some trouble behind you in New York," said Collins, still smiling.

I shrugged slightly.

"I'm innocent," I said, "for whatever that's worth. Anyway, the thing is out of my hands now."

"…and into mine, perhaps," he replied.

"Please explain."

In apparent answer, he leaned to one side and unlocked a drawer or door in his desk—using several keys, it seemed. When he straightened, he brought up a fat manila folder. He proceeded to turn several of its pages.

"It appears," he said, "that you speak German, Italian and French quite fluently, and various other languages with some degree of proficiency…And a solid grounding in classical languages, too. That's always nice."

"I attended school in Europe," I said. "I'm sure your organization doesn't need another interp—"

"Yes," he cut me off. "Tugingen, wasn't it? But it was in Rome that you met Carl Bernini."

When I did not reply, he continued, "On your return to the States you enlisted in the Army, attended OCS and received advanced training in intelligence work after receipt of your commission."

I snorted.

"…you were then sent into combat areas on numerous occasions," he went on, "and subsequently shifted to more sensitive work behind the lines. You were listed as missing in action on four different occasions and twice reported as dead."

"I know all those things," I said.

"I will not suppose that you were ever an art thief," he said, turning several more pages, "nor that you and the late Mister Bernini were once closely associated in such activities."

"Thanks."

"I do understand, however, that you make a considerable number of trips to Europe each year…"

"As an art dealer, I visit numerous galleries and museums, attend exhibits and auctions, meet with artists and private collectors and do nothing illegal. I suppose you can supply me with the dates and places of all my trips?"

He shrugged.

"They are not important. I was merely laying some groundwork."

"If you've laid enough now, why don't you tell me what you want of me?"

"It is a somewhat delicate matter," he said, "but you possess a background in intelligence work, as well as the ability to become unobtrusive overseas, and—"

"No!" I said, standing. "I will not spy for you!"

"I did not say anything about espionage," he told me,

"though from your reaction I feel you must consider it a somewhat dirty business." He sighed and reached beneath his blotter, extracting a sheet of paper. "No, I did not ask you to be a spy," he said, regarding the page, "but for obvious reasons I am quite sensitive about the term. The image is all wrong, you know, what with newsstand and movie fare, with fanatic anti-Communists looking for enemies behind every door. Let me read you something Harold Macmillan once said concerning spies and defectors. It is quite correct, and I keep it around to cheer me up whenever business is going badly—or when someone reacts as you did if he feels the subject is coming up.

" 'Defection of anybody in a policy department is not very important,' " he read. " 'What does he give them? A few memoranda which, from my recollection of government memoranda, never come down on one side of the question or another…The really dangerous espionage is technical. Some machine, some improvement which probably has the life of what—a year at most? I think it's all rather exaggerated, the importance of it.' "

He slipped the paper back beneath the blotter, sighed and said, "So much for spying. If I were a spymaster, Mister Wiley, I would like you to know that the supply exceeds the demand. I would have no need for you. I would employ a professional. I read you Macmillan's words, though, for your own edification. Spying is dull, dry, uninteresting work—and as I began to say, what I have in mind for you is something of a delicate matter."

I reseated myself.

"Please continue," I said.

He nodded.

"Beyond the things concerning yourself which I've already mentioned, it appears barely possible that you may possess another useful quality. I'll let Doctor Berwick tell you about it," he said, turning his head in that direction.

"I am a statistician," said Berwick, beginning to locate me with his eyes. "Years ago, I was involved in a project funded by the military, two science foundations and a major insurance company. The military was interested in survival potential. Why does an Audie Murphy go through numerous battles virtually unscathed while stronger and perhaps cleverer men are dying all about him? Why does an Eddie Rickenbacker live through so many potentially fatal situations? Persons with similar histories were studied by our group, examined psychologically and physically, with hopes of determining the factors which underlie this sort of luck or good fortune or whatever you wish to name it. Conversely, the insurance company was interested in similar information with respect to accident-proneness. The two lines of occurrence seem part of the same thing, whatever that thing may be, so there was a coming together of interests. Upon completion of the project and submission of our final reports, this organization," and he glanced toward Collins, "retained several members of the original team to continue with the research under their auspices."

At this point, the wheels began to turn and I remembered who Doctor Berwick was.

"Did you find what you were looking for?" I asked.

He looked to Collins once more, and Collins wagged his head slightly.

"I'm not permitted to say," he told me.

Thoughts now ricocheting like bullets in the boiler room of my mind, I inquired, "But you have reason to believe that it is somehow chromosome-linked?"

After but a thick moment or two of silence, Collins came back with, "Quite nimble. But I thought you and your brother were not on speaking terms?"

"That's right," I said. "But we were back when he was in grad school, and I remember his telling me about some nutty experiments he was paid a buck and a half an hour to participate in. A Professor Berwick was one of the men in charge. You were fat then, too, weren't you, Doctor?"

He removed his glasses, wiped them, held them up to the light, replaced them, put away his handkerchief.

"Yes," he said. "It runs in my family."

"Well," I said, "since you've conned these nice bureaucrats into believing you're onto something here, and since it seems logical to assume that you used my brother as an example of whatever it is you claim to have proved, why not sic him onto this delicate matter you've got in mind?"

Berwick opened his mouth, but Collins' audible sigh interrupted him. The smile was gone now.

"Mister Wiley," he stated, "you may pat yourself on the back for having correctly guessed that we learned of you through your brother. Everyone in the initial tests had filled out questionnaires, and one item involved a listing of relatives. Only accident-prones and people who alleged several remarkable escapes from harm were accepted for those early tests. It had been suggested that their relatives be contacted to determine whether they, too, exhibited these tendencies. This aspect was never pursued at the time, as the project was concluded prematurely. The government support was withdrawn during a period of budget-cutting and the insurance company lost interest after the preliminary reports. When we picked it up, though, we decided to check out the relatives, on the recommendation of the biological section of the team. That is how we came to locate your record of survival and escapes. I shan't recite it, for I fear that you will reply, 'I know all those things.'"

"Thank you."

"…but on the basis of all these factors," he continued, "when we learned of your present difficulties, it was decided that perhaps you and the agency could be of some benefit to one another."

The left corner of my mouth twitched upward involuntarily. *It was decided.* I have, for most of my adult life, noticed that whenever a large organization gets all impersonal and objective, it is about ready to throw you the shaft. No individual on their end is ever responsible, mind you. *It* is always the culprit, the maker of the sneaky, nasty decision.

"You learned of my 'present difficulties' awfully quickly," I observed. "I want to thank you for being so prompt in attending to my welfare."

Here, he reddened slightly, and I went on, "I can't agree with anything I've heard of this idiotic survival bit, so far. It strikes me as a fund-raising scheme. I just believe in luck—good or bad—and I'm obviously having some bad just now. Also, I couldn't really care less what you know about me. Why don't you just tell me what it is you want of me and what you're able to give me for it?"

But Doctor Berwick had snorted, gotten to his feet, crossed the space that had separated us and was glaring down at me while moving his finger in rapid, salami-cutting motions near my nose, all before Collins could reply.

"Young man!" he said. "To take pride in one's ignorance is a mark of one's stupidity! You do not know all the facts, yet you presume to pass judgment on years and years of careful, detailed research! Who are you to mock probability theory when you are living proof of its operation? You—"

"Doctor Berwick," Collins said softly.

I once saw the same expression and stance—eyes wide, shoulders suddenly stiffened, head thrown back—occur on a man who had just been shot in the back from ambush.

Berwick dropped his eyes and turned slowly toward Collins.

"I fear I was out of myself for a moment," he said, and returned to his chair.

"It is understandable," Collins replied, "as is Mister Wiley's reaction to his situation."

At this point, I wondered whether smoke was beginning to emerge from my ears and spiraling up toward the obscene fluorescent lights. Somewhere inside him, I knew that Collins was smirking at me. He just wanted to keep me dangling. He knew I did not give a damn about any hypothesis of Berwick's. He knew that all I wanted was answers to my questions. He was, I decided, a son of a bitch.

"It should not be especially dangerous," he said. "It will simply be necessary that you take a little trip, speak to a few people, do a bit of legwork and report your findings to one of our representatives. It will most likely turn out to be a pleasant vacation."

While in no position to criticize another's ethics, it was not without a certain indignation that I saw what was about to come.

"And if I undertake this bit of work for you?" I inquired.

"Then," he said, "I am confident that your difficulties in New York may safely be assumed forgotten."

"I see. Where, specifically, would I be taking my holiday?"

"Mostly Italy, I'd say. Though the thing appears to have broader international ramifications."

My palms were suddenly moist and I felt my heartbeat quicken. When I did finally speak, my words came strangely ragged through my throat.

"If you are implying what I think you are implying, I would be a fool to accept. I'd rather take my chances on a homicide conviction here in the States than poke around that organization whose headquarters are in Palermo. No thanks. Send me back to where you found me."

He smiled and shook his head.

"My interest in international crime is purely academic," he told me, "and I have no desire to spy on the Mafia. That is what we pay the FBI for."

"What then?" I asked, feeling my conjecture drop into the sea of false intuitions with a little plopping sound and no ripples.

"The Vatican," he said. "I want to plant you in the Vatican."

III.

Good old Eileen. I lay there beside her, spent, staring at the ceiling. She rested her head on an outstretched arm, her hair a dark splash on a pillow. I drew on my cigarette and watched the smoke curl and wind its way through the half-lit air.

The room was cool and silent. We relaxed, and I said, "It was rough."

"What?" she asked.

"Everything that has happened to me recently," I told her. "I have been sworn to secrecy."

"So?"

"So I want to tell you all about it."

I let my fingers do some walking, and I began telling her.

"I am going to Europe."

She drew nearer.

"Good," she said, and I felt her softness all along my right side.

Then, "When?" she asked.

"Tuesday."

I felt her muscles jerk.

"That's only three days," she said, "and I haven't got…"

"I'm sorry. I didn't mean it that way. I'm going alone."

"Oh. What is she like?"

"Not another girl. It's this business I was about to—"

"You took me once when it was a business trip. I was your secretary for tax purposes."

"It's not that kind of business," I said.

"Oh. You're screwing somebody else."

"No, ma'am," I said. "You're my lovely lady, and I want to keep it at that. I'd like to tell you but you're not listening."

"I'm listening. Tell."

"I have a job I have to do," I said. "It involves a man who was once a priest."

"I know they're smart," she said. "What did he do?"

"He stole three million dollars," I told her, "and skipped Rome."

"Why do you have to find him?" she said.

"Let's leave that out of it," I told her. "I just do."

"Someone's got something on you."

"Maybe."

Finally, "I think you're lying," she said.

"Why?"

"A priest wouldn't do a thing like that."

Finding such logic unassailable, I replied, "Okay, you've got me. I have a date with Sofia Loren."

She slapped me lightly then, and I changed the subject the only way I knew how.

But I had had to tell *someone*, since I had promised my boss I wouldn't.

Good old five feet five, slightly plump, brunette, blue-eyed Eileen. I thank whatever Powers May Be for girls like you, and the fact that I have never been married to one.

Good night, Eileen.

Airports. Enough there already. Stop. After we had broken the smog-barrier and a few windows I suppose, we came at last to be above a green glass, lens-like area that looked as if it went on forever. I can become obsessed with the ocean, just as with an enormous mountain or a vast desert;

for these things are so out of proportion to myself that they seem to represent a cosmic indifference, another order of existence, or both. They make me feel as if something within me belongs to them, and then I desire to share their destinies. Too much thinking along these lines tends to make me morbid. Which is one of the reasons I prefer both nature and art in its smaller guises. So I turned my attention to the magazine I held in my lap and left the ocean to do whatever it is Byron said it does without me as an accomplice.

Arrowing above the clouds and the water, I read till the blue went out of the sky and the night came down, pausing only to eat a surprisingly good meal and drink two Old Granddad and waters. Sipping the second one, I regarded the stars—so bright out here, up here—lit a cigarette and considered my situation.

Collins had taken me to the Office of the Apostolic Delegate in Washington. There, a rosy-cheeked junior counselor had told me of Father Bretagne, occasionally referring to a thick file on the man. Father Bretagne had worked in the financial offices of the Vatican. He had been a thoroughly screened, highly trusted, highly qualified man. All three were standard requirements, he had explained, with special emphasis on the screening—ever since the days of Monsignor Cippico, the only priest from that office ever defrocked and busted for swindling. Father Bretagne had come out with a record the angels might envy and seemed to be doing a wonderful job for approximately five years. It was in the sixth year that they began getting a whiff of what was going on.

There were no irregularities in the books. He had been too clever for that. In fact, everything he had done seemed perfectly legal from the face of the record. He had employed a financial maneuver developed by the late Bernardino Nogara, with a few added twists of his own. The basic difference, though, was that Nogara had used it to benefit the Church.

In 1929 the Holy See had received $90 million as a result of the Lateran Treaty. Pope Pius XI had entrusted the administration of this money to banker Bernardino Nogara, who proceeded to invest it with enormous skill and equal success. At times, though, currency restrictions were imposed on the export of Italian capital. Nogara, however, had set up Vatican accounts with the Credit Suisse of Geneva. When the restrictions were in effect he would order the Swiss bank to deposit money in a New York bank in its own name. He would subsequently apply for a loan from the New York bank in the name of a Vatican-owned company in Italy. The Swiss bank would inform the New York bank that they were underwriting the loan, the money would be lent and, of course, repaid with interest. Thus, additional funds were released from the country despite the currency restrictions and made available for investment elsewhere.

All legal and proper, albeit tricky, for Nogara was an honest man.

In the case of Father Bretagne, however, the funds had flowed from Switzerland to a bank in Rio where a loan was then approved for a company Father Bretagne had had investigated and personally approved. It was only later that several missionaries and concerned laymen had gotten word back to Rome as to the condition of the company. They expressed concern over the fact that it consisted of an old warehouse hardly worth the stick it would take to poke through its moldy walls, filled with non-functional machinery and operated by a staff of two—a manager and a secretary, both illiterate. Oddly enough—or not so, depending on how you look at it— this report was referred to Father Bretagne, who killed it. Subsequent reports came in, however, and were eventually seen by others. In due course, an investigation was begun. The fact finally emerged that the company was wholly owned by a corporation controlled by an Emil Bretagne, the priest's brother. After several pairs of eyebrows were returned to their normal positions, further information was requested. Word of this apparently reached Father Bretagne, though, and he vanished shortly after the inquiry was begun.

I took another sip of my drink, mashed my cigarette, lit another one.

If that had been all there had been to it, I thought. If only that had been all there had been to it I could be back in my comfortable apartment rather than aboard a flight bound for Rome. I could have my shoes off and my feet on a hassock, with some decent music swimming around the room, perhaps a fresh apple and a cognac at my right hand, a good book in my lap...Sigh.

But this was not to be, for a number of reasons. The main one, I feel, was that the Vatican did not want another Cippico affair. I can see the headlines in various anticlerical periodicals: PRIEST EMBEZZLES $3 MILLION, SKIPS ROME. They wanted to keep it quiet to kill bad publicity, which is why the civil authorities had not been notified. But they also wanted their $3 million back, which is why they aroused CIA interest in the case.

The Vatican's inquiry had come up with information showing that Emil Bretagne was once friendly with several revolutionary leaders, both in São Paulo and in Rio. When they were tipped, the CIA was not especially interested in this, as they felt they had matters down there pretty much covered. But some people up the ladder—leftovers from the old OSS days, I guessed—while feeling as I did that the money was the real issue, also felt they owed the Vatican a few favors from World War II times. It apparently was decided that while, on the basis of the evidence presented, they could not get officially involved in the thing, something ought to be done.

I daresay they found some reason for putting a few of their men in Brazil to scrutinizing things a bit more closely. A guess on my part, as is a lot of this, but an educated guess. From what they did tell me it was not too difficult to arrive at conclusions as to things omitted.

Their unofficial involvement obviously extended to digging through files to locate a person with some sort of half-assed background in this area, and then narrowing the field till they found someone who could be blackmailed into taking this stupid piece of a job. As to the job itself, it promised to be quite routine and dull. I was not to get mixed up with revolutionaries or thugs. I was simply to poke around Rome and its environs, speaking with everyone I could who had any knowledge of or association with Father Bretagne. I was to submit a full report concerning this, drawing any conclusions I might as to his departure route and present whereabouts, and then I was to come home. I had a contact man at the embassy. Not a very hush-hush thing: he was a security officer there. I was also to visit a few museums and galleries, to make things look good. Everything completed, my temporary employer would move in his strange ways and the charges which might be made against me in New York would not be made. I did not appreciate this form of coercion any more than I did the fact that the cost of this trip was to come out of my own pocket rather than their fat, secret budget.

I could not help but think that there might be a little more to the job than they had indicated. I cannot subscribe to the notion of sending out a half-armed trooper when he could be fully armed, but I am familiar with the need-to-know business—now observed like a religious ritual in classified matters, but also often used as a cover-up. If I suddenly needed to know something more, I supposed they would tell me at the time, if they could reach me, if I were still living. It seems to be a law of life that whenever there is something illegally obtained and valuable in any given place, the carrion birds tend to congregate at the site. I did not wish to encounter any unexpectedly if I could have been warned. That's all.

"Star light, star bright," I addressed some nameless point of light within the darkness, "it would be nice if Berwick were right on that charmed life business. Just in case."

Rome. Memories. Stuff like that. Gone. Not really lamented. Nostalgia for youth and circumstances past. I guess. At least that is why I had made reservations at the Massimo D'Azeglio on the Via Cavour. My old favorite.

After tipping, unpacking, bathing and changing clothes, I went to walk the ancient streets, to fill my head with happy sights and sounds and my stomach with lunch. It was a sunny though somewhat brisk day, but my clothing was warm and my shades adequate. For a time I simply wandered, up wide, tree-shaded sidewalks and down narrow streets that passed buildings both impressive and dirty. I watched the Vespas weave in and out of traffic and enjoyed the play of sunlight on yellow plaster walls. Here, pigeons bobbed at crumbs before a sidewalk café; there ropes of dark-leafed vines escaped across a garden wall. And the girls—I watched the pretty dark-haired, dark-eyed girls, heels clicking on cobbles and concrete, large breasts thrust almost arrogantly forward, and when they passed near enough I sniffed pungent perfumes and occasionally got a faint smile. I stopped in a small restaurant for soup, chicken cacciatore and some white chianti. Then I walked on, winding up finally at the National Museum, though this had not been my intention when I had begun my stroll. After a while, I lost all track of time and managed, somehow, to forget the messy situation which had brought me to Rome. I was shocked when I happened to glance at my watch and realized that I had spent over three hours in the place. I departed then, the bells of history still chiming in my head, and made my way slowly back toward the hotel. It grew chillier as the sun wandered west, over and out, but I did not mind it. I was happy to be in Rome again, no matter what the reason.

The night was high, cool and cloudless, stars like a bucket of soapsuds splashed across the sky. Heading upward, I eventually reached the inevitable bulk of the Basilica of Santa Maria Maggiore. For a long while I studied it and the area about it. Turning, I regarded the direction from which I had approached. This section, the Monti area, is the oldest and largest region of Rome. It covers three of the famous seven hills—the Quirinale, the Viminala, the Calio—and in times long gone three of my dad's old favorites had lived in the area: Ovid, Virgil, Horace. Also, one of the roughest, most corrupt quarters of the city once existed between the point where I stood and Colle Oppio. I wondered what my namesake would say were he to be released from Elysium to come stand beside me at that moment and share my thoughts. Doubtless, he would chuckle and not be surprised in the least as to my undesired undertaking. The old boy was too sophisticated not to appreciate that while a few of the props have been shuffled, human nature itself has remained unchanged throughout that series of betrayals and calamities we call history. He could appreciate the juxtaposition of genius and corruption, art and crime. Shrugging my shoulders at this profundity, I turned and made my way along the Via Cavour in the direction of my hotel. The sickle moon had risen, clear and clean, was poised before me now as in Time's hand. If I were lucky I might be able to get in at *La Carbonara* for dinner. I'd call and see.

Tomorrow the Vatican.

At ten o'clock the following morning I phoned a number I had been given. After several delays, I was connected with Monsignor Zingales, the man in charge of the investigation. His voice was pleasant, though he had a tendency to wheeze, and after I had identified myself he arranged to see me at three o'clock that afternoon. He was quite aware of who I was and why I was calling as soon as I mentioned my name, but he did not want to discuss the case over the telephone. Bugs at the Vatican? Or at this end already? I wondered. Highly unlikely, but I appreciated his position. I thanked him and hung up.

I stopped for a heavy brunch on my way to the Casina Borghese, where I wanted to view the Berninis once again while my mind was still reasonably uncluttered. I consider him the greatest sculptor who ever lived, and I wanted to see his *Rape of Proserpine* and *Apollo and Daphne* while I was in town, not to mention the rest of the things in that fabulous place. I was often annoyed, especially in recent days, at Carl Bernini being his namesake. Not half so much as at my own situation, though. It makes one feel inferior to wear the name of his better, especially if he has been told about it almost daily, over a period of years. There are those who create things, those who admire them and those who don't give a damn. As my own poetry was dull and my painting, while technically accurate, mediocre—reminding me of Browning's *Andrea del Sarto*: *A common grayness silvers everything*— I was almost driven into the last category by constant, thoughtless and doubtless well-intentioned reminders of these facts. So I became a thief of, and ultimately a pimp for, art. It was only in recent years that I realized I was a second-category man, rather than a third.

This time I kept an eye on my watch and left after an hour and forty-five minutes, pausing only a moment to admire Canova's reclining nude of Pauline Borghese, Napoleon's sister, which had so offended Hitler's delicate morals that he had ordered the figure covered. I am surprised he hadn't reached for his gun. If I'd known his current address I'd have liked to send him a postcard. *Ars est celare artem*, or something like that.

While it was warmer than the previous day and the sun still shone bold and bright, a mass of ominous clouds had appeared on the horizon. I returned to the hotel for my raincoat and umbrella, and took a cab to St. Peter's.

I arrived with tons of time to spare, so I wandered about St. Pete's for a time, slaying minutes. Too much like oceans and deserts and mountains for my taste. I retreated before I got depressed and converted. Smoking, I watched the clouds continue to mass for their assault on the afternoon. Then I hurried on toward the Vatican itself, to locate the Prefecture of Economic Affairs, Office of Administration for the Patrimony of the Holy See, before the downpour began.

I was let in. I did not have to wheedle or poke, but I finally had to produce my letter of introduction before I was shown into the presence of the Monsignor. He rose, gave me his hand, showed me to a seat. He was a brown-haired, youngish, countrified type person, with an engaging smile and strong hands. I had expected an older man.

I smiled back, and he started out by asking about everything from the weather to my trip. I let him lead slowly toward the central question.

"…about this business concerning Father Bretagne…" he finally said.

"Yes?"

"…you must understand our reasons for wanting it to remain—well—somewhat quiet."

"Of course."

"I have several photographs of the man," he said, passing me an envelope.

The man in the picture had dark hair gone light at the sides, a cleft chin and a mouth that looked used to smiling. He wore clerical garb in all of the photos. He looked like a nice guy.

I nodded, handing them back.

"Those are for you," he said. "They're copies."

"Okay."

"He was born in Newark, New Jersey," he told me. "Parents were French immigrants. Very intelligent. Scholarship student. He went through Harvard Business School before he decided to study for the priesthood. Apparently quite devoted to his parents and his older brother, Emil, who took care of him when their parents died. No other children in the family. Emil seems at least partly responsible for his entering the priesthood. Emil had contemplated it for some time himself and probably communicated the enthusiasm. But he changed his mind later and went into business instead."

"I see," I said. "And now he's associated with this—uh—questionable outfit in Brazil."

"That is correct."

"Then that would seem the place to start—the receiving end."

"We have already begun action in that respect," he said. "But we desire more than a simple recovery of the funds. We want to locate Father Bretagne himself. It is still difficult to understand all the details of the operation. We are of course anxious to prevent its recurring."

"I'd bet he's in Brazil right now, or heading that way."

"We feel that he may not necessarily have left Europe yet. Going directly to his brother would be awfully obvious. Also, it would seem likely that he would want to determine the Church's reaction to the theft before traveling very far. Had we released the story, his face would have become quite familiar overnight. With our keeping it quiet this way, he knows we can release it whenever we wish, which might serve to ruin his travel plans. I doubt we can keep it buried forever just to keep him in a desperate state of mind, but I think you can see that part of our reasoning, as well as the obvious displeasure the publicity would bring."

"I follow you—and I'm the one elected to find him."

"No, Mr. Wiley. You are one of the ones we would like to have searching for information concerning him."

"Who are the others?" I asked.

He smiled as he said it, and I could not but refrain from a faint smile myself, as it showed me something about the ghetto area of that place we call the community of ideas:

"There is no need for you to know."

I nodded, held the smile, frowned inwardly, as he continued.

"It has been determined that with your background you would be best suited for the job of interviewing a number of his friends and associates."

At this point he passed me four sheets of paper, neatly typed and sketched. The first was a list of five names, followed by their owners' occupations, whereabouts and apparent relationship to my man. Three of these, however, had no real address. They were clericals located in Vatican City. The other three sheets were maps, indicating the locations of their quarters and approximate times of availability. I've never seen why, in a place that size, they have never seen fit to name or number the streets.

"Have these people been interviewed by anyone else yet?" I asked.

"No."

"Would any of them be aware of the theft?"

"Not unless they learned of it from the perpetrator."

"I see. Is there any special cover story you'd like me to use?"

"Cover story?"

"I'm going to have to give them some reason for my asking questions."

"Oh," he said, then, "I am going to have to leave that to your own ingenuity. I cannot, in good conscience, counsel a person to lie."

As I suppressed a chuckle he blushed and dropped his eyes.

"All right," I said, "I'll manage. Is there anything else?"

"Just do not mention the money or your connection with this office," he said, rising from his chair. "Report any findings you make promptly—to me, personally."

He extended his hand and I took it.

"You'll be hearing from me."

"Good afternoon."

I went off into the good afternoon to find a place to sit, smoke and think, it being still too early to find any of the three listed clericals in their quarters.

One of the names on the list was that of a café owner in Rome—Jacopo Ramaccini. So I decided to taxi to his *Barca d'Oro* for pasta, a glass of wine and maybe some information.

The golden boat was slightly tarnished. In fact, it was a small, windowless basement dive, and poorly lit, I suppose, to conceal some of the dirt. Two men in a far corner had taken time out from their card game and bottle to put their heads down on the table and snore. A fat man in an apron of indeterminate color was the only other occupant. He was seated to my right, holding a newspaper within six inches of his glasses and cursing under his breath.

At my approach he dropped the paper into his lap and snapped his head in my direction, displaying two magnificent scars—one crossing his forehead from eyebrow to hairline and a curving one on his left cheek that might have made for an interesting smile, if he ever smiled.

"Yeah? Yeah?" he said. "What do you want?"

"A glass of white wine," I told him, having reconsidered on the pasta. "Are you Mr. Ramaccini?"

"That's right," he said, rising and moving to a narrow bar. "Why? Who're you?"

I did not watch to see from where he got my glass. I did not really want to know.

"I'm Ovid Wiley," I said, moving to the bar.

He set the glass before me and poured.

He regarded me closely—especially my clothes, it seemed.

"Where're you from?" he asked. "How d'you know me? I never saw you before."

"New York," I answered, glancing from him to the holy pictures tacked to the wall above his left shoulder, then back to him. "I'm in Rome on business. A friend had mentioned your name, so I thought I'd drop in and say hello."

"Ah, New York," he said, smiling for the first time and showing me I had guessed right. The edge of his smile caught the end of his scar, to provide the effect of a clay head being simultaneously squashed and twisted, slowly.

"New York clothes! I guessed, I guessed right," he went on. "What kind of business? What friend knows me?"

"I'm an art dealer," I said. "I come to Rome several times a year to attend art auctions. The friend who mentioned you is named Emil Bretagne."

"Art. Art is good. Art is beautiful and lovely," he said. "I don't know anybody named Emil Bretagne."

I took another sip. It tasted better than the first.

"I know," I told him. "He lives in Brazil. He never met you. But his brother, Father Claude Bretagne, a Vatican priest, talked of you in his letters many times, always as a good friend."

"That is the truth?" he said.

"That is the truth."

His smile became a grin.

"The priest. Ah, that goddamn priest!" he said. "Yes. The priest, he ate here all the time. Maybe he wanted to be a saint someday—or was doing penance for something. The food is lousy, you know. I always eat across the street myself."

Then he laughed, long and loud. One of the snorers tossed in his sleep and resumed in a different key.

"The priest!" he chuckled. "Always he would come here to eat and always we would argue."

"What about? The food?"

"No, no. Not the food. He would eat the swill and never complain. Mostly religion and politics is what we talked."

"Oh?" I said.

"Yes, he loved to argue. He was Jesuit, you know."

"Yes," I said.

"So, he mentioned me to his brother? That is good. Somebody in South America knows my name—and New York. Imagine! *La Barca* has an international reputation now. Maybe someday *Playboy* will recommend it."

He commenced laughing again. I took another sip, waiting.

Finally, he stopped, sighed, then said, "You have seen his brother the priest yet?"

"No, I just arrived. I thought I'd look him up this evening."

He reached out, clapped a hand on my forearm and drew nearer.

"Listen," he said. "Listen. When you see him, maybe you would say the two of you should come here to dinner, huh? I will make a real good one this time. If he says he is mad at me, tell him this one is on Jacopo. Okay?"

"Why should he be mad at you?"

He sighed, removed his hand and turned away. From somewhere he produced a glass and poured himself some wine. He downed it in a single gulp, then refilled both our glasses.

"Because of our arguments," he said, with a belch. "Maybe I offended him. You will tell him I did not mean to if I did. He has stayed away for several weeks now. You tell him he was my best customer."

"What were you arguing about?"

"Oh, politics and religion, like always. You know. Everybody in Italy argues about the Pope's shop, even the priests. He has many big ideas about how it could be changed. So we argued about them. Like always."

We each took a small sip.

"Tell me about some of his ideas," I said, accepting a cigarette he offered. "I don't want to get off on the wrong foot. I never met him before."

I lit both, he drew and exhaled, then said, "Well...You know. He liked the idea of divorce, and a lot of the other stuff—birth control, abortion. He talked about the population exploding and poor people, and I said it was God's will. But we agree about many things, too. So he should not be mad at me for the things we argue about, should he?"

"I don't think so," I said. "Since he was so advanced in his thinking I'd imagine he also had ideas on things like papal infallibility, clerical celibacy…" I let my voice trail off.

"Yes." He nodded. "He always said that the Pope was just the Bishop of Rome. He never talked much about the other, though. But I think I mentioned it once and he did agree." He paused to finish his drink, pour himself another. Then, "Yes," he finally said. "He did. But it was not one of the things we argued about. I did not want to talk to a priest about something this personal. So it was not one of the things."

"I see," I said, finishing my drink. "I will be careful how I talk of these matters when I see him."

I glanced at my watch, then raised my drink.

"I must be going now," I said. "Thanks for your help."

"Tell him what I said."

"Yes."

After finding a decent place to eat I sorted out the dishes that lay before me, then started on my thoughts.

On the face of it, it seemed I had scored something on my first try. Luck? I shrugged my mental shoulders and examined the apparent facts. It seemed that Father Bretagne was something of a radical and had wanted someone outside the Vatican with whom he could discuss his ideas. Almost too neat a tie-in right away. Brilliant priest becomes disillusioned, disgruntled, decides to take the Church for every dime he can before skipping out. It had happened before in other big outfits. Why not the Church? Payment due for long, cheerless years of service to the wrong cause, etcetera. There was that possibility. Unless Jacopo was a good actor, he was not even aware of the man's recent departure. I tended to believe him, as he had no apparent reason to supply what amounted to a motive that went deeper than simple venality. I determined to pursue this angle. For the time, though, I dismissed it and turned my mind to other matters.

What was the CIA's stake in this thing, really? I was supposed to get in touch periodically via the security officer at our embassy. Monsignor Zingales had said I was to report only to him if I found something. At the time, I had assumed he meant for me not to give it to anyone else at the Vatican. But now I wondered. Of course he knew where I came from, and he doubtless was aware that I would tell them everything, eventually. What had Rome and the CIA promised each other, anyway?

Collins' words returned to me: "I want to plant you in the Vatican." Ridiculous. He had never spoken of it from quite that standpoint afterwards. But he had insisted on those reports, prompt and thorough. I wondered what would happen if I mentioned this to Monsignor Zingales. Then my discretion-driven memory had me in New York again and I knew that I would never find out. Oh well. The hell with them all. One master is too many for me.

The next two were dead ends and the third somewhat interesting. I had decided to try calling on all three of the priests on my list that evening. Aware of the Roman habit of dining somewhat later than I usually do, I took the time to return to my hotel for a shower and a short nap.

I did not attempt to phone ahead before I left, as I would not throw a Roman telephone or phone book at a screaming alley cat. They are just not accurate. Also, I did not want to give anyone opportunity to prepare a response.

Lucky and unlucky, depending on how you look at it. I was lucky that the first two priests were in, so that I did not have to call again; the unluck was the results. My first was, I would say, a septuagenarian: stooped shoulders, dark eyes, sparse hair, sandpaper complexion, somewhat hard of hearing. No, he had not seen Father Bretagne for some time, he told me when I finally got the question across. They used to play chess together regularly, once a week ("Very good chess player, that man. Hah!"), until a few months ago when Father Bretagne had gotten too busy to come around much. Did not even know he was gone. Sorry to hear about that. He would pray for him. I should do the same.

The second was younger, heavy, ruddy, watery-eyed, and had a disconcerting habit of tilting his head backward whenever he spoke. Presumably he needed a new prescription and was looking through the bottom halves of his bifocals. Yes, he had heard of Father Bretagne's leaving. They shared an interest in opera, attending some and listening to recordings of others together. No, he hadn't the slightest as to where he had gone or why. Had always seemed a good-natured, devoted fellow. Might even say happy. Hadn't seen him recently. Work pressures and all. He was praying for him, too. Sorry he could not be of more help.

I pounded my way up several streets beneath the grumbling, flashing sky, slick rivulets racing past me now, gurgling, then gone. Reaching the apartment of my final cleric, I shook out my raincoat and umbrella in the hallway.

Finally, "Father Leon Mancini?" I asked the tall, sharp-featured man who had opened his door to my knocking.

"Yes, I am Father Mancini," he said, studying me.

"My name is Ovid Wiley," I told him. "I have been referred to you because I am looking for information concerning Father Claude Bretagne. I am told you are friends."

He cocked his head, raised an eyebrow, squinted

slightly. I did not squirm as he scrutinized me, though I wanted to.

Then, "Yes, I suppose you might say that, Mr. Wiley," he replied. "May I ask why you are inquiring?"

"His brother Emil hasn't heard from him for a time. When he learned that I was coming to Rome he asked me to inquire after him among some of the people he had mentioned in his letters. You were one of them. So if you could spare me a few minutes, I'd appreciate it."

"Well," he said, "I do not really believe that I can be of much assistance to you. But come inside and we'll find out."

He opened the door fully and stepped aside.

"Let me take your things."

"Thanks."

I stepped into a neat efficiency apartment. He vanished, presumably into the john, with my wet coat and umbrella.

"Have a seat," he said, returning and gesturing anywhere. "Care for a cup of coffee?"

"No thanks."

"It's ready, and I am going to have one."

"In that case, yes," I said, seating myself. "I take it black."

After we had settled with our mugs, he said, shaking his head slowly, "I am afraid I do not know where he is or, for that matter, why he left. I was quite surprised when I learned of his departure."

I took a sip.

"Did he give any signs of discontent, dissatisfaction?" I asked.

He paused a moment, then, "No," he said slowly. "I wouldn't say so."

"Something very basic, perhaps?" I suggested. "Such

as unhappiness over Church policies on current issues, rather than anything having to do with his job in particular?"

He looked away, was silent for a time.

"I wish you had not asked me that," he finally said. "I gather from the way you put it that you are already somewhat aware of what an honest answer would entail. It is true that he made no effort to conceal his feelings on matters where silence would have been more in order. He did not approve of the Church's position on many major issues—"

"Would you say 'most' rather than 'many'?"

"I suppose so," he sighed. "What puzzles me is that if he wished to leave the clergy, there *are* procedures for handling such matters. I believe that he always considered himself a good Catholic. I would have thought he would have gone through channels, rather than just packing up and leaving."

He shrugged and took a sip of coffee. I waited until he had lowered the mug before I hit him with the question that might either terminate the conversation of lead me to something of value.

"What would you say his feelings were on clerical celibacy?"

He reddened, looked away and paused too long.

My hunch had been right, I was certain.

"Well..." he began. "It is a controver—"

"He didn't believe in it, did he? He was against it all the way. In fact, he had a girlfriend, didn't he?"

"No!" he said. "I mean...No."

"I am not prying just for the sake of prying," I said slowly. "But it is very important that he be located, quickly. I do not mean to imply an illicit relationship. I just used that as a lever to get you talking. I do have reason to believe he saw a woman occasionally for, let us say, purposes unknown. I need her name. Perhaps she can help me find him."

"Just how important is it that he be found?" he inquired.

"It is very, very important. That is all that I can say. If he did make her identity known to you and you were to tell it to me, I can assure you I will be discreet with the information. I simply want to talk with her, briefly."

He paused to light a cigarette.

"I do not want to see him in any sort of trouble," he said after a time. "How do I know you are not some sort of detective or an attorney?"

"You don't," I said. "But I'm not."

He smoked in silence a while, then rose.

"Wait a moment," he said, and he left the room.

He returned shortly and handed me a small slip of paper he had folded in half.

"Here," he said. "It may be what you are looking for and it may not. All I know is that he gave me this one afternoon and told me that he would not be home that evening, but that if anyone trying to reach him should call me, I was to phone him there, personally, and give him the message."

I accepted it, glanced at it, put it into my pocket.

"Thank you, Father," I said, rising. "I guess I had better be going now."

He nodded, left the room and fetched my things.

"Well, good night then, Father," I said, donning my coat.

"Good night, Mister Wiley."

He did not seem to notice my outstretched hand, so I turned and went out the door, down the steps, through the hallway and into the wet darkness beyond.

IV.

Coincidences are things I distrust. Though they have cropped up often in my life, I tend to regard that with full skepticism when they touch on matters of importance.

This is why I felt uneasy when raising the phone, making the call.

Maria Borsini was the woman's name...

I was certain it would be the same woman. I just felt it coming.

Carl Bernini's girl.

I remembered a dark-haired, dark-eyed, slightly hefty, but narrow-waisted girl who had welcomed us to Naples on our successful return from England. We had had a private celebration, just the three of us. I had uncorked the wine, and she'd made herself comfortable in Carl's lap while I propped the fruits of our expedition in strategic places about the room. Fourteen in all, by Dutch and Flemish artists. We very seldom went after an Old Master. Strictly special-order business there. Too hot to handle normally. The seventeenth century, however, was most obliging. The Dutch and Flemish seemed to love eating and looking at flowers. When they were not doing these things, they liked to look at paintings concerning them. Also, they tended to keep the paintings a convenient, under-the-arm size. Too, many of them would do four or five studies of the same subject. It is next to useless to send art dealers and museums a "reported stolen" list describing the missing-in-action item as depicting a vase of flowers, a bowl of fruit or a gang of peasants sitting about a table eating, and expect an immediate identification. Italy is a perfect place to dispose of such things. They operate under Roman law which makes it just about impossible to recover something purchased in good faith; hence, the buyer has something like a guarantee in those matters.

The paintings positioned, I poured the wine. Carl stopped stroking Maria's hair long enough to raise his glass in a toast.

"To the arts," he said, then smiled.

"…and a good present for the past," I added.

"A prosperous future to their handlers," she said, then drained her glass in a single gulp and giggled.

As I went about the refilling, I could not help but notice the tanned smoothness of her legs, her eyes upon me as I did so. Speculative? Flirting? I do not really know. There is *some* honor among some thieves, advance publicity to the contrary.

She had had a hardy peasant way about her and a slightly slutty appearance, strangely surrounding a mind of which some steel traps might be envious. She had learned and retained an awful lot about art in the erratic up-and-down years of her off-and-on association with Carl Bernini. She even seemed to like some of it. I wondered what things about her were for show, what was for Carl and what was for real.

One morning, she had joined me for my wake-up coffee while Carl was still asleep, and she asked me what I felt like at having been the only survivor of the 747 which had crashed in Athens several months earlier.

"Lucky," I said, sipping.

"Yes," she agreed, after a moment. "Nobody will play cards with you anymore, though it does not seem that you cheat. Carl has had many setbacks in his life, but since he

has been working with you it is all different. You never
get caught. There are few complications. You always get
the best prices. Even Carl, who says he does not believe
in such things, says that you have been his lucky charm,
this past year."

Here, she fingered a holy medal she wore about her
neck, smiled when she realized what she was doing and
let it fall into the valley of her breasts.

When she leaned forward to pour more coffee, the
valley deepened and she did not adjust her robe, a green
thing with orange flowers. Matisse would have used a
single, curved line. I personally preferred the shading that
was there.

When she continued, she spoke more slowly and her
face assumed an inquisitive expression. Her voice actually changed, as well as the grammar and precision with
which her words were delivered. The sophisticated effect
it produced was like an extra cup of coffee in my veins.

"...and one day, perhaps soon, you shall return to your
own country, a reasonably affluent man," she said. "Doubtless, you will purchase respectability; and doubtless, too,
you will retain some connection with the arts, for you
love them."

At that point, she covered my left hand lightly with her
right, and I wondered at her having guessed my intentions so correctly. While I had mentioned it to no one, I
had begun to feel that luck of which she had spoken
might be wearing somewhat thin. I had made up my mind
that this job was to be my last. It would garnish my nest
sufficiently for me to stop taking chances.

I shrugged.

"I might wind up an art dealer one day," I said.

"Soon," she replied, perceptive girl. "I feel that it will
be soon. And when you go, the bad times will return.
Carl can make money, but he cannot keep it. Sometimes,

too, he gets into trouble. A painting is recognized or a dealer cheats him, and he cannot go to the police. Generally, he must hide. I always thought that one day he would make a large commission and be able to keep it. Then he would buy a home and live as other people do. This was my hope for several years. When you and he joined together, I thought that the time might be near. Now I know that it is not so. You are no longer interested in the work. I have watched you and listened to you speak of it. When you leave, it will be as it was before. You possess something that he lacks. I have tried to analyze it, but I cannot."

I shrugged.

"What is America like?" she asked me, leaning farther forward and staring into my eyes, a faint smiling occurring now.

"Big," I said. "Pretty in some places, ugly in others. The same as anyplace else. Its big cities are like most big cities. I like cities."

"I like cities, too," she told me. "I was once ready to become a nun, but I did not take the final vows—I could not—because I like to wear pretty dresses, and I like good food and wine and travel. So I came to the city and met Carl Bernini. He gave me some of these things, sometimes. But more often, it was as if I were back in the convent. He lives from job to job, never thinking of the future."

She laughed then and located a cigarette, held it. I lit it for her. I could give her that, at least.

Then, "You will be a successful art dealer," she told me, and finished her coffee.

It was several days later, after we had disposed of our merchandise, that she and Carl had had an argument, most of which I did not overhear. He began slapping her around, however, and while it was none of my business I did the same to him, on general principles. It turned into a very nasty fight, and I expanded my Italian vocabulary considerably that day. This terminated our partnership, somewhat ahead of my schedule. I did not see him again until I found him in my gallery. I had not seen her since.

The telephone rang, and despite the years I recognized the voice that answered.

"Hello, Maria," I said. "This is Ovid."

"It has been so long…" she said, after a silence that made it about ten seconds longer.

"Yes," I agreed, "but here I am in Rome and wanting to see you. May I come over?"

"Of course," she replied. "But there has been so much time…What of Carl?"

"You haven't seen him lately?" I said.

"No."

I decided then that it was best to be brief and blunt.

"He's dead," I said. "I found his body."

"Oh."

After another pause, "How did it happen?" she asked.

"He was murdered," I told her. "With a knife. At my place."

"Who did it?"

"I don't know. The police have not been able to find out yet. They suspected me, but I didn't do it. They had to let me go."

"Was he visiting with you when it happened?"

"No. I wasn't even aware that he was in town until I found his body."

"How long ago was it?"

"About a week and a half. I'm sorry to be the one to tell you."

"Do not be," she said. "It had been all over between us for a long while."

"Then why did you ask about him?"

"Curiosity," she replied. "He did once mean very much to me, and I wished him no ill. I am sorry that he is dead. I had heard that he was going to America. I had thought that he would visit his old friend—if for no other reason than to ask for money or a place to stay. I am very sorry about the way things turned out for him."

Since I could not see her face or hands, it was difficult for me to gauge her feelings. She was speaking again in that slow, dignified fashion I had heard on but one other occasion.

"So you think he was somewhat down on his luck?" I asked.

"He was when we broke up," she said. "Things were not going at all well for him. He had been in jail for a time. Then he was ill for a long while. He began drinking heavily. Our arguments grew worse and worse. Finally, I threw him out."

"About how long ago was that?"

"Oh, many months. April, perhaps…"

"Have you any idea who might have killed him?"

"No," she said. "I knew nothing of his current affairs."

"Is it all right if I come over now?" I asked. "I'd like to take you somewhere for dinner or buy you a drink or three."

"I am sorry, but tonight is impossible," she said. "I have to work until quite late. I only came home to eat, and I was on the way out when the telephone rang."

"Oh. How about tomorrow then?" I asked.

"Tomorrow is the opening," she said. "We are exhibiting over forty paintings by Paul Gladden, an American who has been living in Italy for the past five years. He is quite good. I work for Bruno Jurgen now, at the Sign of the Fish. You must remember the place."

"Yes. He was a very good fence. Probably still is. Has

branches all over Europe and in both Americas. I like to see a man make good."

"If he had known you were in town I am certain he would have sent you an invitation. There will be dealers and art critics from several countries present. Why don't you stop by around eight this evening? There will be champagne, and I am certain Bruno would be happy to see you again. Who knows? You might even see something you want to buy. We can talk then—or afterwards—depending on how busy things get."

"That sounds like a good idea," I said. "All right."

"How long will you be in town?"

"It's hard to say. I'm not really certain yet."

"Buying trip?"

"Sort of a combination of a vacation and just looking."

"Excellent," she said. "I have to run now. I will see you tomorrow evening then."

"Right. Take care."

"Goodbye."

Click.

I cursed as I smoked and paced. Something was just too neat and cute for other words. It had to be more than coincidence, my connection with the renegade priest through Maria and Carl, with Carl turning up dead at my place and me on the spot this way. My man in Virginia must have known more than he had indicated, and I cursed him for holding it back when it might have been of use to me.

Finished with cursing, I went downstairs and up the street for dinner.

"It is no great wonder if in the long process of time, while fortune takes her course hither and thither, numerous coincidences should spontaneously occur," the historian wrote. "If the number and variety of subjects to be wrought upon be infinite, it is all the more easy for

fortune, with such an abundance of material, to effect
this similarity of results."

Crap, Plutarch! Crap! You and Berwick would have
gotten along fine together.

I ate the food without really tasting it. I lingered over
my final drink.

I found Anna Zanti, the fifth name on the Monsignor's list,
seated on the steps of a building one guidebook describes
as "benin funerary style," her basket of flowers at her feet
and small bunches of them spread, satellite-like, about
her on the stair. She was a very thin, dark woman, with
incipient cataracts and snow-white hair. She wore a shabby,
plaid shawl and long skirts, and the lines in her face deepened as she leaned forward, frowning, to catch at the
words of a customer. Since the conversation could prove
lengthy and the day was young, I passed her on the stair
and entered the concrete monstrosity.

Inside the thing was the altar itself, raised by the
Roman Senate for Augustus Caesar around 2,000 years
ago. When pieces of it were dug up in 1568, they were
believed to be the remains of an old triumphal arch. It was
not realized until approximately three centuries later that
it was the Ara Pacis Augustae. And it was not until 1937
that it was fully excavated and the job of piecing it together
was begun. Marble, atop a pyramid of steps, the outside
screen a bas relief showing the suckling of Romulus and
Remus by their bitch of a stepmother, Aeneus making a
sacrifice, a gala procession, all above decorations of acan-
thus leaves, snakes, lizards, birds, flowers and butterflies.
I mounted the steps and entered, pausing to study the
garlands of fruit, foliage and pinecones strung between
ox skulls that decorated the interior. The altar itself was a
high slab of tufa stone, guarded by mythical animals. I
have always been deeply moved by the Ara Pacis. It had

been packed round by sandbags during World War II, to protect it. Now the whole thing is sheltered by the concrete barn. The windows, some of them 21 by 28 feet, are half an inch thick, specially made by the Saint-Gobain's Caserte glass factory to withstand the rocks and such thrown by demonstrators. Lost, unidentified for centuries, somehow protected, a frail, delicate thing of hope. Poor old Ara Pacis Augustae, they did not have bombs in the days of your youth. I wonder how much longer you will be around, old altar of peace?

About ten minutes later, my respects to the respectable paid, I stepped outside and waited for Anna Zanti's current customer to move away. Then I walked down and said hello, bought a corsage.

"Thank you," she said. "It is very fresh. Your lady will be happy."

I smiled.

"I am certain," I said. "It looks to be a good day, eh?"

"Yes," she agreed. "On days like this I sell more flowers."

"That is good," I said. "Did you know Father Bretagne?"

She gave me a quick face-to-toes-to-face survey, then leaned forward and cupped her ear.

"Pardon," she said. "I do not hear so well."

"A priest. Father Bretagne," I said. "Do you know him?"

She shrugged.

"I know many priests."

"But this particular priest—Father Bretagne...I am trying to find him. You and he were friends, no?"

"Pardon," she said again, leaning forward. "You will have to speak louder."

As I repeated it, she studied my face, squinting. Then she winked and smiled.

"You buy the flowers for your mistress, yes?"

I nodded.

Then she decided, nodding several times herself, "…and you want to divorce your wife for her."

I smiled again. It seemed the right thing to do.

"For forty years I was married to that son of a dog, Antonio," she said then. "Forty years! And he left me after the first! I could not get a divorce then, the way the laws were. Then when they were changed, I wanted one. But the Church still does not approve of such things. So I talked about it with the best priest I knew. That Father Bretagne! He is a saint! So wise, so friendly…Not like the others. No! So one day when he stopped to buy flowers I asked him about it. He talked to me for a long time then. He told me how it was a law of the Church and not a law of God. He made everything so clear that I did not feel bad about going to the lawyer at all. If you talk to him, he will explain it to you as he did to me, I am sure."

"Did he buy your flowers often?" I asked.

"Every few weeks."

"For whom did he buy them?"

She flipped her palms, raised her shoulders and let them fall.

"I never asked him. He never said."

"I would like to talk to him, about my—problem," I said. "Where can I find him?"

"Vatican City," she told me. "He works there. Someone will know."

"Thank you."

She smiled and turned her attention to the flowers, pushing several farther into the shade.

Nothing, or very little, there. As I could see it. I telephoned to Monsignor at the Vatican's Prefecture of Economic Affairs, told him I had nothing to report as yet and asked his assistance on getting into Father Bretagne's quarters for a once-over. He told me how to get there and said that by the time I arrived the janitor would be advised to let me in and leave me alone. He added his doubt that I would find anything of value. I agreed, thanked him and hung up. I had the time, and it was best to be thorough. He was right, though. The small, neatly kept flat showed me nothing that I could use. Nothing at all. It did not seem that he had left it in a hurry.

There was a table full of canapés and conspicuous rows of shiny champagne buckets. The Sign of the Fish is a deep, narrow place, but there are four stories to it as well as a finished basement. The two upper floors contain offices and vaults. The floors were thickly carpeted in a dusky yellow, and I lusted after the cut-glass chandelier in the entrance hall. Someday...

I arrived at approximately 8:45, and no one asked to see my invitation. There were small chatty groups of middle to highly tailored individuals of three or four nationalities and sexes standing about, and a handful of the Bohemian sort who wandered between the food and the paintings. I did not see Maria or Bruno around, though there were two officially friendly girls wearing discreet black gowns and upswept hairdos, moving among the talkers and helping with wraps.

I was only half-surprised to see Walter Carlon, an art critic, off in one corner, sketching in the air with his cigar and moving his lips at a rapid rate before a group of students and old ladies. Short, stocky, near-bald and in his forties, Walt had come into a lot of money and abominable taste somewhere along the line, and he traveled about the world exhibiting both. Over the years, he has demonstrated an amazing ability to back losers and mock the truly talented. His articles and books arouse a sense of wonder in art history and art appreciation classes, where they are held up as models of half-assedness. He is much in demand as a lecturer, though, for despite all else the man is glib. He fascinates as he infuriates. He should have been a politician or some other sort of con man. The power of his words vanishes, though, when they are committed to paper. I do not think he is a phony, however. He seems to believe whatever stupid thing he happens to be saying at any given moment. I cannot really say whether it is despite all this or because of it that I rather like the man.

As I did not wish to get tied down at the moment, I pretended not to have noticed him and made my way to the buffet table. Later, champagne glass in hand, I wandered the gallery, looking for Maria, half-studying Paul Gladden's paintings.

After the better part of an hour, I had grown a bit impatient. Still, she had not said that she would be there right on the dot for the opening—simply that we would meet there. I asked one of the hostesses who said she had not seen her, but perhaps she was working upstairs. At my request, the girl found me a telephone and left me with it. I tried Maria's number three times, but there was no answer.

So, she was probably either upstairs or en route. I determined to wait a while longer before growing concerned or trying anything else. If she did not prove the information source I hoped her to be, I decided that I would write me down as a failure and see whether I could sell the idea to our man at the embassy. I was convinced, though, that they would not let me off that easily. Not after all the trouble they had gone through to recruit me.

But Rome did indeed seem to be a dead end. I was afraid that they would feel, as I did, that Father Bretagne's brother in Brazil would be the next logical person to check out. If they had not already done so, that is. Certainly they had people in Brazil…

Still, the thought came back to me, they have people in Rome, too, and they sent you.

Since I did not know the *why* about Rome, it was fruitless to speculate as to the *if* concerning Brazil.

So the hell with them both. I would run down any local leads Maria could give me, prepare a long report signifying nothing and get ready to go home. What else was there to do?

My subconscious chuckled at this, and forced a list of Portuguese verbs into my head. I threw them back and went after another glass of champagne.

After an hour or so I had grown so tired of Gladden's Wyeth & Water countryscapes that I found myself welcoming a familiar slap on the shoulder and the odor of exhaled cigar smoke.

"Ovid! I thought I saw you skulking about earlier," Walter said. "How the hell have you been?"

"Pretty well," I told him. "Yourself?"

"Fine, fine. When did you get in?"

"A few days ago."

"Business, I take it?"

I shrugged.

"Some business, some pleasure. I like to mix them."

"What do you think of Paul's stuff?" he asked, gesturing.

"Some of it is pretty good."

"Good? He's great!"

He indicated a morningset scene: a farmhouse and some outbuildings, an old tower and yellow hills in the background.

"You can feel the breezes and smell the fields the way he did that morning when he stood there painting it."

"He painted it from a photo," I said, "not that that takes anything away from his field and his breezes—"

"What do you mean? How can you tell?"

"I can tell by the way the perspective is off. Give me a piece of string and I'll show you."

He glared at the painting and was beginning to turn red when he was saved from the string business by the arrival of Bruno Jurgen.

I had seen him coming, passing through the crowd like a dark, white-capped breaker, extending liquid hands in gesture, handshake, salute; smiling, nodding, very neat in his dark dinner jacket, his sandpaper complexion just beginning to crinkle beneath the tan, he flowed, leaving echoes and eddies in his wake.

"Ovid," he said, shaking my hand, "are you here to buy everything in sight?"

I protested that the people would cost a lot to feed, and he added a small gesture to his grin and clasped Walt's hand with an equal professional fervor.

"I was detained in the office," he explained. "Some stupid phone calls. Otherwise, I would have been down here earlier to welcome you. Ovid, I did not know you were in town or you would have received an invitation. There was no difficulty…?"

"None," I told him.

"We have several mailing lists," he went on. "You should receive invitations for all the shows at our New York outlet, and all the ones of international importance from our other branches. I apologize for not knowing of your special interest in Mister Gladden. Are you here on your own or as a representative?"

"Actually," I said, "I'm not here for this specific exhibit," and I tried to let it go at that.

"Oh, a general buying trip," he replied. "Where else have you been?"

"Just here. That's all."

"And where next?"

"Possibly Brazil," I said, with some bitterness.

"You like the climate perhaps?"

"I detest it, but that is of no importance."

He regarded me more closely, then decided, "If you are interested in the work of a particular artist or pieces in a specific style or medium, I can cable our branches in Rio and São Paulo and make arrangements."

"That's quite good of you, thank you, but not necessary. I may not even have to make the trip. Much depends on how things go here."

"Oh? Well, whatever...You must give me your local address, so that I can take you to lunch or dinner while you are in town. Who knows? I may even be able to help you with your local business. You're not up to your old tricks again, are you?"

I shook my head and told him where I was staying.

"I'll phone you tomorrow then, after I have checked my appointments."

"Fine."

"In the meantime, can I sell you some of Mister Gladden's things?" he asked, turning his head in that direction.

"Not just now, thanks."

He shook his head in smiling disbelief.

"That boy will be big one day," he said. "Now is the time to notice that. Not later. Right, Walter?"

"My spirit of the romantic has been sadly crushed," he said. "I have just determined that the man paints from photographs. The perspective, you know. I even begin to wonder whether he snaps his own. Perhaps he is a boon to the postcard industry."

Bruno flushed, which simply had the effect of darkening his tan.

"What of it?" he said. "It is true, but what of it? Many—no, most—modern artists do the same. Would you have them return to the same place every day and await identical conditions? The vision is there or they would not have selected the subject. A photo is only for mundane

details. It is a valuable tool and its side effects are only
incidental."

At this point, his gestures had become violent enough
to cause bystanders to draw back. He turned to me then
and fired, "Is that why you are not interested in his work?"

"No," I said. "As a matter of fact, I think some of them
are very good. It is just that I am not in the market for
this sort of thing right now. My budget, you know, is more
limited than some and I have to be selective when it
comes to speculation. I am certain I could sell the stuff.
The question is—how much? I can't afford to tie up too
much capital while waiting for acclaim to catch up with
his talent. If I had the opportunity to take some of his
pieces on consignment I'd say yes in a minute. But since
you already have that end tied up, I'll just salivate and
swallow."

"You see, Walter?" he said, turning. "Ovid knows there
will be a demand. His judgment has always been good."

Walt expelled a tiny burst of air from between moist
lips, making a little "Phht!" sound.

"Ovid's aesthetic sense rides backseat to the market-
place," he said in a half-joking tone. "Yes, I'll admit to Mr.
Gladden's talent, and its limitations."

He sought out a match and relit his cigar.

"How long have you been in town?" I asked him.

"About a week," he told me. "I'd seen everything current in Madrid, and this is really in the nature of a vacation.

"I *will* mention this exhibit in my next column," he
said to Bruno, "and send you copies."

Turning to me, he added, "...and I'll throw in a plug
for you and your discount house, too. I've got to run now.
That little guy over in the corner—the one with the thick
glasses—is a reporter I have some business with. You'll
do well to nail him before you leave, Ov. And about that

dinner—maybe we could make it a threesome. You two think about it. I'll phone you. If not, give my bests to the Cariocas. G'bye."

And he was gone in a cloud of smoke.

"That man," said Bruno, "is a shithead. Of course we shall exclude him."

I nodded and glanced at my watch. Time was working its way toward eleven o'clock, and I debated making another phone call.

Instead, "I've been looking for Maria," I said. "She told me she was going to be here tonight."

"Maria," he said benignly. "She is an extra right-hand to me. She did more work, part-time, than all of my other employees together, who put in a full week. So I was glad—selfish, but still glad—when she broke up with your old partner, Carl. I think it was good for her, too, by the way. He was a drunken bum, living on her earnings. She came to work here full-time after she threw him out. Now she can meet some nice young man, marry an art teacher perhaps."

At this point, I noticed a small, dark, mustachioed man, hair parted in the middle, who was standing in a doorway across the room, waving ferociously in our direction.

"Someone you know?" I interrupted, nodding that way.

Bruno turned, and the man immediately raised his hand to his ear, as if holding a telephone receiver.

"I am wanted," he sighed. "If it is that ignorant customs officer again I will apply to the Mafia for his removal!" He winked, then, "Yes, Maria was to have been here to-night," he said. "But she telephoned earlier to say that she was not feeling well. I told her to stay in bed. It is a pity. She was looking forward to this opening. She had worked so hard on it. Well…I will call you tomorrow, and we will get together. Till then," and he traced a half-salute.

"Till then," I agreed, and watched him plow his way through the throng.

I headed for the front door then, wondering why she had not answered the telephone.

The cab deposited me before her building, and I located her name and apartment number on a mailbox in the hall. Mounting to the third floor, I found her door and knocked. There was a line of light at the door's lower edge, but no sounds came from within.

I knocked again, then tried the door. It was locked.

It wasn't much of a lock though, so I fetched the picks from my wallet and opened it.

She was lying in a sprawly position, one leg on the sofa and the other hanging over its edge. Her blue skirt was hitched up above her knees and her head was twisted at an unusual angle. There were red stains on her face, her throat, her blouse.

Quietly, I entered, locking the door behind me.

V.

I am the sort of person who overreacts to things. I tend to seek hidden meanings in what people say and do and to erect paranoid constructions upon these. Sometimes I have nightmares where the whole world is a conspiracy, where everything waits for the perfect moment to shatter reality all about me to the sound of cosmic chuckling. I am the sort of person who takes a vitamin pill every day and a tetanus booster once a year. But I have been involved in so many accidents, near-accidents, potential accidents and non-accidental, violent situations that I feel there is some justification for a policy of caution and jumpiness.

I recall one chilly morning when, unshaven, tired-eyed, smelling of beer and tobacco, I emerged from an all-night poker game with my tie loose about my neck and a couple hundred bucks in my pocket. The street seemed to be deserted and the subway station was four blocks away. After walking for a few minutes, I noticed that I was not alone in the world. About 30 feet ahead of me, a man stood in a doorway, drawn well back, looking as disreputable as myself and staring at me. I slowed my pace and kept staring at him. It was too late to run. I reached after my money as he jammed his hand into his hip pocket, hoping that he would be satisfied with a cooperative victim. Instead, he pulled out his wallet as I came up to the doorway and held it toward me with a shaking hand.

"Take it!" he said. "It's all I got! Don't shoot me!"

So I do tend to look for the worst and am sometimes embarrassed when it does not materialize. Usually, the worst strikes without warning, which irritates hell out of me when I think of all the times I prepared for it and nothing happened. I wish the Fates were not masochists, to love one who curses them so.

With these things in mind and a twisted sense of humor to cast out shadows, I sighed back at the telltale odor and advanced toward the sofa. Unfortunately, she was breathing.

I passed her and moved beyond the far wing of the sofa. Lying on its side in a puddle on the floor was an empty half-gallon of Chianti. A broken glass kept it company. She had spilled it all over herself, and I suddenly wished for a head cold as I realized I had also moved nearer the results of an unsuccessful dash toward the sink.

Just to be certain, I checked her pulse and it seemed normal. There were no visible signs that she had fallen and hurt herself. She did not awaken during my brief examination, which was just as well. She did make some soft noises as I adjusted her skirt and moved her into a more comfortable-seeming position. Her face was a mess of wine stains and ruined makeup, cut through with dried tear-streaks; her eyelashes stuck together in little, glistening bunches.

I set some water to boiling for coffee. Even if it would not really do her any good, I wanted some. I opened a window to air the place out, hung my coat, rolled up my sleeves and removed the various messes. Afterwards, I sponged her face with a moist washcloth.

At this, her eyelids flickered.

"…Thirsty," she said.

I took her a glass of water and propped her while she drank it.

"…More."

She took two and a half glasses, pressed the washcloth to her eyes and held it there. She sat hunched forward and her breathing deepened.

"Aspirins…" she said. "…Medicine chest."

I fetched them and poured two coffees while she swallowed a couple of tablets. By then she had lowered the cloth and was running fingers through her long, black hair.

"Ouch," she said as I set the cups on the coffee table. "The world is not as young as it used to be."

She gave me a spasmodic smile as she accepted a cigarette and leaned forward. I seated myself and lit one of my own.

Silence followed.

We sat in silence for perhaps ten minutes. Then she rose, smiled faintly, said, "Excuse me" and left the room. After a time, I heard water running.

A fresh cup of coffee. Another cigarette. Night thoughts.

Maria had not been a heavy drinker when I had known her earlier. But then, neither had Carl. People do change, but this still seemed abnormal. Also, I did not feel that a chronically heavy drinker could have gotten such a sterling endorsement from Bruno, he being a notorious slave driver. No, I decided she had hung this one on for a reason, and it had to be a recent one. I hoped that it dealt with my quarry. Whatever, now was the ideal—perhaps the only—time to get it out of her, while she was still reeling from the blow.

After a time, she returned, turbaned in a towel and wearing a white terry cloth robe. Her face looked much better, though I noticed that her hands shook as she refilled her cup. She sat down, found a cigarette and managed a much better smile than earlier.

"Thanks, Ovid," she said, dropping her eyes.

Then she looked around the room, turning her whole head, not just her eyes.

"And you cleaned up, too. I am embarrassed."

Her survey ended at the door.

"Sorry I didn't hear you knock," she said.

I shrugged.

"I didn't mean to stand you up tonight," she told me.

"No harm done," I said. "How are you feeling now?"

"Rotten," she said. "Were you worried about me?"

"Yes."

"It was one of those bad days. Everything went wrong. I took a couple drinks to relax, then things got worse and I took a couple more. Then I decided, 'hell with it!' and proceeded to drown my sorrows.

"How was the opening?"

"Interesting," I said. "Walter Carlon was there. Bruno told me he missed you."

"I'll bet he did," she said. "I set the thing up practically singlehandedly!"

"Then you decided not to show up for it."

She looked a trifle wistful.

"I'm sorry about that now," she said. "Bruno is an awfully good person when you really get to know him well. I'll have to call him in the morning..."

"Does it happen often?"

"What?"

"Everything going wrong."

She gnawed her lip.

"No, today was special," she said.

"In what ways?"

"I'd just as soon forget about it."

"Of course," I said.

The silence came again and I decided to wait it out.

I studied my shoe tops for several minutes before I heard a soft sob. Looking up then, I saw that her eyes were moist.

"It's difficult, isn't it?" I said.

"Y-yes."

I offered her my handkerchief, but she shook her head and used her sleeve.

I wanted whatever was causing this, but I did not know how to go after it. There seemed to be no handles. It could be a delayed reaction over Carl. It could be something quite different. I could not tell.

"You are a success now," she finally said.

"That is a very relative term."

"But you are, and I am glad for you."

"Thanks. I guess I chose a poor time to come to town, though. I wanted to find you happy, to take you someplace where there is laughter. I wanted—"

"You sometimes thought of me after you left?" she interrupted.

"Oh yes. Often."

She smiled weakly at this, so I went over and sat down beside her, put an arm about her shoulders. She did not resist. She began to cry again, though, and she leaned against me. I let her go on this way for a long while.

"It could have been so good," she finally said, her cheek against my chest. "...Then everything went wrong. I am born to lose, always."

It reminded me of something long gone by, but I said nothing. There followed a seizure of hiccups, then more tears.

"...It was just about perfect," she said. "Perfect..."

"Until today," I speculated.

"Until today," she agreed. "Now, both of them...Both of them!"

"Sad."

"I don't know what to do. I really don't."

"You are still young, pretty, employed."

"Rotting," she said. "Everything has gone rotten. To lose another. We were so close, so close to it."

"Now…" I ventured.

"Now," she said, "I feel an ancient widow all in black. Now it is over."

"Twice," I said, catching the drift with hackle-raising suddenness. "This time Claude Bretagne."

The alcohol had slowed both her reflexes and her thinking. It took several seconds before I felt her stiffen.

"How…? How did you know?" she said softly.

"I know many things," I told her. "I even know about the money. First you lost Carl, now Claude. How did this one happen?"

"I don't know," she said. "I don't understand what happened."

"How did you find out about it?"

"What does it matter to you?"

"A great deal," I said. "I'm in trouble, and you can help me by telling me about this."

"Will I get in trouble, too?"

"No."

"All right," she said, pushing away from me and sitting up straight. "All right."

She lit a fresh cigarette, then rose and walked to the window.

She stared out for a time, then began: "Yes, we were lovers, Claude and I. Does that make me seem wicked? To have seduced a priest? Or to have let him have his way with me? It wasn't that way at all. We met by accident one day, in the gallery. We were showing the works of several South American artists. He came to look and we began talking about them. He knew quite a bit about South America, and I was interested. He seemed very lonely, and I was lonely, too. We began talking of other matters then, and later we had lunch together. He came to the gallery quite often after that, and each time we would go for a walk or a glass of wine. We would do something, together. This simply went on, and on. Until finally we became lovers."

She paused and flicked an ash out the window.

"The details are none of your business," she said then. "We were in love, we were happy for a time.

"I forgot about Carl. I forgot about the old days and the things we did then. Claude talked of giving up the priesthood to marry me. But there was a thing that stood in the way. For a long while, he would not tell me what it was. I knew it could not involve his feelings or beliefs so much, for he was quite radical in his views on most of the Church's policies. Then he told me of the nature of his work, and if he left there would be an auditing of the accounts he handled. If they went into them very, very deeply, he said, there would be trouble. I was shocked. I had thought that such things were out of my life forever. He did not explain any more for a time, but he told me to trust him. I did."

Then she turned and faced me.

"You know or you have guessed this much?" she asked.

"Yes."

"What else do you know about it?"

"Very little."

"And you really need to know more to keep yourself out of trouble?"

"Yes."

"I trust you. I have always trusted you," she said. "But I must have your word if I am to tell you more."

"My word as to what?"

"That you will help me to find his killer," she said.

I thought rapidly, suppressing all physical reactions, then said, "Very well. You have my word."

She studied me for several long heartbeats.

"How long have you known he was dead?" she asked.

"Just since you told me."

"All right," she said. "Now I know why you are a good card player. I believe you.

"About a month ago," she went on, closing her eyes and massaging them with thumb and forefinger, "he changed. In a single day. He seemed very depressed, but at first he would not tell me what was bothering him. This went on for several days. He began using my telephone to place calls out of the country."

"Where to?"

"South America. Brazil. He has a brother there."

"What did they talk about?"

"I don't really know. I am not even positive it was always his brother he talked to. I just assumed that—as I assumed the calls themselves dealt with the money."

"Why?"

"Because he later told me he had become depressed because it seemed his superiors were growing suspicious. He began to worry about their finding him out. Then he began making plans to leave the country."

"Do you know how much money was involved?"

She shook her head.

"A large sum. That is all he told me."

"What happened next?"

"He came and stayed with me for a time while we made arrangements, long enough for him to obtain identification papers under another name. Then we made reservations at a small hotel in Lisbon. He went on ahead and telephoned me when he was safely checked in. I waited then for him to notify me when it would be safe to follow."

"Why the delay?"

"He was to obtain new papers for both of us as man
and wife, under another name. These would show us to
be Portuguese citizens. Since we did not know how long
it would take to obtain them, I was to wait for him to call
me—and to tell anyone who asked after him that I did
not know where he was."

"*Did* anyone show up to ask?"

"Yes. Two men. They said they were from the Vatican,
that they wanted to locate him. I told them I knew nothing.
That is all. They never returned."

"I see. Then what?"

"When the papers were ready, he was to make flight
reservations for us, either to São Paulo or Brasilia—it
depended on information he was going to obtain in the
meantime. Then he was to notify me, so that I might join
him in Lisbon and we could leave together."

She dropped her eyes then, turned her back on me
and stared out the window once again.

"Then everything went wrong," she said.

I decided on silence, waited.

"He telephoned and said there had been a new development, and he would have to change our plans. He was
going to go alone. After he arrived and dealt with certain
matters, he would contact me and tell me where to meet
him, what to do. He told me not to worry. Said that he
would take care of everything."

"When was all this?"

"Yesterday."

"Yesterday!"

"Yes. Just a little while before you called. I was still
deciding what to do when you rang."

"Did he tell you why he was doing this? Did he say
what these new developments were?"

"No. He would not tell me."

"Did he sound worried? Agitated?"

"Yes. Both. But again he would not tell me why. So I decided to discover the reason for myself. I was able to get passage on a late flight to Lisbon. I took a cab to the hotel. That is were I found him…dead."

"How was he killed?"

"He was shot," she said softly, "in the head."

"How did you get into the room?"

"The man at the desk gave me a key. He had left word when he checked in that his wife would be joining him. I carried a small bag. I wore a ring. I went up and found him lying there."

"Any signs of a struggle?"

"Yes. The room was in disorder. Things were broken, thrown about…And he was lying there on the floor with blood on his face. He—he'd been shot beneath the left eye."

She raised her hands and muffled a sob.

"Was the gun there?"

"I didn't see it. I didn't search the room, though."

"What did you do then?"

"I was feeling scared and sick. I backed out of the room and closed the door. Then I left. I didn't go past the desk. I took the back steps."

"Did anybody see you leave?"

"I don't think so."

"Did you leave anything behind in the room?"

"No."

"Or take anything out of it?"

"No. I just wanted to get out."

"What did you do then?"

"I dropped the key in a mailbox and called the police on a public phone. I gave them the name of the hotel and told them that there had been a murder in Room 333. Then I hung up and returned to the airport. I caught a flight back to Rome, and it was morning when I came in. I phoned the gallery and told them I was ill. You know the rest."

"I see," I said, and I rose and crossed the room and put my hands on her shoulders and kept them there until she stopped shaking.

Then we returned to the sofa and sat there for a long while.

"What should I do?" she asked me in a faraway voice.

"Nothing, now. I have to think about it, and I'm a slow thinker. I'll let you know tomorrow. Where…?"

"I will be here," she said. "You have not forgotten your promise?"

"No."

And we sat there until she began to yawn, which of course made me do the same thing.

"Do you think you'll be able to sleep?" I asked.

"Yes," she said. "If I can't, I'll take a pill. I don't think I'll need one, though."

I rose, fetched my jacket.

"I left my number on the pad beside your telephone."

She nodded. She got to her feet then and accompanied me to the door.

"Be sure to bolt this thing after me."

"Yes," she said, tilting her head and studying my face, "just like the old days."

"Good night."

She squeezed my hand.

"Good night."

I went away then, counting new questions, wrong answers and funny feelings, step by downward step.

I was awakened by the ringing of the telephone before I was ready to get up. But then, if there had been no telephone, I still would not have been ready to get up. I never am. Consciousness is a cold statue in a pigeon-infested park, scoured each morning by the mysterious and not altogether benign processes of certain bodily fluids whose existence I resent daily. Asked by a psychologist I once knew what animal I would most prefer being if I could not be a man, I immediately replied, "A tapeworm." He had asked me before I'd had my morning coffee.

Between obscenities, I snatched up the receiver and told the caller to go away.

"Did I awaken you, Ovid?" came Bruno's polite voice, with the smugness of one who has been up for hours and is proud of the fact.

"No, but you interrupted my jai alai game."

He chuckled, then asked me whether I would join him for lunch.

"All right," I said. "It's the least you can do."

"Fine. I will pick you up at the hotel at one o'clock."

"Good. See you then."

"Goodbye."

"Goodbye."

My fluids refused to reverse their mysterious and ungentlemanly actions, so I staggered off to the bathroom to start the day on a clean foot. By the time I had finished my work, so had they. So I dressed myself and went out for coffee and rolls.

Eating and meditating, I organized my thoughts around my mission and the information I had so far collected. I would have to beat it all into shape and get it to the man at the embassy before too many hours passed. My own status would doubtless be influenced by it. I hoped that upon checking my report with Portuguese authorities, someone would be satisfied that I had done everything asked of me by locating the priest, would thank me in a cold, stiff fashion, so that I could feel ever more resentful, and tell me I was off the hook and could go home now. If such were the case, certain things about this business would always bother me; but then, I've learned to live with the fact that lots of things do and more doubtless will. As for my promise to Maria, it would be kept to the letter, when my report stimulated further investigation requiring the apprehension of Claude's killer.

Enough to somewhat brighten my morning, there. I decided to leave it at that and take a walk, while I made up my mind as to the things I was going to say and the manner in which I was going to report them.

Later, I telephoned the embassy, and after two rigmaroles and one wait got to talk to the security officer, who was named Martinson. I began telling him the story I had heard and he interrupted and told me he did not want to hear it over the telephone, that I should come to the embassy immediately and report in person. I told him that was impossible, but that I could make it later in the afternoon or in the evening. He asked me why.

"I can't tell you over the telephone," I said, with perverse delight.

So we made arrangements to meet in the early evening at his apartment, which bore a respectable address on the Via Veneto. He sounded as if he had correctly assumed that I was putting him out on purpose.

Why not? He was just another arm of my persecutor, so far as I was concerned, to be jostled whenever I could get away with it. Besides, I'd be damned if I'd miss that free lunch with Bruno. He liked good restaurants and good food, and he might have some interesting shop talk or gossip.

I telephoned Maria then, sympathized with her over her hangover and told her that I would be in touch with her later in the evening. She made affirmative noises to this, which I took as a good sign.

Then I strolled, slowly, back toward the hotel. The sun was warm and cheerful in a smooth, kind sky. Upon reflection, I noticed that I was almost happy.

"...and so, what do you hope to find in Brazil?" Bruno was asking me, having just finished a ten-minute rundown on the current state of the arts in that country.

At his last word, I removed my gaze from the rear of the retreating waitress and executed a small shrug I had learned in Naples.

"A change of scene, romance, exercise...Who knows?" I said, toying with my wine glass. "Perhaps this trip will hold me for a time. I may not even need to go to Brazil."

"Oh?"

He raised his glass, sipped from it and lowered it slightly.

"Then you will be returned to New York soon?"

"Possibly," I said. "It depends on so many things. I do not know for certain yet."

"But it is likely to be within the next few weeks?" he persisted.

"I simply do not know."

"Damn it!" he said. "You are just as secretive now that you are a legitimate businessman as you were in the old days!"

I smiled before I shrugged this time.

"You misread me," I said. "I can't tell you what I don't know myself."

"I inquire," he said, "because there is something I wish to ask of you. If you were going back again soon, I wondered whether you would be interested in taking

Gladden's unsold works, exhibiting them and keeping them on consignment for a time?"

I sipped my wine and thought about it.

"What about your own operation there?"

He shook his head.

"It is a matter of space and time," he said. "We are filled to the brim and booked solid with exhibits. It would be close to a year before we could set him up properly."

"So? He may be worth more in a year's time."

Bruno frowned.

"You know there is more to this business than the commercial end of things," he said. "Paul Gladden is ready for a good exhibit in New York. He is an artist, not a piece of merchandise. I want to see him receive the recognition he deserves. You have been building a solid reputation in recent years. Since I cannot give him that publicity at this time, you would be a good choice. Are you interested?"

"What sort of terms are you thinking?"

"For me?" he said. "Nothing. At the moment, I am only interested in furthering Mister Gladden's career. I like his work, I like him personally. I feel that one day soon he will be acknowledged as one of the great ones." He smiled at this. "Perhaps then, he will remember that I helped him along a bit," he finished.

"In other words, I would handle his works on a straight percentage basis—no strings attached?"

"That is correct, and fair. You would be doing all the work."

"Quite altruistic of you," I said. "I wonder what Mister Gladden would say?"

"He was quite enthusiastic when I mentioned the possibility to him last night," he said. "I would have introduced you, but you had already left the gallery by then.

Still, I can arrange a meeting before you leave town. What are your feelings?"

"Yes," I said, "I'd like to meet him."

"...and you will have an exhibit at the Taurus—soon?"

"Yes. I can do that fairly soon after my return. My calendar is nowhere near so filled as yours."

"Excellent!" he said, raising his glass and clicking it against my own.

As he refilled them, he said, "My heart would have been heavy, but if you had told me 'no', it would not have been the first time I had had to turn away a talented individual after a brief exposure, to make way for better known artists. It is sad, but then there are the stern realities of business. One can only accommodate so many."

"Space and time," I agreed. "Truer for you than myself right now. I must confess I somewhat envy you your quandary."

"Why," he went on, as if not having heard me, "there is a boy in Greece—only seventeen years old—who has done grotesques worthy of Goya. I have sold several of his things, but politics..." He grimaced. "And there is a woman—Aleda, she signs herself—a schoolteacher in Belgrade. Primitive. Very powerful. And two French women—sisters—who did not begin painting until quite late in life. How they do the female figures!" He kissed his fingertips and smiled. "They are lesbians, of course. But this is good. It is always a labor of love that way. And an old man in Denmark with a house full of eerie statues he has made...Beautiful! When he dies who knows what his relatives may do with them? He is eccentric—mad, perhaps. Who will ever know or care but a few such as ourselves?"

"It is a pity."

"Another man might say, 'Since I cannot handle them,

let them be. Else, they may cause me difficulty one day.'
But I am not such a man. I have been thinking…"

He paused and took a sip of wine.

"Would you be interested?" he said then. "It sounds as
if, having snatched up the best, I am offering you what
remains—and this is true. Still, what remains is of considerable value, and some of it of intrinsically greater worth
than much that I am forced to handle. I love art sufficiently to abet its recognition, though."

"What would you want for all these leads, Bruno? We
are still competitors."

"Not really, not at the same level," he said. "I would
not think of touching some of the things you handle, nor
you some of mine. This does not preclude our appreci-
ating their merits, however. If I would—and I must—
pass along news of such items, I might as well give it to a
friendly competitor, to someone I have known and trusted
for a long while—"

"What do you want in return?" I interrupted. "I am not
—repeat, *not*—in the old business any longer. I have a
clean record in my own country. So if you're leading up to
something along those lines, forget it."

He sighed, then smiled.

"It would be hypocritical of me to take offense," he
said, "and I do not despise my own roots. But I was hon-
estly not thinking of anything of the kind. I wish to see
these artists receive some real public exposure, because
they deserve it. If I am to do someone a favor of throwing
business into his lap, I would rather it be a friend than a
stranger. That is all. I can see how you would misunder-
stand, though. If it will make you feel any better, please
feel free to do me favors also, whenever you wish."

He smiled then and finished his wine.

"My apologies," I said. "Of course I am interested."

"I have photographs of some of their works with me,"

he said, still smiling, "and the names and addresses of the artists."

He produced a large, heavy envelope from inside his jacket, opened it and began spreading pictures.

Then I could tell why he was grinning. Even from photographs I could tell.

They were all of them good. Very good.

After many long minutes I looked up and said, "You're right, of course. They deserve to be shown."

"Then you think you will handle them?"

"Yes," I said. "Certainly."

He poured us the last of the wine. We drank it and he picked up the check.

The day faded into evening: Buildings and foundations raked and dappled by well-placed lights. A full, clean lunatics' or lovers' moon high in the sky. Prospect of candlelit cafes. Violins and flowers. Stuff like that.

My mood had advanced sufficiently so that no real rancor remained when my cab deposited me in front of Mister Peter Martinson's small villa. He answered my ring himself, and while I could not tell much from the brick wall that kept the world outside, the interior proved to be a comfortable bachelor's lair.

My thoughts of maintaining a cold politeness faded after a moment or two. He was an affable enough fellow, somewhere in his mid-fifties, somewhere between husky and fat, white eyebrows matching what remained of his hair, remnants of a military manner about him. He had on sandals and wore a dark green dressing gown over slacks and a shirt. We shook hands and moved into his living room, where I decided to accept a drink after all.

He hooked a leg over the arm of his chair, took a healthy slug of his drink, smiled and said, "Okay, tell me about it."

"Is this being recorded?" I asked him, for curiosity's sake.

"Yes," he said. "I find it easier than taking notes. The recorder is part of my stereo setup and the mike is under that table." He gestured, indicating both pieces of furniture. "If it really bothers you, I can make do without. But it's strictly for my own use and I'll erase it when I've finished."

I shrugged, said, "Academic curiosity," and began telling him about the people with whom I had spoken and what they had said.

At first, he interrupted only occasionally, with small questions to clarify small points. Then we were both interrupted by a telephone call to which he said, "Sorry, you have the wrong number," and hung up. When I got to Maria's story his expression changed, and he leaned forward and did not say anything until I had finished. Then, "Damn it!" he said, punching his palm. "Why didn't you get word to me sooner?"

Since I couldn't come up with a good lie fast enough, I told him the truth.

Then hellfire flashed in his eyes, spread across his face in an instant, red sheet. His mouth tightened and his cheeks rose. He proceeded to demonstrate that years of desk work had not robbed him of a first-class military vocabulary.

Despite my earlier mellowness, there was plenty of fuel inside me and a spark leapt the gap. I do not like being pushed around, by anybody. Especially for reasons unknown.

So I waited, I lit a cigarette and waited. I composed myself while he chewed me out, ignoring his words and waiting for them to stop.

Finally they did, and I spoke very softly then.

"So fire me," I said. "Or dock me my next paycheck."

He started in again, then stopped. He stared at me as if I had suddenly become a different person, then seemed to collect himself and address the new guy.

"You don't understand…" he said, and it was somewhere halfway between a question and a statement.

"Why not tell me? All about it," I said. "I might be a lot more useful if I know more."

He shook his head.

"You know why," he said.

"The old need-to-know bit?"

"The same. I'd like to tell you more, believe me. Hell! I don't even know the whole story!"

I shrugged, drew on my cigarette, swallowed some more of his excellent bourbon.

"Well," I said, "if Maria's story checks out—and I'm sure it will—I'm pretty much out of the picture, aren't I? I mean, they wanted me to find the priest. Okay, I did. Mission accomplished and all that. Right?"

He appeared to ponder, for the space of a drink and the lighting of a small, evil-looking cigar.

"You may well be correct," he finally said. "I simply do not know. I'll probably have definite information for you after I've relayed what you've told me so far. I'll include your query when I send things along."

"How long do you think it will take?"

"A day. Perhaps two," he said, the blue-white atmosphere of his exhalations creeping toward me. "I don't know what my opinion will be worth, but I'll recommend patting you on the head and sending you home. I don't see what more they could expect of you—unless I'm missing something they had in mind. You were one person the girl was likely to talk to—an old friend with no particular fondness for the law—and talk she did. My guess would be that that's all they will want of you.

"In the meantime, though," he went on, "I want you to

continue to keep an eye on her. Be with her as much as possible, and learn everything else that you can about Father Bretagne. Friends, enemies, likes, dislikes. Anything that can help us—"

"...get back the money," I finished, as the doorbell interrupted him.

"Exactly," he said, rising. "Excuse me a moment, will you?" and he passed into the small entranceway, turned toward the door, moved out of sight.

I heard him take hold of the doorknob. Then for some reason he paused and said, "Who is it?"

"Embassy messenger," came the partly muffled reply.

"All right."

I heard the door open then, followed by a puffing sound I had not heard in ages. I might not even have recognized it had it not been followed by a sharp cough and a wheeze, unlike that of one who is simply clearing his throat. There was a brief moan and a crash, as of someone falling or being pushed to the floor.

I sprang to my feet, knowing it was a gun with a silencer that had made the noise. By then, though, the man was already in the room with me and the gun swinging in my direction.

He tried to say something as I tried diving forward, and neither of us was very successful. The gun did not puff this time. It emitted the peace-pulverizing blast guns generally do, right before I slammed into the floor near the man's feet.

He had missed me, I learned several heartbeats later.

It was either my loopy luck, my stumbling swan dive, his half-aimed shot, or all of these. But he had missed.

As I scrambled to regain my footing, I was knocked to my knees by a heavy blow on my right shoulder as he swung the gun downward, using it as a club.

As I caught myself with my hands, he swung the weapon

sideways, striking me a mean blow near the top of my head.

I skinned my left elbow as I fell toward that side, trying to roll with it…

…and as I looked upward through the spark-shot, dancing piece of reality that separated us, trying to make my muscles drive me upward, forward and through him, I saw that he had swung the muzzle toward my face and was smiling as he pulled the trigger.

The click was deafening.

Then he made a mistake in choosing between two possible reactions.

Instead of bashing me again, he made a quick attempt to unjam the pistol.

He managed one oath before my already-aching head struck him below the belt and sent him sprawling backward, the weapon falling from his grasp and landing beneath me where I fell.

I seized it to use as a club as he doubled, then rolled onto his hands and knees, facing me.

I found myself pointing it as he reached out with his right hand, and my reflexes jerked my trigger-finger toward me.

This time it did not jam. Perhaps the impact when it struck the floor…

He slumped forward, face down, and sprouted wet, red antlers upon the rug.

The bullet had entered his forehead and emerged at a sticky looking point behind his right ear…

Rapid footfalls in the entranceway caused me to raise the weapon in time. I had a glimpse of an ambiguous expression on the new man's face and of the pistol in his right hand—thankfully held high, in anticipation of a standing target—before I squeezed the trigger again and caught him in the shoulder.

His weapon clattered to the floor and he turned and ran as I scored the far wall with another round and heard it ricochet.

By the time I managed to get to my feet and out into the entranceway, I heard a car door slam. He had parked his car right beside the curb, with its engine running. I leaned back against the door frame as his tires screeched, and resting my right wrist upon my left forearm, took aim and emptied the weapon at the retreating vehicle.

The second shot shattered the rear window. I don't know what the final one did.

The car continued on, gathering momentum as I sagged. Then, four long seconds later, it swerved suddenly, crossed pavement, curb, sidewalk, and struck the side of a building near the corner, shaking loose bricks down about it. After a few moments it began to burn.

I knew that the street would not be deserted much longer. Except by me.

VI.

I stepped back inside and locked the door. Automatically, I wiped the pistol on my jacket before dropping it to the floor. I stared down at poor old Martinson, then stooped and felt for a pulse. There was none.

I tried to stand, grew dizzy and dropped to all fours. My right arm almost gave way then, and my shoulder felt ready to explode. Perspiration suddenly beaded my forehead, and when I was able to wipe it away I saw that it had mingled with blood. I strove to control my breathing, succeeded, crawled forward.

Then I took my first real look at my assailant. Despite deep creases between his eyebrows and along his cheeks, I guessed his age at around twenty-five. He had a dark complexion, black hair, flaring nostrils. All the pockets of his cheap, dark suit were empty.

Regaining my feet by stages, I crossed the room and raised the telephone from its cradle. I heard the sound of a distant rock band and a subdued murmur of voices. Whoever had phoned earlier had not broken the connection at his end, effectively tying up Martinson's line. I replaced the receiver and headed toward the rear of the dwelling.

I located his kitchen and discovered a door that let upon a small, walled garden. A brief exploration there led me to a gate which opened upon what appeared to be a narrow alleyway.

I paused before unlatching it.

It did not seem likely there would be another of them

in the alley. No. With two unsuspecting victims, one driver-backup man and another to do the actual meat work was all that would seem necessary.

Still, I shuddered. I wanted to be away, far and fast. I wanted to fade from the world and come back on a sunny day. The gate seemed to lean in that direction.

Taking several deep breaths, I flung it open. I tucked my shoulder and gritted my teeth as I did so, went through and hit the ground rolling.

Nothing. I was alone.

I lay there shivering and aching for several moments before I climbed to my feet. I dusted off my clothing, wiped my face and hands with my handkerchief and ran my comb though my hair. I almost screamed at the last. Once my comb was in my hand, my reflexes had taken over. But my hand was no longer its usual self. I settled for a light brushing back with my fingertips.

Then came the old one foot after the other business as I turned right, heading away from the corner where the smashup occurred.

Between silent curses, walking, I was able to think once more, as my spinal nerves slowly returned control of things to my forebrain.

Three dead men, two of them by my hand, behind me; a fourth, the priest, getting stiffer in Lisbon; a fifth, Carl Bernini, whose choice of a deathbed had served to get me into this thing…

That was one thought.

Now an attempt had been made on my life. Which made no sense at all. I knew nothing that would so jeopardize anyone that he should consider my removal necessary. I eliminated coincidence from my calculations. I simply could not believe that my visit with Martinson just happened to coincide with the time when someone was planning to remove his name from the list of the living. No. I had been sitting quietly in the living room and the man with the gun had come to me, as if he had expected to find me there.

But if it was me he was after, why not go for me sometime when I could be found alone? Ditto for Martinson, if he were the only target. A double killing is always more risky than a single one.

It indicated they were after both of us, and the only reason I could see for a combination like that would be an assumption that I had something important to tell him and had gone there to do so. It had become necessary to destroy the information at that point.

Information. I needed it now, to keep alive. Someone had already drawn a line through my name, stuck a pin in my doll and driven a nail into my coffin.

That was thought number two.

I walked for perhaps twenty minutes before I began making my way back toward the main thoroughfare. By then, the sound of sirens was a thing of the past.

I crossed the street immediately when I reached it and began making my way south. After a time, I located a cab, decided against returning to my hotel, gave the driver a fake address several blocks from Maria's place and closed my eyes.

I once spent a day looking after my sister's kids. I took them presents to keep them amused and settled down with a book I was reading. Only I had made the mistake of giving my nephew Timmy a toy drum. After a couple hours, I gave him my pocketknife and told him that drums were usually filled with candy. This solved the problem for a small while, and I still remember shaking my head and telling him, "Yours was one of the ones that wasn't."

My head was a toy drum with no sweets inside.

°

I walked past Maria's place several times, pausing periodically to skulk in doorways. I spent a good half-hour doing this. Passing beneath the window before which she had spent so much time the previous evening, I could see that her apartment was lighted. No one else seemed to be surveying the place.

Finally, I entered her building, hoping she had gotten everything out of her system and wasn't off on another bender. I wanted her full, fast, sober cooperation in what I suspected was necessary to preserve both our lives.

No one below, no one on the stair, the landings empty…

I waited outside her door, listening. Her radio was playing—a piece of an opera I did not recognize. I heard no other sounds.

Five or six minutes later I heard her walking about. Then came the sound of running water and the clinking of dishes and cutlery.

Softly, I knocked.

Her face broke into a smile when she opened the door and saw me, a smile that immediately reversed itself.

"You've been hurt!" she observed, reminding me of something Eugene O'Neill once said concerning the emergence of appropriately trite words at times of pain and emotion.

"I cut myself shaving," I said, pushing away her hand and stepping inside.

She followed me to the sofa and watched me flop down. "Coffee?" she asked. "I have some hot."

"Yes. Please."

While she fetched it I adjusted my position, arm behind my head, so that I would not stain her upholstery.

I watched her move about. She was wearing brown slacks and sandals, a white blouse, a dark apron printed with a peaceful harvest scene. Her long hair was brushed and shiny now, her face clean and composed. Moving on, I also saw that the apartment was now in trim shape.

While much better to look at, her face had a certain clamp-jawed determination about it which made me cast her as one of the Furies. While it was good to see that she seemed physically normal again, I was not unhappy over her probably still bruised feelings either. They might come in handy.

But she smiled again, faintly, when she brought the coffee.

"Our situations seem reversed," she said. "What happened?"

I ignored her question and asked, "Has anyone phoned or stopped by since last night?"

"No," she said. "No one."

"What about you? Did you go out or phone anybody?"

"Only the gallery," she said, "to tell them I was not able to come in today."

I lit a cigarette, leaned over the coffee cup.

"Your head!" she exclaimed. "You need a doctor!"

"I could use one," I told her. "But not now."

She held her thumb and forefinger about three inches apart as she leaned forward.

"It is about this long," she said, "and it looks deep. You should probably have stitches. I did not realize—"

"You should see it from this side," I said, gulping coffee. "Listen. There is no time now. I am in danger. Someone just tried to kill me. The only reason I can see for it is my interest in Claude. Since you are my source of information on the subject, I believe that you are in danger also. I have no idea how they learned about me so quickly or who they are. I am going to fade from the scene now, though, and I think you had better come with me."

"I do not understand," she said. Then she indicated my head. "But that is real enough. You feel that we are in immediate danger?"

I nodded.

"Every minute that we stay here—in this place, in this town. In this country, for that matter. That is why I want you to pack two suitcases immediately and be ready to leave with me in fifteen minutes."

"That is impossible," she said, meeting my eyes for a moment, then nodding, "but I will do it.

"You are somewhat conspicuous," she added.

"I'll clean up while you get your things together."

"There is blood on your jacket and shirt. Your trousers are torn and stained."

"I can't go back to my hotel to change. Someone may be watching for me now."

She looked away, then said, "Claude left a gray jacket here. He was about your size."

"Oh? He liked to run around in civvies?"

"When we were together, yes."

"Did he leave anything else?"

"Just some handkerchiefs, hose and underwear that were in the wash. An extra pair of shoes that would not fit in his bag."

"I see. Yes, if you would get me the jacket and hunt up a couple of safety pins for my pantleg, I'll start getting ready."

I sat up straight. I ingested more smoke and coffee and tried to translate them into thought.

I had a pocketful of travelers checks, a small amount of Italian currency, assorted credit cards and a thousand dollars, U.S., in a money belt I wear when I travel. For a time, therefore, there would be no pressing need for cash. My passport, fortunately, was still in my pocket. No problem there. I was in a position to move quickly.

I watched Maria rummage through her closet, emerging

at last with a dark, shaggy jacket that looked as if it would do nicely. She brought it to me, and as I tried it on for size she asked me, "Where is it we are going?"

"Brazil," I replied. "Not a bad fit."

"Brazil? To see Claude's brother?"

"Most likely. The answers are probably where the money is, and he happens to be in the same place. By the way, do you have his address?"

"No, but I have his telephone number. Claude wrote it in my directory."

"São Paulo?"

"Yes."

"Good. Get it, find those pins and go pack."

She hesitated.

"Ovid," she said, "I trust you, or I would not be going with you. But I want to know more about this. What is happening, and why are you involved? Why was Claude killed? For the money he took?"

"I do not know why Claude was killed," I said, "though I am certain it has something to do with the money. This is one of the things we must find out."

"How much was it, Ovid? How much did he take?"

"Three million dollars, give or take a few cents."

She drew away from me, then sat down and stared at the floor.

"I do not believe you," she said finally. "They audit those records. There are many ways to check. A man would be found out—quickly."

"Claude was found out. That's why he ran. Also, he was very clever and in a position of extreme trust. That's why it took them so long to find out."

"So much money…" she said. "It is fantastic."

"Yes."

"Why was there no mention in the papers? Or on television?"

"The Church is keeping it quiet. Bad publicity."

"What is your part in all this?"

"Too long a story," I said, shaking my head. "It will have to wait."

She smiled as she turned away.

"It is good to know that he was the best," she said.

It took us more than fifteen minutes to get ready. It took a little over twice that time. I spent a large part of it soaking, sponging and rinsing my scalp. I succeeded in removing most of the blood, but I also got the thing to bleeding again several times. I finally staunched it with a wad of toilet tissue which I left in place till we were ready to go. Regretting the lack of a hat, I settled for slicking my hair back to cover the offending area. I pinned the tear in my pantleg and sponged off most of the dirt. I tried soap and water on my shirtfront, but once a blood-stain always a bloodstain. I would have to keep the jacket buttoned.

A telephone call assured us two seats on a morning flight out. We called for a cab then and locked up the apartment. Emil Bretagne's number in my pocket, I hefted both suitcases—the lighter in my right hand—and we started down the stairway, me leading. We had made the turn at the landing and were partway down the second when we heard the distant ringing of a telephone.

"It's mine," she said, turning. "I can tell. Should I get it?"

"Go ahead," I said, "and you're still sick, you haven't seen me and you're not planning any trips."

She nodded and hurried back. I continued on to the next landing, rested the luggage and my arms, waited. There was no one at the foot of the next stair.

As I debated lighting another cigarette, I heard a door slam overhead, then the sound of descending footsteps.

"Nobody," she said, swinging into sight. "There was no one there when I answered it."

"Was there a dial tone or a click?"

"No. Just silence."

"Any sounds of breathing, shuffling of feet—little noises?"

"I could not tell. I was breathing rapidly myself. Possibly, though."

"Come on," I said, hefting the suitcases and moving toward the stair. "Is there another door to this place?"

"At the rear of the basement," she replied. "What is wrong?"

"Later," I said, moving fast as I could.

There came a tingling in the soles of my feet, the palm of my hands and the nape of my neck. As I reached the ground floor and headed toward a door Maria indicated at the rear of the hall, I noticed that my mouth had already gone dry. I read somewhere that this is a very old reflex, a device to help kill your scent when fleeing predators. It is instructive to consider the body's attitude toward a few thousand years of civilization.

I slowed when I reached the door, let Maria open it, find the switch and lead the way down toward the faint light that occurred. The steps were rickety and steep. The single light bulb hung like a dirty piece of fruit above a tool-cluttered table. We picked our way among damaged furniture, broken appliances, filthy cartons tied with dusty cords, a bust of Mussolini and stacks of moldering periodicals, occasionally encountering an untenanted spider web.

At last we reached a door, which Maria unbolted with some effort. I led the way up a crumbling brick stair and into a wide alley, illuminated here and there by the spillage from rear windows.

"Which way?" I asked. "I don't want to make it easy on them."

"Go right," she said. "What was it about the phone call?"

"My evening began that way, and three men are dead already."

"Did you…?"

"Yes. Two of them."

She guided me up the alley and into a side alley then, silently.

After several more turnings, I was not certain as to my direction. I was cold and my shoulder throbbed each time my heel struck the ground. My headache kept my mind off it part of the time, though.

A few rats hurried to avoid us. The sound of traffic was a faraway thing. I counted two hundred more paces, then said, "Wait."

I lowered the suitcase to the ground. I stood panting and rubbing my shoulder. My armpits were damp and my feet were sore.

Suddenly I felt her hand on my own. Her touch was cool.

"You are shaking," she said. "You were hurt and you are tired. I will take the suitcases now."

"Just let me catch my breath," I said.

But she picked them up and I did not protest. I was not sure how far I could have gotten with them.

"How much farther to a main drag?" I asked, following her.

"Oh, it is not far," she said.

But she lied. At least, it seemed a good distance before we emerged on a lighted street and I was cheered by the sight of people and the passage of traffic.

"There is a café in the middle of the next block," she said, turning left.

"Good."

It was a quiet, neighborhood bar, only partly filled. We took a corner table near the door and stashed the luggage behind us.

"Quickly," I said, "get to the phone and call the police. Give them your name and address and tell them you think someone is trying to break into your apartment. Then hang up. We may be able to discomfort the enemy. Then call us a cab."

"Very good," she said, and left me.

I ordered two brandies in her absence and drank hers too, before she returned. I ordered two more and lit a cigarette.

"All right," she said, sliding into the seat across from me, "I've done as you said."

"Good."

"What *is* going on?" she whispered. "You never used to get involved in things like this, Ovid. Million dollar thefts...Killings..."

"I know—and I don't much like the idea now. It's too late, though. Something I've done has apparently scared somebody besides myself. It seems you're included— because of Claude, because of me. You were safe till I showed up, though, so I must be the catalyst. Why, I don't know—and I need to know. I've been searching my mind, going over everything I've done since I arrived in Rome, and I can't find the answer. Maybe I'm too sleepy, or it's something too obvious. We have to find out though, so we can stop whoever it is before they reach us. That means we have to run now, keep them at a distance until we can strike back."

"You mean, kill them?"

"If necessary," I said, "though I hope something less strenuous will suffice."

"Will they pursue us out of the country, d'you think?"

I took a sip of my brandy.

"My guess is yes," I said. "If they find out where we are, I'm sure they'll make another try. If it is so important as to warrant drastic action, they will be looking for us. The thing has international ramifications and the trail leads to Brazil."

"You are certain of this?"

"Fairly."

"Then we may be heading toward something even worse than what we seem to be leaving behind."

"Possibly. But this time I'm forewarned."

"They will be, too—and you say they almost got you tonight."

"That's right."

"What saved you?"

"Luck. A gun jammed."

She dropped her eyes and stared at my hands. Her hair was somewhat out of place, her face soft in the dim light of the table lamp. At that moment, I realized she looked quite lovely.

She glanced up and smiled self-consciously when she realized I was staring at her.

"Luck," she said, then raised her glass in a small salute. A moment later, her face clouded once more.

"Did you know either of them?" she asked.

"No."

"Who was the third?"

"A man named Martinson," I began, then wondered how much I should tell her. I trusted her, but—Well, she was a part of the thing and I was not certain where all her edges met with the rest of the picture. I could see no real reason for not telling her, but then I saw no reason for telling her either. When it came to the fact that I was an unwilling shill for the CIA, she had no real need to know.

"…he was a friend," I finished. "I was visiting him when they came for the hit."

"Oh," she said. "Then it is a matter of vengeance also?"

"Hardly," I said, "now. There were only the two of them. They've paid."

Her eyes flashed, something primeval, and she licked her lips twice as I gave her an abbreviated version of what had occurred. A childhood filled with vendetta chronicles? A passion for elementary justice? Or just plain violence? I could not tell. But her face had become more animated, had changed completely from the Madonna-like aspect she had worn moments earlier. She had cursed softly when she realized the significance of the dead telephone.

"I hope the one in the car was the man in Lisbon," she said.

I took another sip of brandy and sat there, wave after gratifying wave of numbness washing over me, in the coat of the dead man I had come to Rome to find, until the cab came for us and I forced my bones erect, unwilling last-minute Lazarus, and into the world again.

I'd slept, in the cab that took us to the airport, in the rimless peace symbol that slit the Atlantic skies. Maria had shaken me awake for breakfast; I had growled, mumbled, eaten, taken two aspirins, leaned back in the seat and closed my eyes again. Somewhere there had been a small nightmare which I could not remember. There had been no problem in obtaining the tickets, we had stashed the luggage and made ourselves inconspicuous till flight time. We had opted to remain in the terminal rather than ride around in a cab or take a room for the intervening hours —the idea being that even if we were spotted there, we would be safer with lots of humanity around us. No one apparently spotted us; or if someone did, all the things I hated about airports had rendered him impotent. Maria had removed her makeup, bound her hair beneath a scarf, donned glasses and hidden behind a book. We sat near to each other, though not together, while we waited, and I managed to doze behind a newspaper. Between then and boarding, when the shops were opened again, we obtained a small flight bag, shaving equipment, several handkerchiefs, a beret and a cheap, blond wig. While they were not much, the last two were the best items I could come up with in the way of disembarkment uniforms.

Now came a gentle nudge.

"*Do* you want another cup of coffee?" Maria was asking.

"Yes, please," I said, opening my eyes and raising my cup.

After I took several sips, she said, "Did you know that you snore?"

"Only when I can't sleep on my side," I said. Which is how I always do it, unless the alternative is unavoidable.

I sighed, lit a cigarette and stared out the window, hoping she would take the hint. I did not feel like talking.

She did, as moments later I heard the flutter of a magazine in her lap.

I do not like having to trust anybody, and I had thus far been forced to make an exception in her case. I had had no opportunity to check on her Lisbon story. For a time now, I would have to operate on the assumption that it was correct. Though I wanted details, I was in no position to get them. I would have to trust to my own feelings that a girl who had once hinted that she felt some affection for me, who now shared a peril with me, could be trusted. Shaky. Full of holes. But it was all I had.

I speculated as to my own status. For all I knew, the corpses of Martinson and his killer might not have been discovered yet. I had left the place closed up, and if no one had seen me firing after the car, it was possible that they were still where I had left them. With my fingerprints all over the place and the tape of our conversation on the recorder, of course.

…which meant that the Roman authorities would be wanting me for questioning, at least.

On the other hand, the embassy would be notified, which might result in their arranging to have things kept quiet while they screamed to Foggy Bottom for advice.

…which, of course, would result in some clucking and preening, as the chicken eventually marched in, perched on Collins' desk and laid its egg.

Either way—by Roman cops or the CIA—the passenger lists for outgoing flights would be checked. As my passport bore my name, so did the passenger list. But the initial chores of finding the dead man and identifying me as the person wanted would have delayed them sufficiently, I hoped, for me to have landed and faded by then.

I had wanted out of Italy before I ventured any contact with the CIA again. They had done such a lousy job taking care of me, as well as their own man, that a communications lag seemed a good idea. For all I knew, the information leak that had led to the killing could be in their own shop. Whatever, I was not about to extend any trust in their direction.

I took another sip and another drag.

I had been to Rio once, but I had never been to São Paulo. I knew nothing of the town and I knew no one in it. I would have to get some guidebooks and maps as soon as we landed.

"Have you ever been to São Paulo before?" I asked Maria.

"Yes," she said. "Years ago. With Carl."

"Oh?"

"Business," she said, with a slight smile. "This was after you had returned to the States."

"They can't miss our foreign accents," I said. "Do you recall whether they ask for your passport when you register at a hotel?"

She laughed.

"I do not know about the big hotels there," she said. "We did not stay at any of them. We stayed at a small place in Santos, about an hour's drive from São Paulo city. It was not such a good hotel, but there are hotels and boarding houses on every street. Santos is a weekend resort place on the ocean. I liked it. No one asked us for papers when we stayed there." She shrugged. "The ones we had were forged, anyway."

It sounded like a good idea. Carl's usually were. Except for his last one, of course.

"Do not worry about our accents," she added. "São Paulo is full of people with foreign accents."

"Then Santos it is," I said, and she nodded.

I returned my attention to wingtip, water and cloud.

I was revived and somewhat elated when we passed through the baggage pickup and customs without any difficulty. We purchased a stack of maps and tourist materials, consulted them quickly and sought a cab. I had found that the American Express office was on the Rua 7 Abril, located it on the map and told the driver to take us there. When we arrived, he wanted to wait for us, but we dismissed him, went inside and cashed a whole book of travelers cheques. I gave about a third of the money to Maria, then hefted the luggage and started walking.

We turned at the corner, walked a block, hit the Rua São Luiz and headed down it till we came to the Municipal Library. There we found a busy bus stop and waited for a bus that was only partly filled to come along. We boarded the first one that did and spent the next hour and a half changing busses.

I remembered Rio as a vast melange, combining all the races, containing vast riches and miserable poverty, featuring ultra-modern hotels and office buildings, colorful provincial enclaves and hillsides full of *favelas*—the most squalid slums I have ever seen; all of this bounded by mountains and ocean beaches, strewn with flowers, coursed by maniac drivers, spitted by the Tropic of Capricorn, cycling between lethargy and frenzy, infused with voodoo and sprinkled exotic appetites, concrete Christ on the Corcovado dashboard above.

São Paulo, on the other hand, reminded me of Chicago. From the air, it had seemed a great, prickly mass. Now that I moved among its high, serrated ranks, my first impression was that I was surrounded by an army of massive, glass-eyed robots, enormous energies churning their innards. I did not find this disenchanting, nor did I doubt there was more to it than a monarchy of masonry and metal. It aroused my curiosity as to the real city that lay behind this façade. In the case of Chicago, the removal of its mask proves a disappointment; with New York there is more, much more, to excite one's wonder, to hold it for a span of time. I lamented the brevity of life and the possibility that my own was about to become a special example of this rule.

We had not intended to ride the busses for as long as we did, but getting back downtown proved more complicated than we had anticipated. At the train station, Maria picked up a pair of tickets for Santos while I waited. The blonde wig made a difference in her appearance that was not unpleasant, though I liked her better the other way.

Fortunately, we did not have a long wait for a Santos-bound train. We boarded, found seats and cultivated patience. If the station was too busy for me to tell whether we were being observed, I consoled myself that it probably made us a bit more difficult to spot, also. We had moved and stood with groups of people most of the time, and we seemed to look like many of the Paulistas we saw, off for a holiday by the sea.

Before very long, we moved, rattling and swaying, into evening and the southeast. I studied the maps and booklets for a while, pretended to study them for a while longer as I scanned the other inhabitants of the car.

A family group of six, a very old couple, a rather attractive girl reading a magazine, three chattering women and a middle-aged man working a crossword puzzle were all that I could see without turning my head and staring. There were others toward the rear, and several empty seats.

I relaxed, sighed and lit a cigarette.

"How long?" I asked.

"The man said about an hour. Perhaps less."

I nodded.

"Good. I'm getting hungry."

We watched the town, then countryside, speed by. After a time, the moon rose. I was beginning to feel safer.

The following morning, I bought all new clothing and disposed of what I had been wearing in a convenient trash receptacle. Then I succeeded in renting a car and returned to the concrete block and stucco hostelry called The Plaza, where Maria and I had registered as Paul and Madeleine Timura, of Piracicaba, after some taxi-switching and walking, the previous evening. We had taken a room with double beds, the only one available, and walked to a small restaurant we had passed three blocks up the road. From there, I tried to telephone Emil Bretagne, but no one answered. I obtained his address from the operator then, learning that it was a "Mr. & Mrs." listing. I managed to get the number for Bassenrut Development next—the suspect organization which listed him as an officer. No answer there either, though again I obtained the address. After a large meal and a long, hot soak, I fell into bed and knew nothing till morning.

I tried Bassenrut again then. This time I got through, but was told that Emil was out of town and, no, they were not certain when he would be back—perhaps another week—and they did not know the details of his itinerary.

Rather than ringing his home again, I decided to visit it. We located his street on the map and marked the route. Then we set out driving, through what promised to be a beautiful day. The most recent day to have made such a promise having proved a liar, however, I remained skeptical.

The way was somewhat hilly, splashed with green and possessed of amazingly red soil. The air, through the open window, came clean and cool, and for a long while I could smell the morning and the sea we were leaving behind us. Wave-like, we mounted a continually rising plateau as we headed toward the city, and glancing back, I could see for a great distance.

When we neared the city's outskirts, we bore to the left, following the map, and we eventually entered a suburban residential area. About ten minutes later, we came to a small shopping complex and stopped there for lunch. I visited a hardware store afterwards and purchased some tools I thought might come in handy. I was not going to let something like absence of the owner keep me out of Emil Bretagne's place.

We continued on then, in a generally southern direction, and the residences began to grow larger and the distances between them greater. This progression continued as we drove on, and although the day grew warmer, increasing numbers of massive, roadside trees cast sufficient shade to compensate for it. Traffic eventually thinned to the point where we encountered other vehicles only occasionally.

Soon it became difficult to tell whether we were passing residences or sections cleverly landscaped to hide them. We continued to trust the map and wound our way through the rolling, colorful landscape until we came to a marker that proclaimed Emil's street. Turning there, we passed through more of the same and decided after a while that we had missed the place.

I was beginning to think of turning back to try it again when Maria spotted the upper portions of a house, high and far off the road to our left.

I slowed, seeking a driveway, and through a sudden gap in the trees saw that the house was a large, two-story place set on the crest of a small hill. The road curved, kept curving, almost seemed to be making a physical effort to hurry us on past a narrow driveway that suddenly appeared to the left. I hit the brakes then and regarded a post that stood beside it, bearing a small sign that contained a single word: Bretagne.

Turning, I proceeded down a mixture of white gravel and red soil that quickly bore us out of sight of the road. After a few moments, I heard running water and came to be driving beside a small stream. Further along, we came to a sturdy wooden bridge, gate bar upraised, and crossed over. Then it was upward, with several switchbacks, and into an oval—a flagpole and flower beds on its island— before the house itself. Two cars were parked there.

We parked near them, and having rehearsed our stories earlier, we headed up the walk prepared to tell them.

The door was opened partway by a small, dark, fat girl who seemed out of breath and partly crouched. When I took a step forward, she drew back, eyes widening, and the door moved several inches in our direction.

"My name is Paul Timura," I said, "and this is my wife, Madeleine. Is Mister Bretagne in?"

"No," she said. "He is away."

"Oh my," I said. "That *is* too bad. I hope his wife is in?"

She paused a moment, then opened the door and admitted us into a dark, cool entrance hall with a stained glass skylight.

"Please wait," She said, and vanished through the nearest of several low archways. There followed a murmur of voices, though I could not distinguish what was being said.

"I am frightened," Maria whispered.

"Why?"

"There is money here. Power too, perhaps. I did not know that Claude's brother was wealthy. If he wanted to, he could cause us more trouble."

I squeezed her hand, releasing it when I heard footsteps approach.

The girl appeared in the archway and said, "Come this way, please."

We followed her into a sitting room done up in French Provincial, which always makes me uneasy. Three men and a woman stood and faced us as we entered. The woman was small-boned, pale and around fifty. Her platinum hair looked as if it had just been set and she wore her makeup well. I found myself wondering how she had looked twenty years ago. She was still quite attractive.

"Mister Timura...?" she said, an uncertain smile on her lips, quick lines of puzzlement traced about her eyes.

"Yes," I said. "Paul Timura. This is my wife, Madeleine. I met Emil some time ago, on business, and we hit it off pretty well. We exchanged addresses, but we never did get together again. I just happened to be in the neighborhood and thought I'd stop by and say hello."

"I am afraid that he is out of town," she said.

"I knew I was taking a chance, but it was a nice morning for a drive in the country."

She continued to smile and indicated a short, pudgy

man whose tinted glasses did not conceal the puffiness about his eyes, nor their thick frames the fact that he lacked eyebrows. He had thin hair, wore a comfortable looking lightweight suit and his handshake was firm.

"This is Inspector Morales," she said, "and—his assistants."

"Victor and Dominic," he supplied. "I am pleased to meet you, Mister Timura." He nodded at Maria. "…and your lovely wife," he finished.

I shook hands with the other two—darker, larger, younger, more heavily muscled—and we mumbled the usual pleasantries.

Turning again to Mrs. Bretagne, "I am sorry to have interrupted you," I said. "I really should have telephoned —but it was one of those spur-of-the-moment things. If you will just give your husband my best wishes when he returns, we won't keep you from your company…"

I edged back a pace. I wanted to get the hell out of there.

"Oh no," she said. "Their call was professional, not social, and we've just about finished. Please be seated. Rose will bring you drinks. What would you care for?"

"Well—" I glanced around the room. No glasses were in sight. "Anything," I said. "Perhaps a beer."

Maria nodded.

"A beer, also," she said.

"Very good. And bring me a scotch and ginger ale," she told the girl. "Are you sure you gentlemen won't have anything?" she asked the three.

"Quite sure," said Morales, retreating toward the chair he had vacated. "We are still on duty. It is a rule."

We seated ourselves. Morales was studying me quite closely.

"Where are you from, Mister Timura?" he inquired.

"Piracicaba," I replied, making it sound more conversational than his question. "I hope that nothing serious has happened here."

"I am afraid that something did," he said. "There was a robbery."

"Oh? How unfortunate."

I turned toward Mrs. Bretagne.

"I'm very sorry," I said. "What was stolen?"

"I don't know," she replied. "I wish that I did."

Morales tamped a cigarette on the edge of his fist. Dominic struck a light for him as he raised it to his lips.

"What happened," he explained, "is that someone broke in last night and forced Mister Bretagne's safe. Mrs. Bretagne has no idea what he kept in it, and he is unavailable at this time."

"Terrible!" I said, mentally adding a curse for whoever had beaten me to it. "The man must have been awfully quiet."

"Ah!" he said, expelling smoke and narrowing his eyes. "This is the interesting part. The night before last, Mrs. Bretagne received a telephone call from a man who identified himself as her husband. It seemed a long distance call, for the connection was poor. Also, the conversation was quite brief. Also, the caller said that he had contracted a cold. Enough! She believed it to be her husband and she did as he said."

"Yes," she interrupted. "I had not seen him for a time and the trip sounded like a good idea. It has been a long while since we had anything like a vacation together."

I lit a cigarette of my own as Morales went on:

"He asked her to meet him at a hotel in Brasilia the following day—yesterday. He said that they had just been invited to a wonderful party—government officials, officers, celebrities—and that he wanted her there with him. He said they might stay for several days afterwards."

"So I gave Rose time off and flew to Brasilia," she said.

"Only we had no reservations at that hotel and there were no messages for me. I took a room and waited. I must have phoned every other hotel in the city, to make certain I had not misunderstood. But there were no reservations, no messages at any of them…"

She paused a moment, looking as if she were about to cry.

"Then I phoned some friends we have in Brasilia," she continued, "and they helped me inquire around town. There was no such party planned! The whole thing was a lie! I was sick and humiliated. I would not even stay overnight in that town! I took an evening flight back and got home quite late. Then I learned that it was more than just an evil joke. While I was away, the house had been burglarized!"

She drew a handkerchief from her sleeve and turned away while she did things to her eyes and nose with it.

"I'm terribly sorry," I said. "We chose a wretched time to drop by, and I hope you'll forgive us. We had no way of knowing…"

Rose arrived at that moment and I seized my beer and took a swallow, grateful for the diversion.

The fact that Emil's whereabouts were not even known to his wife was interesting. The fact that someone had taken advantage of the situation as he did was even more interesting. The nature of the object or objects stolen or sought was positively intriguing.

"Any fingerprints?" I asked Morales.

"None that we were able to locate," he said.

"Sounds professional," I observed.

"I think not," he said, shaking his head. "It was cleverly set up, yes. But the safe itself was opened quite crudely. It was an older model, and it should not have proved too difficult for an experienced safe man. Whoever did it, though, literally tore the thing apart. He employed a variety of power tools, and he made a number of false starts.

"By the way," he said, uncrossing and recrossing his legs, "where did you say you had met Emil?"

"Rio," I replied.

"I see. What was the subject of your mutual interest?" he asked, his tone becoming less conversational.

"I was trying to sell him an insurance policy," I said. "He was interested, but not enough to buy. So we dropped the subject and just sat around talking. We had dinner together, had a very enjoyable evening."

"What company are you with?"

"I *was* with an agency," I said. "Bundsky and Company. They are no longer in business."

"Oh. Who are you with now?"

I ransacked my mind for something unverifiable. The last thing I needed now was a smart cop, even if he was curious for all the wrong reasons.

"I am writing a book," I said.

"For whom?"

"For any publisher who is willing to pay for it."

"Oh."

"Did you find any clues at all?" I asked, in a quick effort to direct the conversation away from myself.

"I am afraid not," he said. "He cleaned up after himself quite thoroughly, and there do not appear to have been any witnesses to anything unusual hereabouts."

"How unfortunate," I said, forcing the faintest of smiles. "I hope that he had adequate insurance coverage."

He seemed to lose a momentary struggle against it, and then smiled himself.

"I do not know," he said, shrugging. "A recovery, an arrest, a conviction—these are my aims. I am still at the information-gathering stage. For instance, I'm asking everybody—even people of somewhat remote connection with the family—such questions as, 'Where were you last night? What were you doing? Who were you with?' "

"Very thorough," I said, nodding. "Very thorough."

All eyes focused upon me for a moment then: Maria's, betraying nothing, but looking to me for some sign; Mrs. Bretagne's, with sudden speculation and nascent fear; Dominic's and Victor's, like those of hunting hounds who know their prey will soon break cover; Morales', dark and placid, patiently expectant, like those of an ikon.

"Would you answer those questions for me, Mister Timura?" he asked, producing a pencil and notebook from inside his coat. "Just for the record."

"Certainly," I said. "We were staying at a hotel in Santos called The Plaza."

"We?"

"My wife and I. In fact, we are still registered there. We only drove up here for the afternoon."

"I see," he said, making a note. "Then of course there must be witnesses?"

"The clerk who checked us in was also on duty when we went out to dinner later. We stopped to ask him about a restaurant we wanted to try and he told us they had good food. He was still on duty when we returned later, and we spoke with him briefly then. The restaurant was called Two Sails, and I heard our waitress addressed as 'Rita' several times."

"What time did you check in?"

"Around sundown. I didn't look at my watch."

"What time did you return from dinner?"

"Sometime between ten and eleven, I'd say."

"What did you do then?"

"We went to bed."

"You remained there till morning?"

"Yes."

"Where had you been before you checked into The Plaza?"

"In Piracicaba. We came down on the train."

"How long were you there?"

"A year. We had a furnished apartment. Our lease came up and we decided to travel rather than renew it, now we are not tied down."

"I see. What was the address?"

I gave him a phony one and he wrote it down. Then he closed the notebook and put it away.

"That seems to cover everything," he said, smiling. "Thank you for your cooperation. Oh, one more thing. Just to tie all the ends together, may I see some identification?"

I grinned.

"I was hoping you wouldn't ask me that," I said. "When I was partway up here I discovered I had left my wallet behind at the hotel."

As I said it, I could not but exult slightly, knowing that Maria's purse was in the rear seat of the car with the tools.

"No matter," said Morales, rising and glancing toward Maria. "Your story sounds quite plausible. I am not a traffic patrolman, that I should be concerned about your not having your driver's permit with you."

I nodded, trying to look sheepish.

"Thank you, Mrs. Bretagne, for your time," he said. "I shall telephone you as soon as there is something to report. If things go slowly, I shall still call you in a few days, to tell you so."

She rose, looking brave.

"Thank you, Inspector—and your men."

He nodded, turned and extended his hand in my direction.

"Mister Timura."

I rose and shook it.

"Inspector."

As I did this, Victor stumbled and lurched against me.

"Sorry," he said, then, "Oh. You must have checked the wrong pocket. Your wallet is there."

I controlled my face and patted my hip pocket.

"You're right. So it is," I said. "Thank you."

I flipped an ash into the ashtray and waited. Nobody else moved.

"Would you be so kind as to produce it, Mister Timura?" Morales asked.

The cage door clanged shut, and any pacing I did now would be of a purely ritualistic nature.

So I opened my coat very slowly, letting him see there was no gun inside, withdrew my U.S. passport and handed it to him.

He studied the photo and the description, glancing up at me several times as he did so. Then he leafed through it, closed it and passed it back.

"I'm afraid I'm going to have to ask you to accompany us," he said. "There are a few more questions which have occurred to me."

I nodded.

"Very well."

He glanced at Maria then. I could not see the look he gave her, but she rose to her feet.

"Thank you for the drink," I said to Mrs. Bretagne, who was looking quite frightened now. "Tell Emil I'm sorry I missed him. I hope everything gets straightened out soon. It's nice to have met you."

She nodded sharply and looked away.

Morales gestured and his men escorted us outside. They searched us on the far side of the cars, out of sight of the house.

"You will ride in the rear of my car," he said. "Dominic will drive yours. Give him the keys."

I did this, and we entered his vehicle. It had looked like an ordinary four-door Chevy sedan from the outside, but there were no door handles on the interior in back and an elaborate metal mesh affair that clung to the roof looked as if it could be swung down to further isolate us. They did not lower it, however.

Morales took the passenger's seat and Victor made a show of passing him a .38 revolver. He lowered it to his lap without taking his eyes off me.

Before Victor could enter on the driver's side, Dominic reappeared with Maria's purse and my bag of tools. These were passed inside and Victor followed. Morales searched through both and shook his head slowly.

"You are planning to repair something?" he asked, smiling.

I shrugged.

"You never can tell when something might go wrong."

He chuckled.

"I am about to flatter you, Mister Wiley," he said. "I am certain that I have heard of you. It was years ago, but a name like yours tends to stick in one's head. I am not certain as to the details, but I believe it involved Spain and some missing paintings. A lookout request perhaps."

"You have a good memory."

He beamed.

"Thank you. I have heard nothing in recent years, though. Have you been in jail?"

"No," I said, "and I was cleared in the matter you referred to."

"I believe you," he said. "It would be stupid to lie to me when you know that I will check everything you say, and I do not believe that you are stupid."

Victor had started the engine and we were moving around the oval now.

"You have not yet told me that it is all a misunderstanding," Morales said, "and that you can explain everything."

I sighed.

"It is, but I can't," I said.

"How unfortunate. That Timura business was not really bad, though, for a spur-of-the-moment thing."

"Thank you."

"*Did* you break in there last night?"

"No. We really were in Santos, at the Plaza, under the name Timura. The thing will check out, as I described it."

"I rather thought it might. How far back will I have to go?"

"It stops about there."

"Then what?"

"I haven't decided yet."

We were on our way toward the bridge by then.

"It does not matter," he said. "We will give you time to think about it and we will repeat the question."

His gaze shifted to Maria.

"...unless your—companion wishes to answer it now," he added.

Maria shook her head.

"She talks even less than you," he observed.

I nodded.

"All right. There may be some unpleasantness, though," he said. "I cannot be with you at all times if the questioning should be of long duration."

"Are we under arrest?" I asked. "If so, what are the charges?"

He raised his hand.

"We merely wish to question you concerning an illegal entry and possible larceny," he said. "You must admit, in all fairness, that you are very suspicious characters."

"That's true," I acknowledged, "but for all the wrong

reasons. We knew nothing of the crime. We only wanted
to see Emil Bretagne."

He rattled my tools in their bag.

"With these?"

"I would like to speak with a representative of the
United States government," I said, "and Maria with an
Italian one."

"I should think so," he said.

We crossed over the bridge.

VII.

It was not exactly the same as in the States.

After a brief conversation with Morales, a husky, blue-jowled, young man received the contents of all my pockets and sent me to be photographed. I was separated from Maria at that point.

My trio of arresters vanished during the picture-taking, and two other men conducted me to a dirty, barred room and locked me in. They refused to answer any of my questions. They did, however, permit me to keep my belt and shoelaces, which at least allowed for comfortable pacing.

We had been driven way out in the boondocks, and the station, precinct, office or whatever, appeared to be the converted main building of an old farm-complex. My toilet facilities consisted of a bucket in the corner, and there was a jug of water beside my cot. Otherwise, the room was bare. Its one window looked out on a flat area of perhaps a hundred feet, where the weeds had been scythed down, followed by many acres of wild shrubs and tangling vines, with some trees way off in the distance. I found myself more than a little depressed.

They did not feed me dinner, but I was not especially hungry. I had been doing what they had probably wanted me to do; *i.e.*, thinking. This, in turn, made me feel the way they must have wanted me to feel: scared.

The whole setup smelled as badly as the bucket.

Morales had produced police identification at my request, and he acted like a cop. The desk man had made the elaborate display of his credentials, and he seemed a meticulous fellow.

But no one had been in uniform, and the flunkies had been unnecessarily quick when it came to shoving and seizing arms and shoulders.

And the place did not look like any station I had ever been in. There was no flag, no dusty photos of judges, politicians, supercops on the walls...

And while I was supposedly there for questioning, and they had not seemed particularly busy, I had not been asked a single question yet.

I had been caught in a series of lies and cover-ups under very suspicious circumstances, they had doubtless discovered the lockpicks in the lining of my wallet and if they had checked with the authorities at the most recent place of departure indicated on my passport, they may or may not have been told that I was wanted for questioning in connection with three killings. New York—if they had checked there—might have mentioned my recent involvement in the Bernini case. I could not even guess as to my actual status on that one.

I could see no reason for the delay in questioning me.

...Except to throw a scare into me.

I wondered about them—their motives, their purposes. They were not behaving the way good cops should, and I did not like the alternative this suggested.

I stretched out on the cot and watched the room grow dark. There was a wall fixture bearing a single bulb which had long ago burnt out, a featureless skull streaked with dirt. I had a drink of the water. I kicked off my shoes. I clasped my hands behind my head.

I was a U.S. citizen. I had not committed the crime under investigation. Once they realized this and saw that I knew nothing about it, they would have to let me go.

Wouldn't they?

°

I was shaken awake, and once I'd made the mistake of
opening my eyes they were assaulted by a beam of light. I
shielded them, but my arm was taken and I was half-
dragged to my feet.

"What…?" I began.

"You will come with us," said the man with my arm.

"Let me get my shoes."

"Forget your shoes. Come!"

They conducted me back to the front room. Its only
illumination was a reading lamp on the desk of the blue-
chinned man, who sat studying or pretending to study
the contents of a manila folder. They showed me to a
chair and retreated to positions somewhere behind me.
We were the room's only occupants.

I sat there for perhaps ten minutes before he looked
up and pretended to become suddenly aware of my
presence.

"Ah! Mister Wiley!" he said. "You do acknowledge that
Ovid Wiley is your correct name, do you not?"

"Yes," I said, and cleared my throat.

"I would like your help in clarifying some matters."

"Gladly."

"Then I would like to know why you and your companion were using false names."

"The reason," I said, "is because she is not my wife. I try
to be as discreet as possible in certain matters."

"Admirable," he said, tapping his pencil against the
blotter. "Why did you present yourself at the home of
Mister Bretagne and attempt to deceive his wife as to
your actual identity?"

Back in my cell, I had decided how far I would go on
that one. It represented one of the few occasions in my
life when I was unable to come up with a good lie. I
simply could not think of a plausible alternative for what

I was really attempting. I had to settle for a part of the truth, as much as it might nettle my bosses.

"It is a bit complicated," I said, managing to fight down a near-irresistible impulse to burst out into maniacal laughter at the words. "First, I've never met Emil Bretagne. I don't know him from Adam. I went to his place to obtain information concerning his brother."

"Brother?" His pencil paused on the upswing.

"Claude Bretagne, a priest who worked at the Vatican."

He reversed the pencil and began scribbling on a legal-size pad.

"Claude was murdered," I said, "four days ago. In a hotel room in Lisbon. I was in Rome at the time. I am an art dealer, and I was on a buying trip which would bring me to Brazil after I left Europe. Claude and I had mutual friends. Maria is one of them. With all due respect for Portuguese authorities, there are limits to the amount of time and effort that can be expended in any one case—particularly that of a stranger in one's country. It was known that Claude kept in pretty close touch with his brother. So, since I was headed this way and have some background in investigative matters, we thought it might be worthwhile for me to speak with Emil—to see whether Claude might have mentioned anything in his letters that would prove useful. We weren't certain that Lisbon would pursue matters this far."

"Who, specifically, is this 'we' of whom you speak?"

"Maria, some of his priest friends and his boss—Monsignor Zingales of the Prefecture of Economic Affairs, Office of Administration for the Patrimony of the Holy See."

"Please repeat that, slowly," he said.

I did, and he wrote it down.

"This Monsignor—he suggested this on his own? Or in his official capacity?"

"On his own."

"So you were actually doing this as a favor, rather than as an authorized representative."

"That's right."

"And you brought this girl with you…"

I smiled.

"She was willing to come. I have nothing against combining business with pleasure."

"…and that explains the assumed name. Very neat. Your story can easily be checked, you know."

"If it will help to get us out of here any sooner, I'll be glad to pay for the telephone calls."

"That will not be necessary," he said, making another note.

He leaned back in his chair then, picked up half a cigar from a cast iron ashtray, lit it and stared at me. He pulled his nose a few times, then asked, "You wish to smoke?"

"Yes."

He fumbled in a drawer, located my cigarettes and matches, made a sharp gesture with his head.

One of the guards approached, took them and brought them to me. I lit one and looked about for an ashtray.

"Use the floor," he said. "Now, about the breaking and entering at Mister Bretagne's place…" He paused and puffed his cigar slowly. "We sent a man to Santos. The desk clerk and the waitress both identified you from your photos and supported your story of being where you said you were last night."

I began to smile and he raised a hand.

"This of course does not preclude your having departed the hotel by its rear entrance during the night and driven up here," he said. "Or, for that matter, you might have done it before going to Santos. Mrs. Bretagne was gone all day, and we have no way of knowing precisely when the crime was committed. However, your story has a surface appearance of the truth at this point."

"That's something anyway. How much longer are you going to keep us here?"

"I cannot answer that," he said. "The decision is not mine to make."

"When may I speak to a representative of the United States government? And Maria to one of hers?"

He shook his head.

"Again, I have no say in the matter and I can tell you nothing."

"All right," I sighed. "I understand."

"Do you have any knowledge of anyone else who might have committed the crime?"

"None whatsoever."

"Could you venture any guesses that might be of help to us?"

"Of course not. How could I?"

"Inspector Morales thinks you have a shady background."

"Even if he were right in his guesses about things that might have happened long ago," I said, "there would still be no tie-in here."

He returned his attention to the folder. I smoked and waited. It occurred to me that he had run out of questions and was mulling over what I had said so far.

"Excuse me," I said.

He looked up immediately.

"Yes?"

"Something has been bothering me. Namely, the fact that no one seems to know where Emil Bretagne is. Not even his wife. Does he go away like that often?"

"Mister Bretagne is not under investigation. You are."

"It just sounds rather odd. That's all. You'd asked for

a guess, and I was looking for some guessing material."

He appeared somewhat mollified.

"I understand that he does make several business trips a year," he said.

"Without telling his company where he is going?"

"I understand that he has a fairly free hand in what he does."

"What *does* he do?"

"I believe he is an investment counselor."

"Access to other people's money," I mused, "and no raised eyebrows when he wants to travel. Now no one knows where he is. When they do it in the States, they usually head for South America. Where do Brazilians go? Switzerland?"

He snatched his cigar from his mouth and stood.

"Mister Bretagne is a highly respected businessman! A patriot!" he snarled. Then, to the guards, "Take him back to his cell! And give me his cigarettes and matches! He may start a fire!"

I thought the last bit rather petty, as I handed them over. Still, I had gotten what I had been fishing for.

They didn't seem to know where the hell Emil Bretagne was either.

Not only that, it seemed I might have prodded a small area of doubt in the local psyche. Curiouser and curiouser, said the man.

In the morning, I was brought some corn flakes and warm milk, long after the sun and I had risen. I slopped them down, paced, stared out of the window. Standing by my door, I listened to distant voices and the occasional ringing of a telephone, but I could never make out any of the words spoken. I wondered about Maria. I hoped they were treating her a bit better than me, but I doubted it. I wondered what she had told them when they had spoken with her, as they must have by now.

I was grateful that I had kept my real reason for being involved in the whole mess to myself. Maria was intelligent and strong. But how long they could keep us incommunicado and what they might do to us while they had us was a matter on which I did not wish to speculate at great length. People are frail things, and while I would confess to anything to avoid excessive discomfort this fact would come to be noted before very long, and the credibility of anything I said would be destroyed. While this would make it easy to get a confession from me, it would make it difficult to tell whether what was being gotten was the truth. And I had the feeling that the truth was what Morales and his fellows wanted. I mean, if someone were to punch me in the stomach and say, "Confess that you are an agent of the CIA," I would say, "Okay, I am an agent of the CIA." After a time, this would tend to pall. I would not see anyone asking me this question without a reason, though. So I was hopefully safe from having the whole story pulled out of me. That would be terrible. Not because I gave a damn about the agency, but because the story was unbelievable and would just lead to further questions for which I had no real answers. Hell, I found it hard believing it myself.

On the other hand, if Maria were to mention those three magic initials, I could see us either being released quickly or detained indefinitely. I did not wish to gamble on the former, because I was certain that I would lose. The agency would disavow me and nobody here would buy it. There is a strange, sad Limbo for persons like that, I understand. In the meantime, I could feel them taping the electrodes to my *cojones*.

If I seem to overdramatize, there were several reasons. First, what we were receiving seemed pretty strong treatment for foreign citizens who were only suspected of a possible connection with what might have been a robbery. They claimed they did not know what, if anything, had been stolen; and the allegedly injured party seemed a pretty suspicious character himself. In the absence of any real evidence against us, the logical, civilized thing to do would be to take our statements and keep tabs on us. Then there was the matter of the lockup itself; the place just didn't seem like a police station, isolated as it was, staffed as it was, looking the way that it did. No, there had to be more to the situation than we had been told, and I feared those goblins in the dark corners.

A lunch of dreary-looking cold cuts came and went, and my water bottle was refilled. My jailers remained uncommunicative.

Dinner was something of an improvement: juice, soup, bread, fish, milk and coffee. The guard gave me a cigarette and lit it for me—whether out of kindness of his heart or pursuant to an order, I could not guess. He would not answer my questions, though.

Either the wait was meant to be a psychological pressure or they were checking on some of the things I had said. Or they were checking on something completely different. Circle any number of the above. Or none of these. Hell.

The following morning, I worked several pieces of wire loose from the cot's frame and spent over an hour working with them and the lock on the door. It was old, as was everything else in the building, and I got it partway once, but the wires were too soft and kept bending. I stuck them down behind the baseboard then. Maybe I could get it open with them, with a bit of luck and bit of time, but what would I do then? Get into more trouble, probably. I doubted I could get out of the building, and even if I did I had no place to turn for help. I didn't even know where we were. And what about Maria?

We had to wait, hoping they would find something to vindicate us or implicate somebody else.

I did not have to wait very long, though. Two guards—a different pair this time—came for me and conducted me back to the room where I had been questioned.

The same chair, the same routine. The guards took up positions behind me while the captain shuffled papers at his desk. When he finally looked up, he stared at me for several moments, then nodded several times.

I continued to meet his gaze as he said, "You appear to have told us something of the truth, Ovid. But we want all of it."

I did not say anything, since he had not asked me a question.

After a pause, he went on; "We have checked with Lisbon. There is indeed a record of a Claude Bretagne recently found shot to death in a hotel room in that city. They are still investigating. So far, there have been no arrests."

"I hope that proves something to you," I said.

"Yes, it proves that you know about it. Nothing more. In fact, it raises questions. The obvious one, of course, being whether there is a connection between the death there and the housebreaking here."

"And Emil's disappearance," I said.

"He did not disappear! He is on a business trip!"

"Well, his business trip then."

He slapped the folder with the flat of his hand.

"That is not an issue!" he said.

"Then perhaps it should be—" I began.

A very heavy hand fell upon my shoulder, and I shut up. The fingers dug in beneath my collarbone and squeezed.

Collarbones are very fragile things, and I did not doubt
that the hand could demonstrate this if it squeezed much
harder. The captain saved me this lesson, though, with a
gesture. The hand withdrew.

"I was not soliciting your opinion," he said.

I rubbed my shoulder.

"So I gather."

"The connection, as I see it, is yourself," he continued.
"I cannot believe your story of investigating a murder at
the request of a few friends of the deceased. You do not
seem that sort of person. I would be more inclined to
believe that you see a profit somewhere in this. Perhaps
you even killed Claude Bretagne yourself."

"I can prove I wasn't in Portugal at the time."

"…or had him killed," he said, shrugging. "No, I do not
believe your story. You will tell me now what you did with
the items you removed from Emil Bretagne's safe."

"If I had broken in and stolen something," I said, "would
I not have been a fool to return the following morning,
laying myself open to questioning and arrest?"

"You miscalculated," he said. "That is obvious. Perhaps
you thought you had something he would not report missing. Perhaps you want to sell it back to him."

"Blackmail? Was he engaged in criminal activities?"

"Enough!" he said. "You are here to answer *my* questions! Not to question me! What did you do with it?"

"What?"

"Whatever you removed from the safe."

"Nothing," I said. "I took nothing. I was not even—"

The hand returned to my shoulder and the fingers
began to dig once more.

"Then who did? Who took it?"

"I don't know."

He stood.

"I am going to take a walk," he said, "and smoke a cigar. You think about my questions. Perhaps when I return you will be able to answer them."

"I would tell you now if I knew," I called after his retreating back.

Then the grip on my left shoulder was transferred to my bicep and my right arm was similarly seized. The second man moved around to my right and stared down at me. He smiled, removed a heavy ring from his right hand and put it into his pocket. I took a small measure of solace from this indication that they were not ready to scar the merchandise yet.

Then, still smiling, he slapped me.

It was not a hard slap. It was a get-acquainted sort of thing. A promise, as it were.

As I jerked from it, he pushed my shoulder and the other pulled back on my arms. Then he slapped me and pushed me again.

He waited a moment after that, then punched me in the stomach. As I snapped forward, my arms were jerked again, wrenching my shoulders, and he seized my hair and pulled my head back. He spat in my face and shoved me against the back of the chair.

I gasped and shuddered at the same time. He allowed me to catch my breath, then repeated the performance.

I did not say anything. A curse? A threat? They are laughable responses, and I had nothing else to say.

The pummeling continued. He was careful not to strike my ribs with any of the low blows, though they came harder and faster now. I passed out twice, briefly, and pretended to remain that way for as long as I could. I tried to roll with it whenever he cuffed my head, but was only partly successful. He pressed my right wrist against the arm of the chair and used his lighter to singe the hair off the back of my forearm. I clamped my teeth and watched. He kept smiling the whole time and never said a word.

Then he pulled a watch from his pocket, glanced at it, hit me in the stomach again and returned to his little corner of the world. My arms were released then and I sagged.

My face tingled and felt flushed. My breakfast lay between my feet and in my lap. Coming or going, it hadn't been a very good breakfast.

I was still slouched forward, breathing heavily, when the captain returned. I heard him rummage in the desk.

"Would you care for a cigarette, Ovid?" he asked.

"Yes."

He brought me my pack and I took one. He lit it for me.

"You have had some time to think now."

"Yes."

He strolled back to his desk, rested his rear on its front edge.

"Now do you recall what you took and what you did with it?" he asked.

I took a long, deep drag on the cigarette, feeling it would probably be my last for a long while.

"No matter what you do to me," I said, "I can't tell you something I don't know."

He sighed.

"I cannot accept that as an answer," he said. "Give me a better one."

"I would, if I had it. Believe me."

He rounded the desk and reseated himself.

"I do not believe you," he said. "I fear that I will have to ask you the question in many different ways. You will not like some of them."

"I want to speak to a representative of the United States government," I said.

"You have already told me that. Now tell me what I want to hear."

"I'm sorry. I don't have the answer you want."

"I am sorry, too—for you. You could make it very easy for yourself, and of course the young lady."

"She knows nothing, either."

"She was the priest's whore," he said. "She told us that this morning. She learned of this thing from him and told it to you. Then you had him killed and the two of you came and stole it."

"You know that isn't true."

He shrugged.

"I know only what she told us."

"Have you let her speak with a representative of the Italian government yet?"

"You will get to speak with your people eventually. After you have spoken to us. They will not be happy to learn that you came here to abuse our hospitality."

"How is Maria?" I asked.

"She is unhappy," he said. "Unhappy because you will not tell us what you took from the safe."

"Oh. Wasn't she there with me, holding the light?"

The hand fell upon my shoulder again.

"She does not know this Monsignor Zingales," he said.

"No. She doesn't."

"But you said a group of Father Bretagne's friends prevailed upon you to speak with Emil."

"I said that a number of his friends were concerned. This was as individuals, not as a group. They are not all acquainted with one another."

"And they asked you to come here and question Emil, and you said yes."

"That's right. It wasn't much out of my way and it would only have taken me a short while."

"What did you hope to learn?"

"Anything his brother might have mentioned to him concerning difficulties, problems, enemies."

"And what would you do if you came across such information?"

"Turn it over to the authorities investigating the killing. I still think the inquiry should be made. Perhaps you should make it. The Portuguese authorities would probably appreciate whatever you can find out. Perhaps Mrs. Bretagne would remember her husband's mentioning something about this."

He jerked his chin upward and the hand left my shoulder. Then he found his pencil and made a note. After that, he leafed through the file for several minutes.

Then he raised his eyes and gave me a smile.

"You know," he said in a more confidential tone, "if you were to tell me what I want to know and the object were to be recovered, I believe that something could be worked out with the Bretagnes. It might be that my department and the family would agree that it would not be necessary to see you charged with the crime. You and your girl would be free then, to enjoy our beautiful state for as long as you wish to remain."

"I wish I had something to give you," I said, "but I don't."

He sighed again.

"You are not a stupid man. Why do you cause yourself so much difficulty?"

"I wish that I had something to give you," I repeated. "Since you do not believe me, I fear you will maim me or kill me. I do not want either one, but I see no alternatives. Do you not have some truth drugs—amytal, pentothal—or a polygraph? They will show you I am telling the truth."

"Drugs are not dependable," he said, "and we do not have a lie detector. But do not talk of death or of maiming.

We are not like that. All that we want is the truth."

I said nothing. I finished the cigarette and added it to the mess on the floor.

"You have nothing more to say?"

I shook my head.

"Very well."

He rose and departed again.

I felt a hand upon my shoulder.

I awakened sore and weakened. I was lying face down on the cot in my lockup. My thoughts were a jumble, and I didn't try to order them. I just let them go by like figures on a dance floor at 3 A.M. during a drunken masquerade as the ship slowly sank.

After a time, I moaned and the band quit playing. I rolled over and pressed the back of my hand against my forehead. This was a mistake.

When I was able, I sat up and took a long drink of water, waited, took another one. Then I cleaned myself as best I could. The smell was nauseating and I felt filthy. I went to the window and stared outside, trying to figure how much time had passed. The air was cleaner there, though the day was hot and getting hotter.

I reviewed my earlier thinking of forced confessions. I realized that a willingness to confess to anything was not the answer here. They wanted something that could be verified locally, quickly. If I constructed a tale, it had better be a good one. I considered and rejected one where I had broken in and stolen some papers, precise nature unknown, and mailed them to a person in, say, Santiago, Chile. I didn't think they would buy it—and if they did, it might land me in prison. I knew nothing of their penal system and wanted to postpone learning about it until I could read something on the subject in the New York Public Library.

If they were really cops, as they claimed to be, I had a feeling they would have informed our State Department by now that they were holding me. Someone should have been around to see me. If they were not cops, their reasons for wanting whatever might have been taken from Emil's place were doubtless illicit. This being the case, an unverifiable story on my part might result in something even more unpleasant than prison.

Whichever, they seemed to want it awfully badly.

Since Emil Bretagne seemed party to his late brother's financial doings, it seemed safe to assume that his disappearing act had to do with their discovery. The rifling of his safe and the zealous investigation of this act could be seen as connected with the missing three million.

Which meant there was absolutely nothing I could say that would get me off the hook, and poor Maria was in the same canoe up the same smelly creek, watching our paddle disappear behind us.

Doubting that there would be any help coming from his direction, I damned Collins for the thousandth time and decided that I would have to try to escape. It would have to be soon, too. A few more questioning sessions and I'd be unable to leave if they left the doors open.

I reexamined the bars on the window, but they were too firmly set in place. The walls were solid, the ceiling out of reach, the floor firmly nailed where it belonged. That left me the door, one way or another.

I needed a weapon. Perhaps one of the legs of the cot could be worked loose…

I tried them and got one to the point where I could remove it in a hurry.

If I could manipulate the lock properly, say late at night, I might be able to take someone by surprise. I wanted a gun. None of my jailers bore any visible arms, but there had to be a weapon somewhere about. I wished

I had an idea how many people there were about the place.

A little later, they brought me some stew and a piece of bread. As usual, one man brought it in while the other waited at the door. They were the same two who had worked me over. We said nothing to one another.

I stretched out then and watched a spider begin a design in the window. Before very long, I fell asleep.

I was awakened, not for dinner but for a repeat performance.

The questions were unchanged, as were my answers. I didn't get a cigarette this time, and I congratulated myself on being able to pass out more quickly than I had on the previous occasion. One of them explained that this was the last time things would go easily for me. I believed him.

Back on my cot. Darkness all about me. Pain inside.

It had to be tonight.

I couldn't move, though.

I drifted in and out of sleep—briefly, I think—several times.

I grew a bit stronger and ordered my muscles to move me.

Protesting, they obeyed. This brought me wide awake, and I sat on the edge of my bed and drank water. It tasted terrible.

I rose and fetched my wires from behind the baseboard.

Through the small opening set at eye-level in the door, I could see that the hall was empty. A bulb of low wattage burned in the ceiling a few yards off to my left. I knelt and began working on the lock.

I was interrupted once by approaching footsteps, and returned to my cot. Whoever it was seemed simply to have taken a stroll up the hall and back again, however. The steps approached, passed, turned, retreated.

I took up my position again and began fumbling with the too-soft wires. Perspiration collected in my eyebrows and small, flitting things came to bug me. Then the lock moved and clicked softly.

Shaking, I returned to my cot and waited to see whether the sound had carried and been noted. Somewhere between five and ten minutes later, I decided that it hadn't.

I stuffed my shoes as far down into my hip pocket as they would go, then returned to the door and checked the hallway.

Nobody.

I removed the leg from the cot, held it in my right hand and edged the door open, slowly and quietly. Stepping through, I closed it behind me and moved up the hall.

I passed several closed doors with dark eyeslits like my own. I glanced through each as I went by. Two of them contained sleeping forms on cots not unlike mine. I thought the second one was Maria.

I passed the interrogation room. It was dark and empty, its door open.

I moved through silence and took it as a good sign. While I had no idea as to the time, it seemed late. I was headed toward the room where they had received me initially. If more than one man were on duty, it would seem there might be some conversation going on. Of course, there could be others—bored, reading, asleep.

I approached the door. It was open, and light flooded the hall around it. About twenty-five feet beyond was the front door to the building. I edged my way along the wall on that side of the corridor until I stood directly beside the puddle of light. Then I stood still and listened.

Perhaps ten minutes passed. I heard small movements, a sigh, the scratch of a match, a belch, the rustling of paper, the squeak of a chair. I shifted my weight slowly, preparing to rush in and start bashing.

I almost gave myself away when the telephone rang.

It was taken before the second ring. A gruff voice answered, spoke briefly, then said, "It's for you."

I heard a grunt, the *bang* of what might have been a chair leaned against a wall as it came forward, then footsteps.

I did not stay to eavesdrop. I turned and hurried back in the direction from which I had come. I was not about to try jumping two of them.

I made it back to the door of my room without being discovered, continued on past it and entered a dark, open room that appeared to be something other than a cell. It was packed with old furniture—dressers, beds, chairs—and smelled of must, dust and urine. I worked my way through it, for there were two unbarred windows in its far wall.

Neither was nailed shut, but both were stuck. I went to work on the one that had yielded a bit. I managed to raise it a few inches, and stopped short of a major noise when it began to bind again. Cursing, I worked it slowly. There was a mass of unkempt shrubbery beyond it and an incline that looked to descend six or eight feet fairly rapidly.

I was certain there was a rear entrance farther back. But it would doubtless be locked and possibly guarded. I knew nothing of the layout at that end of the building, so I would be risking too much to try there what I had planned doing up front. I had wanted to take Maria with me, but now I would settle for just getting out myself and bringing our embassies into the picture.

I eased the window past the tight spot and got it up another eight inches before it stuck again. Then I began working it from side to side, gaining perhaps an eighth of an inch each time. The growing things outside smelled sweet. The night air was cool and delicious.

When the opening was wide enough I slipped my shoes back on and went through it. I hung a moment by my hands, then dropped a couple of feet to the ground.

The stuff was thick and a bit thorny, but I worked my way down through it, keeping low. Then I moved a good distance away from the building and headed toward its rear. I wanted to circle the place, to get a better idea what it looked like.

There was a rear door, but it was boarded shut. I passed on, eventually locating my own window. I drew nearer. It was still dark and silent within. Good. I counted down then and found the one I thought to be Maria's. It, too, was dark and silent, but I worked my way to a position beneath it and tossed a pebble inside.

After a long wait, I tossed another.

Six stones later, I heard soft sounds and a figure appeared behind the bars. I studied it and remained silent until I had satisfied myself.

"Maria?" I whispered.

"Ovid?"

"Yes. Have they hurt you?"

"Not—much," she said. "But they have made me tell them—things."

"Don't worry. Tell them anything that makes them happy."

"But they ask things we do not know."

"Keep telling them that—and keep asking to see the Italian ambassador. I'm going to call for help from the first phone I can reach. I'm going to try to steal a car now."

"Did you get a guard or did you pick the lock?"

"The lock."

"Oh."

"Why?"

"I was hoping you got the small one with the moustache."

"I'll be back," I said. "He'll get his. You hold tight and stall. Start pretending to faint."

"I already have. Be careful."

"Yes. Goodbye, Maria."

"Goodbye, Ovid."

I retreated then and moved on toward the front, the metal tube clenched tightly in my fist. I began hoping for someone to hit.

I still wore my money belt. Strange that they had not thought to check for that. Things would have been so much easier if I'd had my lock picks in it.

I hated leaving her that way, but it was the only out available.

I slowed, dropped to the ground and began to crawl as I neared the front of the building.

There was no one in sight, and two cars were parked beneath the trees. There were two outside lights on the building and one on a pole about a hundred-fifty feet up the driveway. There was also light from the office, coming through the window to the left of the doorway.

Keeping low in the high weeds, I headed toward the vehicles, frightening myself and a rabbit in unequal proportions.

I reached the cars, moved between them, trying to decide which one was going to get its ignition jumped. This was quickly settled. Neither was. They were both Fords and the one on my left was newer, but the one to my right had a key in the ignition. I released the air from the tires of the one on the left, using my lock-pick wire.

Too good, it seemed. But with all the lousy breaks I had been getting recently, I was not about to look a good one in the carburetor. I eased the door open and slid inside, pulling rather than slamming it shut. It was not completely closed, but the latch had caught. That would have to do.

With a quick glance at the building, I started the engine, backed up, shifted gears and headed for the long, narrow driveway that led to the road. There was a brick retaining wall to my left and a tree-filled gully on the right.

I switched on the headlights and fed it gas. I entered the driveway, took a turn and passed through a small clump of trees. Something—either a bird or a bat—dislodged itself from a tree and fled by me. Then the world came to an end as I took another turn.

A pair of headlights was coming straight toward me.

I wanted to tear out the steering wheel column by the roots and throw it at them. Instead, I gripped the wheel and pushed the gas pedal to the floor.

There was no place for me to pull off on the side. If I stopped, they had me; if I backed up, they had me.

I stayed as close to the wall as I could, hoping that the driver's reflexes would cause him to swerve away toward the gully. My hitting him then might help him along in that direction, leaving me room enough to get by.

It didn't work that way, of course.

He leaned on his horn and began slowing as soon as he saw me. I didn't want it to be a head-on collision, but I was ready for one. I leaned on my own horn and kept going.

The distance between us narrowed rapidly, and he finally swerved. But it was too late.

We hit. He was partly off the driveway and I pushed him farther, but not far enough.

I scraped along the wall, pushed partway past him and came to a halt. I tried plowing through. I tried backing out. But I was wedged in place.

I seized my cot leg club from where it lay on the seat to my right. A glance at the other car showed me that it contained three occupants. The door on my side was jammed against the wall; the one on their side would only open a few inches before it bound against their vehicle. Without hesitating, I covered my eyes with my left hand and swung my club against the windshield.

They make them pretty tough these days. Windshields.

The three of them piled out of their car. All of them held guns. They emerged from the far side, and two approached me from the front while one went around to the rear.

The two pointed their weapons at me and one of them yelled, "Drop that and raise your hands!" He emphasized his request by shifting the muzzle slightly and putting a bullet through the windshield.

I dropped the club and raised my hands. I had never liked the idea of dying in an old Ford in Brazil.

One of them kept me covered—it was Dominic, I just then realized—while the other two tried moving their car out of the way.

The engine wouldn't do it. Neither would muscle power. I heard them cursing.

I began to laugh. Hysterically, I think.

Then Dominic said, "Come out through the windshield."

"There's still a lot of glass."

"Clear it with whatever you were using—carefully!"

I did this, then crawled over the dashboard and out onto the hood. He backed off several paces and I climbed down to the ground.

"Turn around. Lean against the car," he said.

Then, to one of the others who turned out to be Victor, "Search him!" he ordered.

This turned up the pieces of wire in the lefthand pocket of my trousers.

"How did you get out?" he asked me.

"I opened the door."

"With what?"

"Those wires. It was an old lock."

The driver, a small man whom I had not seen before, approached. "Damn! Damn! Damn!" he chanted. "Look at the cars!"

He drew back his fist.

"Stop!" said Dominic. "If you knock him out, you are going to carry him back yourself. I've had all I can take tonight. Leave the lights on in this car. Let's get down to the house."

The driver nodded curtly and turned away. Then, "Make him get the ignition keys," he said. "This engine is still running."

I returned and fetched them.

Flanked and followed, I rounded the massed mess then, cutting down through the gully, and moved back along the driveway. Some awakened birds made grumpy noises in the trees. It had been a good dream while it lasted.

The questioning continued. In fact, it began as soon as I was taken back inside. This time, though, there were added refinements, such as being beaten across the soles of the feet. There were new questions, too, such as who had sent me to steal whatever I had stolen and how much I had been paid for the job. After each negative reply, a sock full of sand across the belly became the rule. For variety's sake, I guess. I was tied spread-eagle to a table-top at this time, and whenever I passed out a bucket of water was sloshed over my head and shoulders. I lost track of time and the number of dousings.

The next two days came to seem like the product of delirium to me. I won't say that they filled a tub with water and forced my head under until I could hold my breath no longer, then gave me artificial respiration and resumed questioning me. I won't say that they finally applied electrical shocks to my testicles until I finally babbled the entire story over and over—from Carl Bernini through the CIA—and that they only laughed at me and said I was telling lies. No, I won't say any of these things.

For part of a night and half of a day, I lay naked on my mattress on the floor, shaking and drifting between nightmare and spells of consciousness that were no improvement. They had removed the three-legged cot when they brought me back, and they had not returned my clothing after a subsequent session. I had stopped worrying about internal injuries. Occasionally, I speculated as to how much longer I had to live. Ironically, there was not a mark on me.

Whenever I found myself wondering when they would come again, I would retreat from the thought by reviewing what I would do to them if I had the chance. I kept pushing everything else out of my mind and dwelling on the details.

Then, sometime in the afternoon, they came again. They came several times, in fact.

They brought in a table and a chair, set them by the window and went away. Moments later, they returned and set a hot, decent-looking meal on the end of the table. One of them paused and glanced at me as they were leaving.

"Lunch," he said.

I crawled across the room to reach it. My feet were too sore to bear my weight.

I got into the chair and began eating. Before I was very far along, they were back again. I shuddered, but did not even turn around when I heard the door open. Then I bolted another mouthful, in case they had come to take it all away and laugh.

But Dominic said, "Excuse me," as he set a basin of water at the other end of the table and laid a towel, a washcloth, a bar of soap and a razor beside it.

As he walked out, he said, "Your clothing."

I turned around and saw that my clothes, nearly laundered and pressed, were lying folded upon the mattress.

I did not allow myself the luxury of thinking. I finished the meal quickly and washed it down with a glass of clean water. There was a small glass of what appeared to be wine that I had saved for last. I sipped it, and it was.

I scoured myself afterwards, remaining seated as much as possible. They had not provided a mirror, but I managed what afterwards felt like a passable shave.

I hobbled back to the mattress and dressed myself. I was surprised to find that no one had disturbed the contents of the money belt.

A large envelope had lain beneath my clothing. Opening it, I discovered everything they had taken from me— passport, wallet, comb, watch, etc. I postponed lighting one of my remaining cigarettes until I had combed my hair and stowed everything where it belonged. I winced at the list of artists Bruno had given me. It had been the subject of numerous queries.

I left my shoes off and went and sat by the window, using the table as a footrest. I was beginning to feel slightly human again. I even entertained the notion that I might be allowed to live. After my second cigarette, I grew sleepy and dozed off there in the chair.

About half an hour later I heard the door open and was instantly awake and wary.

Victor nodded and flashed a smile.

"If you will come with me, please," he said.

I nodded back, struggled into my shoes, rose and accompanied him into the hall. We walked along until we came to the front room. He indicated that I should enter, but remained outside himself.

Inspector Morales sat behind the desk. Before it, to my right, Maria was seated. She appeared to have been the object of a cleanup campaign also. But her face was pinched and her glance furtive, despite the scrubbing, the combing, the makeup. There was a vacant chair to her left and Morales gestured toward it.

"Please have a seat," he said, "Mister Wiley."

I did this thing and waited, staring at him.

"First," he said, "as I have already told Miss Borsini, I apologize for any discomfort you experienced during your stay here. I understand that several of your questioners exceeded their authority. They have been reprimanded and they will receive departmental discipline."

I thought of Victor's smile and said nothing.

"After further investigation," he went on, "we find your statements quite acceptable. It was an unfortunate coincidence that you happened to appear at the scene of the crime the morning after it had occurred—under what I am certain you will admit were suspicious circumstances."

He paused, as if expecting us to agree, then shrugged.

"Such mistakes do sometimes occur," he continued, "and this was one of those times. Again, I am sorry. It is over, though—the inconvenience, the distress…We are releasing you. I am certain that the remainder of your visit in our country will help to erase the memory of—the unpleasantness. You must understand that a policeman's first duty is to be thorough."

I continued to stare at him.

"We had your car returned to the rental agency," he said, "shortly after we took you into custody. Since we had no idea how long you would be with us, it seemed senseless to let the charges accumulate. As it is, you owe nothing on it. We also checked you out of your hotel in Santos, for the same reason. That is your luggage in the corner."

He gestured, but I did not turn my head.

"Again, you owe nothing," he added.

He produced a pack of cigarettes, smiled and offered them around.

"No," said Maria.

I shook my head.

He lit one, snorted smoke around it, leaned back in his chair.

"Since you lack transportation," he said, "I will have you taken wherever you wish, whether in Santos or in São Paulo."

I felt Maria's eyes upon me then.

"Then take us to the Othon Palace in São Paulo," I said, it being the only one I remembered from the Highly Recommended list in the guidebook, because of its simple name.

"An excellent choice!" he said. "I recommend it highly. You will find their restaurant quite good."

I withdrew a cigarette from my pack. He extended his lighter and snapped it on, but I ignored it and used a match.

"You are of course angry," he said, "and justly so. That is regrettable. I regret having around ill-will even more than I regret having made a mistake. However, what is done cannot be undone. There are many things in this country which will provide you with happy memories. São Paulo is a world in itself, a world of the future. You will see. There is much beauty and power, and the future of all South America is being forged here daily. When you leave, it will be this that you remember. These memories should serve to mitigate your most recent ones. Let us speak of them no more. Have you any questions? Is there anything that you want?"

"Did you find it?" I asked him.

"What?"

"Whatever was taken from Emil Bretagne's safe."

"No," he replied.

"Did you find Emil Bretagne?"

"Not yet," he said.

I smiled.

"This, however, should come soon," he added.

I permitted my smile to deepen.

He looked away.

"Miss Borsini?" he inquired.

"No. Nothing," she said.

"Very well, then," he said, rising. "I am going into the city now myself. I will drop you at the Othon Palace."

Neither of us said a word, but we rose and followed him. Maria immediately seized my hand, and I realized that she was trembling on the verge of tears. I put my arm about her shoulders and we walked out to the car that way.

Dominic followed with the bags and Victor slid into the driver's seat. We had the rear of the vehicle to ourselves and she cried silently, all the way to the hotel.

On the way in, I committed every twisting and turning of the road to memory, as well as the position and the name of every elevated and ground-level roadway we traversed once we achieved the city proper. The drive lasted well over an hour, but at the end of that time I was certain I could retrace the route.

"It is beautiful, is it not?" said Morales at one point, a concrete-crowded section of the city burning white beneath us.

We did not reply. We had not replied to any of his attempts at neutral conversation on the way in.

He sighed and gave up again.

Relief and continuing fury were my only emotions, mixed with surprise that the ordeal had ended as abruptly and strangely as this. It seemed weeks, rather than days, that they had held us. Now they decided they had made a mistake, said, "Sorry about that," and were acting as if hardly anything had happened. Beyond the fact that it made little sense to me, their attitude almost seemed calculated to infuriate. Pain, humiliation, indifference and dismissal—signifying that our only value in the universe was whatever information we might possess that they wanted. Very well, then. I hoped it would not be too long before they learned the value this had caused me to place upon them. They were quite special to me now.

"...I suppose you will complain to your embassies," Morales was saying as we drew up before the hotel. "This will result only in our explanation and regrets being cast in the form of a letter. I say this only to save you time better spent in viewing our lovely country and enjoying its capital."

We stepped out of the car. Dominic fetched the luggage from the trunk and placed it beside us on the walk. He was smiling.

Morales stood before us.

"Enjoy yourselves," he said, and extended his hand.

I looked at his hand, looked at his face, turned away. I picked up the luggage and took it into the lobby. Neither of us looked back.

I sketched a quick map of the route and jotted the car's tag number as I waited to check us in. We were given a room several floors up, toward the rear.

When our luggage was on the racks and the door had closed behind the departing bellhop, Maria and I stared at each other for a moment and then she was in my arms. She was shaking and she sobbed aloud now. I held her tightly, rubbing her neck, stroking her hair. It was several moments before I realized that I was also kissing her. I didn't stop. It was a reflex, a release for both of us.

Things simply progressed without a word being said. We were on the bed within minutes. Then came the wild ride down the best of roads, dream-silent, through a hot landscape of flesh, her hair knotted around my hand, her softness flowing beneath me. For a time there was nothing else that mattered.

Later, as we lay there, I stared at the ceiling and smoked and she clutched my left bicep to her breast.

"What are we going to do now?" she finally whispered.

"Find out what happened," I said. "It's too soon to kill Morales. I may have to wait a few months. Possibly even leave the country and come back again. But I'll get him."

Then, after a long while, she asked, "But what of the other matter?"

"It's all connected," I said, "somehow. I'm certain of that."

Her grip on my arm tightened, then eased.

"How shall we begin?" she asked.

"By reporting what has just occurred to our embassies."

"What good will that do?"

"None. But I think it is expected of us. Let us seem predictable for a time."

I put out my cigarette and stroked her hair.

After a while we slept.

VIII.

Donald Mason was his name. He was in his late forties, I'd say, and his black hair was only lightly sprinkled with gray. His dark eyes were steady, his movements slow and deliberate. He was well-tanned, and there was a reassuring air of competency to his clipped, Boston accent.

It was early afternoon and the two of us sat in a small office at the American Consulate, a bright day's traffic making noises below the window.

It was two days after our release. I had telephoned the Consulate that same afternoon, identified myself as a U.S. citizen connected with a certain government agency and requested a meeting with a security officer. I added that it was urgent, gave my name and telephone number and hung up. Then Maria and I had ordered dinner from room service and waited in our room.

It was early evening before Mason called. It was a long distance call. From where, he didn't say. We'd made arrangements and met in that same office that following morning. I had told him the whole story then. He had listened, then said that he would check into it and get back in touch.

Now we were there again, a little more rested.

Now he was telling me that it was all over.

"You mean I am not wanted in connection with the killings in Rome?" I asked.

"That is correct. Our people are handling that investigation, with the cooperation of the Italian authorities.

The Italians might put it the other way around, but it amounts to the same thing."

"Any luck yet?"

"There have been no arrests so far."

"What about Father Bretagne's death?"

"We have been assisting the Portuguese authorities in looking into the matter."

"Anything there?"

"No arrests yet."

"What is my status in connection with Carl Bernini's murder?"

"You appear to be off the hook."

"The agency cooperation with New York authorities? Or is it the other way around? I forget."

"Let us say you are pretty much out of the picture now, and the investigation continues."

"Any arrests?"

"No."

"What about our storm trooper treatment by Inspector Morales?"

"There is an Inspector Morales on the local force, and he fits your description. However, he denies the entire story. He says he has never heard of you or Maria. His department backs him up, to the extent that their records show nothing concerning your being arrested or held for questioning."

"*Is* he the one investigating the Bretagne robbery?"

"Yes."

"I gave you a description of the building where we were held and a map showing its location. What's there?"

"A deserted farm, with a main building more or less fitting your description."

"Signs of recent occupancy?"

"Some."

"Who owns the place?"

"An old couple, living in a retirement hotel in Poços de Caldas. They've had the place up for sale for some time now."

"What about the license number I gave you?"

"It's police, all right. And the car is assigned to Morales."

"So?"

"It stops there. Anybody could write down his license number and describe an old building. It's your words against his, and he's theirs and you and Maria are foreigners. You certainly don't look as if you've been abused recently."

"Do you believe Morales' story?"

"Of course not. I'm just telling you to forget about it."

"That will take a lot of forgetting."

"Take the rest of your life if you care to."

"Thanks. What about Emil Bretagne? Has he turned up yet?"

"No."

"You *are* looking for him, aren't you?"

"Ovid…"

"Yes?"

"You do not seem to understand what I have been saying. It does not matter whether he is being sought or whether he is found. Not to you. Not now. I have just accepted your final report. You are out of the picture now. I thank you on behalf of the agency. You are free to go about your own business as you would."

"That's just peachy keen," I said. "Do you mind telling me what it is that I have accomplished for you?"

"I would like to," he said.

"—but I have no need to know?" I finished.

He nodded.

"That, basically, is it," he said.

I nodded back.

"I understand. Very well. Since you can do nothing for me and you want nothing more from me, I guess that about winds things up. Doesn't it?"

"I'd say so. What are your plans now?"

I shrugged.

"Since I'm here, I might as well enjoy it—see some of the sights, visit the galleries and museums. Things like that. Why?"

"Just curious," he said. "I would hate to see you get involved in any more difficulties—now that it would serve no useful end."

"Are you trying to tell me that it would be dangerous for me to remain here?"

"No, I was not implying that at all. You can find danger anywhere if you go looking for it."

"I see," I said. "I wasn't planning on hunting for any. Why don't you tell me where I can find it, so I'll know what places to avoid?"

He smiled, showing teeth almost too perfect to be his own.

"The thought simply occurred to me," he said, "that you might have become so involved in this thing that you would wish to follow through on it on your own. I would recommend against this."

"I wouldn't know where to begin," I said, returning his smile and lighting a cigarette. "No, I intend only to spend a couple of weeks visiting this lovely country, then return to the States, pick up the reins of my business and sell my story to *Rolling Stone*."

His smile went away.

"I would not joke that way," he said, slowly, softly.

"Of course you wouldn't. You're an employee. But then, I'm not joking. Somebody, somewhere, should be interested enough to at least pay me for my expenses on this trip. I make out, but I'm hardly what you would call wealthy. This running around is costing me and hurting the gallery."

The edge went out of his voice.

"I believe your expenses are reimbursable," he said.

"Nobody said anything to me about it," I said. "But in addition to my expenses, I lost what business I could have been doing."

"I am certain something can be worked out. Submit your bills for the trip and an estimate of your losses to the man who will get in touch with you about a month after your return. He will take care of the matter. Does that sound satisfactory?"

"I suppose."

"Give me a definite answer. We get enough bad press without you adding this to it."

"All right: yes. My answer is yes."

"Good."

He sighed.

"Now I believe we have covered everything," he said.

"It seems that way."

He rose and extended his hand. I took it and shook it.

"Thank you," he said, "and I apologize for not being able to specify for what. I doubt that I will ever see you again. So have a pleasant vacation and a good trip home."

"Thank you."

As I turned away and headed toward the door, he added, "Good luck."

Maria and I dined that night at an overpriced fish house that the guy who wrote the guidebook claimed was good. For me, it was an obscure sort of celebration. I was free of something, according to Mason. No matter that I did not understand what that something was. It had influenced my actions for the past several weeks, gotten me shot at, shuttled between countries and beaten up. Now that phase of my existence was ended, according to Mason, and this seemed to warrant an evening in an overpriced fish house.

Physically, I was feeling fairly normal again. My feelings toward large, impersonal organizations with lots of power were unchanged, but then I've always been an anarchist. Now, but for two promises, I was free to tend my gallery.

Maria either did not remember, did not care or had dismissed as hysterical my ravings about the CIA during the worst stages of our questioning. Just as well, that. Our connection was meaningless to me, and such things are generally difficult to explain. An inquiry by an Italian official had gotten her the same story I had received concerning Morales. I had telephoned the Bretagne place. The first time, the maid had checked and told me Mrs. Bretagne was unavailable. The second time she simply hung up. I filled my mouth with fish and thought of Kafka.

Maria had just finished asking me her what-are-we-going-to-do-now? question for the sixth or seventh time and I was preparing a variation on my wait-a-while-and-let-me-think answer, when I heard my name spoken, prefaced by a polite obscenity.

Walter Carlon's hand fell upon my shoulder as I turned.

"...and well-met," he finished.

"Don't I know you from somewhere?" I said, shaking his hand.

"Maria, you're looking well," he said.

"Thank you," and she smiled.

"May I join you?"

"Sit down," I said. "How long have you been in town, Walt?"

"Got in the day before yesterday," he told me. "Came up from Rio. Spent a couple days there. Galleries and the

Press Club, mostly. Then I heard there was a lot of good stuff being shown here."

He lowered himself into a chair and sighed.

"There's a lot to see. My feet are killing me."

I nodded and grunted a noncommittal reply. He returned his attention to Maria.

"Too bad about your boss," he observed.

"What?" she said, "Bruno?"

"Yes. You mean you hadn't heard?"

"No. What happened?"

"Auto accident. A little over a week ago. I was at the funeral."

We had stopped eating. Maria's face was tight, and she was staring at him. He dropped his eyes.

"Hell of a way to start a conversation at dinner," he said. "I thought you knew. Sorry."

"How did it happen?" I asked.

"Just like I said. He was up in the hills and he went off the road. Maybe he fell asleep at the wheel."

"I take it there were no witnesses?"

"No."

"Had he been drinking?"

"I don't know, but *I'm* about to." He turned and ordered a drink from an approaching waiter. "Let's talk about something else, huh?"

I nodded and resumed eating. Maria did the same.

"You know, you're what brought me here," he said.

"Oh? How?"

"That night in Rome, talking about Brazil," he said. "You got me to thinking about it. I'd been wanting a change of scene, and I didn't feel like visiting the States. So I packed up and came here."

"How do you like it?"

"Fine! I've seen tons of stuff by Portinari that I never knew existed—and Camargo, Bandaira, Scliar, Elsas,

Carybé, Eurydice. Great! You were right. I'm glad I came. I felt like doing a year's worth of columns yesterday. Don't you feel like spending at least a month in the Museum of Contemporary Art?"

"I haven't been there yet."

He laughed.

"Really," he said.

"I'm not joking," I told him. "I haven't seen it."

"What have you found that is so much better?"

"Nothing."

"I don't understand."

"Neither do I. We've been locked up for days and interrogated by maniacs."

"You mean kidnapped? One of those terrorist things?"

"That explanation seems as good as any."

His brows worked themselves together as he studied me.

"You're not joking?"

"No. I'm bitter as all hell."

"Did you report it to the American Embassy?"

"Of course. No satisfaction there."

"That's terrible!"

"We agree."

"What was it like?"

"Not now. I'm eating."

"But what did they want? How did it happen?"

"We were just lucky enough to visit the home of a guy named Emil Bretagne the morning after it had been burglarized. We gave some so-called cops a phony story, and that's how it all started."

"Bretagne," he said, nodding. "No wonder."

I glanced up.

"What do you mean, 'No wonder'?"

"Well, everybody wants him."

I lowered my fork.

"How so?"

"My God! Don't you read the newspapers?" He paused to accept his drink, sample it and ask for a menu. "He is a much sought-after man," he said then.

"Why?" Maria inquired.

"Money," he said, gesturing simply. "The story broke while I was in Rio. He was a big wheel at the place where he worked—Investment Director or something like that."

"Bassenrut," Maria said.

"Yes, that's the outfit. He's been gone a couple weeks now. He did a lot of traveling, keeping tabs on their investments, so nothing seemed unusual about his taking off on another trip. It was several days before they got wind of what he was up to—and then they wasted several more days trying to be discreet about it. By then it was too late. He moved very fast and was able to clean out some accounts and liquidate a few assets before they could freeze him out."

I had to swallow before I could sigh.

"How much did he get?" I asked.

He received his menu at that point, glanced at it, ordered. Then he looked at me and shrugged.

"Some of the guesses run into the millions," he said. "Bassenrut hasn't given any figures. They may not be able to."

"What do you mean?"

He smiled.

"Not paying your taxes is a great tradition in this country, and enforcement of the tax laws is nowhere near as efficient as it is in the States. I understand some outfits down here keep four sets of books."

"Four?"

"One for the officers themselves, one for the shareholders, one for foreign investors and one for the government. Now if Bassenrut had something like this going, they wouldn't be too quick to start specifying accounts and amounts."

"And Emil, I take it, had access to whatever books they kept?"

"Hell! He was in charge of their accounting department!"

"Sounds like a talented fellow."

"Second in his class at Harvard Business School."

"Only second?"

"Yes. But they kept the honors in the family. His younger brother was first. He didn't go into the business world, though. He became a priest."

"And the whole business is common knowledge?" I said.

"Most of it. The story broke last week. My fellow journalists in Rio filled me in on some of the details."

"Where do you think he is?" Maria asked.

He shook his head.

"There aren't even any good guesses. He could be in Switzerland by now."

She raised her napkin and bowed her head. She began to sniffle.

"Then they were just shoo—shooting in the dark," she said.

"What do you mean?" he asked.

"When they arrested us," she said.

"I don't understand…"

"When they pulled us in," I said, "they were kind of rough, and that was a touchy point."

"You say that nothing at all came of it when you complained?"

I could not even manage a cynical smile.

"That's right."

"And there is no record?"

"No record. We just imagined the whole thing."

"How rough were they?"

"Let's change that subject."

"What was the business about a phony story? Why the hell were you at Bretagne's in the first place?"

"A good question," I said. "Answering it could take a long, boring while."

"I've got plenty of time."

"Why not?" I said. "Just remember that you asked for it."

Our fourth cup of coffee had grown cold and we were sipping after dinner drinks when I finished. For a time, the two of them just stared at me.

Then Walt said, "That is unbelievable."

Maria said nothing.

"I agree," I said. "Only the guys who started the ball rolling and the guys who kept it moving would believe it—and they seem to have dismissed me from the whole thing. I don't know what function I served or why, and nobody seems to care. That's why I told you. Nothing that I did or that I say about it matters. It is as if nothing had occurred. Also, I wanted to cry on somebody's shoulder."

"Now I wish I hadn't asked you," he said, the corners of his mouth growing tight. "Now I'll be seeing Saci in every doorway."

Maria continued to stare at me. It made me somewhat uncomfortable.

"Saci?" I said. "What's that?"

"A nasty chap who throws bombs and kidnaps diplomats, holds people against their will."

"I'm afraid I never heard the name."

"It's a nickname," he said. "There was a small write-up in the *New York Times* some years ago. He may not really be an individual. It is a name that has appeared on ransom notes, been painted on buildings and shouted at demonstrations."

"How long has he been around?"

He chuckled.

"Oh, a couple hundred years, I'd say. Saci-Pererê is the full name. He's a minor figure in lots of legends, a small black elf who wears a red nightcap, smokes a long pipe and hops about on one leg. He is invisible most of the time. He takes great delight in all sorts of mischief. A good name for a revolutionary leader—though it is not exactly revolution that he seems to have in mind."

"What then?"

"I guess secession would be the best word. For years there has been an on-again, off-again movement for the States of São Paulo to break way from the rest of Brazil and become an independent country. The last time it made world headlines was in the early sixties. I think it was around then that Saci was first mentioned. The revolutionary, I mean. Not the elf."

"How strong is the movement now?"

He shrugged.

"I don't know. Nobody knows. This is because nobody understands Brazilian politics, least of all the Brazilians. I do understand that the State of São Paulo has the best militia in the country, and it is axiomatic that whoever controls the military can control the country. But then, nobody can be certain who controls the military, least of all the military commanders."

"It sounds somewhat screwed up."

"Face it, this is a feudal country in a post-industrial world. São Paulo sticks out like a hitchhiker's digit. It's big, rich, industrial, urbanized and growing. It's an anomaly, and there is a faction that wants out. Hardly a Marxist dream. Somewhat the other way around, I'd say. Though I'd also guess that some elements of the group—the ones who get stuck with all the dirty work—are snapping at the carrot of a Workers Republic of São Paulo or some-such. Saci may be the carrot-wielder. Or a dupe. My friends' theories varied on that."

"You think it was people such as this who had us prisoner, who questioned us?" Maria asked.

"Frankly," he said, "yes. Political activity costs money at all levels, and there was a lot involved in the Bretagne thing. You showed up in a bad place at a bad time and started lying to them. They wanted whatever you knew. From what you said, you will have to admit that if you knew more they would probably have gotten it."

"If your guess is correct," she said, "I am surprised that they released us at all."

"Why not?" he asked. "You're harmless. What have you been able to do to them? Nothing. What can you do to them? The same. Such men are not always complete monsters. To some, violence is a scalpel, not an axe. If that was the case here, you are fortunate."

Maria laughed softly.

"How lucky we were!" she said.

"I'd say so," he agreed, lighting a cigar. "Actually, it might not have been human decency that spared you, though. Ovid's mentioning the CIA might have frightened them. If he was indeed working for them on a different matter, they would not be too anxious to arouse the agency's interest in their business. The last thing they would want is a gang of U.S. snoopers investigating the death of one of their own people by those who oppose a U.S.-supported government. Your release produces a haziness as to the motives and even the identity of your captors. Any number of guesses might be made. Death, on the other hand, would have narrowed the field and drawn unwanted attention. Either way, whatever determined your release, you are fortunate."

"But we can identify them—Morales and the others," she said.

"So what? You'll probably never see them again, and if you were to it would be your words against theirs. For that matter, your Morales may not even be the Morales on the local force."

"True," I said, "and we are left with a fistful of water."

"It's better than being dead."

"What are we to do now?" Maria said.

"I believe you should let me take you to some of the museums tomorrow. You haven't seen any of them yet, and you really should, you know."

"That sounds excellent," she told him, then added, "Why don't we, Ovid?"

"That would be nice," I said.

"I meant—" he began.

Maria gave me a somewhat nasty smile.

"We might as well do something," she said.

I nodded. Hell, I wasn't looking for an argument.

Things grew quiet then and we settled up and found a taxi, agreeing to meet at the Museum of Contemporary Art in the morning. Maria did not speak to me on the way back. I picked up a newspaper in the lobby, for something to do later.

We moved from canvas to canvas, room to room, wing to wing. Maria clung to my arm and we moved slowly, not always noting everything that was before us, not always hearing everything Walter said. The museum was a glorious place, I think.

We had had our argument the night before. I hoped the rooms were soundproof.

Since she wasn't talking to me, I'd decided to return the compliment. I'd hung my jacket, seated myself and began to read the paper. She was in the bathroom for a time, then out of it. Then pacing. Then sitting. Then sitting and smoking. Then sitting and smoking and staring.

I had located, read and was re-reading an article on Emil. It contained nothing that I did not already know, complete with photo. It was not a good picture, but it was clear enough so that I could see the strong resemblance recalling those I had seen of Claude.

…Then sitting and smoking and staring and making a noise like a pre-whistle hiss of a boiling teakettle.

I glanced up and was hit by a wave of Italian adjectives, some of which I could not catch, as they were in an unfamiliar dialect. I did catch several versions of "liar!", "pig!", "slanderer!", "coward!" and "stupid!", though.

When she paused to inhale, I asked her what she was talking about.

This gave me time to light and enjoy a cigarette, then begin another.

It grew more interesting when she added pantomime to the words and gestures. A not-too-loose black slip in motion is an undeniable asset when it comes to getting points across.

I was many things for not telling her the full story of my forced involvement in the Bretagne case, and many more for telling everything to someone else—especially with her sitting there. I had made her seem a woman of the streets, even if I had not said she was sleeping with Claude. What other conclusion could anyone draw? I had done nothing intelligent the whole time we had been together. I had gotten us arrested and tortured. We had learned nothing we wanted to know, and it was unlikely now that we ever would. A brave man would be out learning what had happened and righting wrongs. She detested São Paulo, and I was another pig for taking advantage of her innocent young body at a time when she was not really responsible for its movements…

The gods had seen fit to grant me a vision at that point, in response to some feeble speculations during the previous few days as to what married life with Maria might be like. I shuddered and drew back from the abyss, flames singeing my hair and eyebrows, scorching my crepe-soled shoes.

I waited till she paused again, then said, "Is that all?"

She threw back her head and let out an animal-like bleat. Then I dropped my newspaper and seized her wrists as she sprang at me. I avoided her kicks as best I could. Fortunately, she was not wearing shoes.

Then I thrust her back onto the bed and stood over her. "Three things," I said, over her noises. "Hear three things, and then I'll go away and you can yell all you want.

"First," I said, though her sounds did not diminish, "I told Walt much of what had happened because I felt like it. I will also tell anyone else I feel like telling now. You are free to do the same. It doesn't make a damned bit of difference, and it made me feel better. In fact, we learned something as a result.

"Second," I said, and she was merely whimpering now, "I didn't tell you everything because I never anticipated our getting this involved together. Once we did, it was too late. We were moving too fast, and I still wanted to keep you out of it as much as possible. Now you know anyway, and what difference does it make?

"And finally," I told her silence, "if I seem to be doing nothing right now, it is because there is nothing to do at the moment but waiting and thinking."

"Waiting for what?" she spat. "Thinking of what?"

"Waiting for more news of Emil. It will determine what I do next. If you don't care to do it my way, I can get you a ticket on the next flight back to Rome. In fact, that sounds like a good idea anyway."

"No!" she said. "I am with you until we find Claude's killer."

"Well, you are not helping to find him by bitching over

everything that's happened. You used to give me credit for having some brains and some luck. The luck seems temporarily out of stock, and there's not much for my brains to chew on. If you can't understand that, you might as well leave. Or I will."

"I am not leaving."

"All right," I said, shrugging. "Shall I?"

"Where would you go?"

"Down to the desk, to get a room on another floor. A quiet room."

She studied the carpet.

"No, do not go," she said softly. "You must understand how it is with me when I am upset or when I am depressed—or both—as I am now. I must do something. I must complain to someone. I grew disappointed over the way that things had gone. I did not mean it the way it sounded. Do not leave me."

She took my hand and looked up at me.

"I only scold at people I care for," she said, and she pressed my hand to her cheek.

My eyebrows grew cool and I slipped off my shoes. The abyss seemed to have closed somewhat.

I held her hand against my side and stroked her hair.

"I understand," I said, turning then and seating myself beside her.

I put my arm about her. I raised her hair and kissed her neck.

I kissed her lips, her throat, and after a few moments with the straps, her breasts.

She leaned back and I felt the tenseness go out of her.

"I understand," I said.

The black nightgown fell to the floor and did not move again that night.

…The museum was a glorious place, I think. We moved

in a half-high, dreamy sort of way through corridors of color, contour, crystal and light. That morning all artists were great, and the birds of the mind made invisible music in the bright air.

That day was good for both of us. Walt was a shadow-figure, a genie with good suggestions and a rented car, as useful and unnoticed as electricity or air. I had almost forgotten what it felt like to be without responsibility and cares for a time. A small, rodent-like thing at my mind's roots called attention to the fact that every other time I had felt good recently, the day had ended in disaster. I decided not to pay it any heed.

This time it had not been a coupling of desperation, like the congress of frenzied baboons, but something pathetic and tender. Such things seem to occur with less and less frequency as the world grows older about me, so my pleasure was not unmixed with gratefulness. We walked and we saw what we would. We touched one another frequently and laughed often.

The day was controlled by the old Time:Joy equation—the more of the latter, the less of the former—or something like that, and the sun was forked by towers and masticated by concrete molars after what seemed but the briefest of whiles. When the shadows flowed together and the lights of the city came on, we found ourselves in a small café.

We laughed and talked, not really caring what was said so much as enjoying the sounds and the echoes of the day's colors. There was music in the little place, and the window beside us opened upon a small garden where the flowers slept now but left a bit of their sweetness behind, to come cool and occasional on a stray current of air across our table. We ate thick sandwiches and drank beer and were happy.

We smoked and made noises and listened to the music and sang along with it, and after a time I excused myself.

On my way to the restroom, I picked up a newspaper that was lying on a vacant table.

It was a long while before I returned, and when I did I did not sit down. Instead, I slammed the folded-back paper down onto the table, upsetting Walt's beer glass. For some reason, it did not break, and he caught it before it rolled over the edge.

"What the hell!" he said, his arm wet, his head snapping upwards. "What's wrong?"

"You son of a bitch! That's what's wrong!" I said, pointing.

He looked down at the paper, stared a moment, then smiled.

"Yes," he said. "I see it. I repeat, 'What's wrong?' "

I repressed an impulse to take a swing at him.

"I told you something in confidence," I said, forcing my voice soft and steady, "because I've known you a long while and because I thought I could trust you. Thanks a lot!"

The article—complete with a fuzzy photo of me—occupied one of the inner pages. It stated that I, an agent for the CIA, had been kidnapped and questioned under torture by local terrorists, then released. It said little concerning my antecedents, other than that I was an art dealer; it did not mention Maria and there were several paragraphs as to how the government was continuing to crack down on such groups. All of this under Carlon's byline.

"Mm," he said. "They cut a lot and they added a lot. In fact, they rewrote the whole piece, dammit!"

"That's all you have to say about it?"

"It's a lousy picture, too," he added.

I hit him then and called him every name in the book.

It knocked him over backwards, but the table behind him saved him from going to the floor.

There was an instant of silence followed by a babble of voices, then a number of people converged. Patrons, employees or both. I don't know.

My arms were seized and I did not struggle. No one attempted to hit me. The bartender was shouting that we would have to leave.

I did not resist as they escorted me out.

Maria joined me moments later.

"I paid the bill," she said.

"Great."

I was looking up and down the street for a cab then.

"I'm going back inside now to see how Walter is."

"Like hell you are!" I took her arm. "You're coming back to the hotel with me—now!"

She jerked free of my grip.

"Like hell I'm not!" she said, her eyes flashing dangerously as she backed away. "I do not have to be your accomplice in bad manner, too!"

"Then go ahead!" I snapped, and she turned and I was alone on the outside of a closing door.

I walked on up the street then. I found a cab and returned to the hotel.

After ringing up a drink, I sat by the window, staring out, with just a small light on, thinking things over.

I felt hurt. The only two people in town who I thought I could trust were against me. Walt had always seemed to have a newsman's background from somewhere or other, but I had thought those days were far behind him and had assumed he was beyond the point of betraying an obvious confidence for the monetary pleasure of a byline. So I was wrong, and that hurt.

I could call Mason, Collin, et al, mad as hell. This did

not serve to cheer me up. They had wanted no publicity, and here was a fractured piece of my story in a big daily, with a photograph yet. I wondered briefly how it had gotten in, and could only conclude that the government had wanted it to appear, with comments cautioning Saci's people to ease up and reassuring everyone else that something was being done. It seemed I was off the CIA's hook now, but I did not want to do anything to antagonize them. Walt was therefore welcome to keep them company in hell.

The thing that really caught in my craw was Maria's going back to apologize to the bastard, keeping him company, doubtless sympathizing with him. And she was taking a long time doing it, too. Even now they were probably sitting together, mumbling nonsense and assurances, smiling occasionally. Perhaps their hands lay together...

My God!

Was I getting jealous?

Of course not. She was just another girl, and I happened to like her. We had a few things in common. That was all. I had no intention of keeping her around on a permanent basis when this whole thing was over. So what did it matter what she was doing at that moment?

Nothing.

When this whole thing was over...

It was over now, so far as I was concerned. I was done, finished, dismissed. I had made Maria a promise, true. But such things are only good if they can be kept. The way things looked now, I was in no position to find Claude's killers and never would be.

So there was no real reason to stick around, and several good ones for going away. I had a business to take care of, I had things to do in New York.

I took a big swallow of my drink and these things

seemed even more true. I had no real reason to be in Brazil at all now.

Nothing I had done that had brought me here had been a matter of real choice on my part. Now the pressures had abated and there was nothing to keep me here.

Nothing, except for the fact that since I was already on the scene it would be a shame to waste the opportunity to see the rest of the local museums and galleries worth seeing.

I took another sip.

Yes, that was the answer. I would remain in Brazil for a few days, perhaps a week. Then I would go away and encourage my memories to do the same.

…for about six months, I'd say. That should give him plenty of time to forget, also.

Then I would come back and kill Morales.

I finished my drink, mixed another.

Everything was settled now, so far as I was concerned.

I lit a cigarette and watched the city.

Four days passed. There had only been a few nut calls. I had told the callers that I did not speak Portuguese—or English either, when they tried that—and hung up. Then I had told the desk to stop putting through telephone calls and the problem went away.

Maria had come in later that night, after I had retired, and slept on the couch. I took the couch on succeeding nights and let her have the bed. We were still on speaking terms, but that was about all. She felt that I had been mean to poor old Walt, who she insisted had not really done us any harm; I'd done all the harm myself when I'd told him my story, and he'd done no more with it than I should have expected. She also recalled once more that I had not given her Claude's killer's head yet and did not seem to be taking its quest as seriously as I should. I told

her she was out of the picture now, so far as I was concerned, and she could damned well do what she pleased.
As for me, though, I was gong to spend the next few days
enjoying myself. She was welcome to join me if she
wished. She was not too keen on the idea, but she went to
a couple places with me—just to keep an eye on me, I
suppose. She did not tell me what she was doing the rest
of the time and I did not ask her. I knew she was seeing
Walt, though. He had picked her up at the hotel on a few
occasions. I had not spoken with him myself since I had
hit him, and he had made no effort to get in touch with
me. In this, I would say he was wise.

Four uneasy days went by in this fashion. Otherwise,
though, I had a fairly interesting time. After all, I had not
been playing for keeps.

I found myself unaccompanied in the Museum of
Brazilian Art. It was only mid-morning, but I had already
achieved an old, familiar fatigue. I was growing jaded.
Too much of a good thing. There was a lot of great stuff
hanging on the walls about me. But I appreciate strawberry sodas and martinis, too, and I would not care for a
steady diet of either.

So it was that I found myself contemplating the end of
my sojourn in São Paulo. Another day, I decided, and I
would fly to Rio for a quick look. Then I would go home.

"Mr. Wiley. Oh-vid Wiley," a somewhat nasal voice
intoned behind my right shoulder, and I felt a hand touch
my sleeve.

I turned slowly and regarded the small apparition
which had addressed me. Vaguely female in form, it was
about five feet in height, the color of uncreamed coffee,
had on a bright red blouse, a skirt of everycolored paisley,
enormous riding boots that had seen better days, huge
circlets of copper through the earlobes, no fewer than
ten bracelets of various materials—most of them kind of

snakey—and a yellow scarf over long, streaked hair. The
eyes that met mine were the darkest I had ever seen.

"Oh-vid Wiley?" she repeated, thrusting a folded-back
newssheet toward me and indicating a section with a
pudgy thumb.

I did not look at the paper. I simply nodded.

"Yes," I said.

"I wish to speak with you," she said softly, lowering the
paper.

"Go ahead."

She glanced quickly about the room. There were a few
other people at its opposite end.

"Not here," she said, and gestured with her eyes toward
a doorway.

"Please," she added when I hesitated. "It is very important."

"All right."

I followed her about the wing until we came upon a
deserted section. Apparently satisfied, she steered me
out of range of an overhead television camera, drew close
to me and said, "Emil Bretagne wants to see you."

"Oh? Why?"

"He has something to give you."

"What?"

"I do not know. He did not tell me that."

"Why me?"

"He did not tell me that either."

"Okay. I'll talk to him," I decided. "Where is he?"

She shook her head.

"I may not say. I may only take you to him."

"When?"

"Now. We should go now."

"Is it far?"

"Yes."

"Will I be gone overnight?"

"Yes."

"Then I want to go back to my hotel and get some things."

"No," she said. "There is no time."

"Well, I'm going to take the time," I said, "whether you think I should or not."

"If you do," she told me, "then I may not take you to him."

I suppressed a sigh and immediately considered the consequence of my going. I had already written myself out of the script and I knew that if I went alone with her it would somehow lead me into more trouble. Also, I had been dismissed by the people who had gotten me involved in the whole stupid business.

On the other hand, being a primate endows one with a certain curiosity, and when one has wasted as much time as I had on a fool's errand one is often willing to go another step if it may serve to remove something of the foolishness. Pride, I'd call it.

So, "All right," I said. "I will go with you now."

She took my arm.

"Then we must hurry," she said.

We did.

IX.

I just sat and smoked and watched the jungle unwind about me. It was maddening. My new companion, whose unpronounceable name we compromised to "Vera," had the window seat. She was not very talkative and she alternated her chewing between gum and snuff. Maria had a seat across the aisle and stared continually out the window, either ignoring me or fascinated by vegetation. The driver was a demented clown with a bottle of beer in one hand and a missing ear. He only lowered the bottle when we passed another vehicle, at which times he exchanged an elaborate series of hand-signals with the other driver. I learned later that this "language of the road," so to speak, is somewhat common in that mad country. He manipulated the groaning bus by occasionally adjusting its passage to roughly coincide with the direction the battered road-bed was taking. At times, he sang to us. I could not tell whether the vehicle possessed brakes.

I had with me several paperbacks I had managed to pick up at the last minute, but I could not get interested in reading. Neither of my companions was especially communicative. The jungle was monotonous and the heat oppressive.

Maria was an accidental fellow traveler. Vera and I had encountered her as we were leaving the museum. She had been on her way in, unaccompanied. She was, she explained, at a loss for anything better to do, so she was seeking my company. She recalled the itinerary I had announced that morning. And where was I headed now?

So I told her. Over Vera's protestations, of course. It was the only safe thing to do. Pity.

She then insisted on accompanying us to the bus station and purchasing a ticket for herself—again, sending Vera into a pout. The little woman appeared to be weighing the situation for several moments, then agreed to this addition to her plans.

We caught a shuttle bus which took us to a stopping point where we met and boarded this horizontal roller coaster whipping us through the Matto Grasso on its day-and-a-half run.

When I had suggested that it would be considerably speedier and more comfortable to fly, rather than take that thousand-plus-mile road I understood to have been mainly napalmed through the jungle, Vera had simply said, "No," and she would discuss the matter no further. So I watched that damnable green unwind and lit another cigarette.

In a way, I was glad that Maria was there. I felt a certain responsibility for her, since I had brought her to Brazil, since I was instrumental in those things which led her to suffering here. I did not want her to think I had deserted her. I was troubled, though, by the rapid change in feeling she caused in me. I was annoyed to find myself alternating between affection and anger on a schedule I could almost chart. She—either fortunately or unfortunately—displayed similar rhythmic behavior, and our cycles did not coincide. I considered this with a combination of pique and thankfulness. I was not certain whether I wanted to fall in love with her, felt that perhaps I was doing so and was annoyed with myself for my uncertainty.

We stopped several times, for food, fuel and to attend to basic human needs. The places where we stopped—and the ones we simply passed—represented a dissertation's worth of material in their progression from the ramshackle to the truly primitive. I saw very little cut lumber after the first several hundred miles. Delimbed trees supported roofs of corrugated metal or thatching. I saw jeeps, junkers, burros and pickup trucks about some of the clusters of buildings we passed. The emptied oil drum appeared to be the basic unit of furniture. The most common garb was khaki shorts, with or without an undershirt, and boots or sandals. Children ran naked as often as not; grizzled faces grinned at us; bright birds perched on rooftops and rails.

There were dark-skinned Indians about at several of the later way stations. They seem to be constantly finding new tribes of them about. I believe they are even beginning to run out of names for them. A while back, during some road building in the north, the workers came across a previously unknown tribe whose language was unintelligible even to other tribes in the area. They were duly dubbed "West of the Road Indians" and ignored or exploited as circumstances warranted.

It was quite late in the day when we stopped at one of the way stations and were informed by the driver that we had an hour in which to eat. He indicated a long, low building to our right, and we headed in that direction.

The place had a dirt floor, picnic-style tables, benches and a crude counter. Cooking odors drifted from the doorway behind the counter. There were flies all about, and I tried hard not to visualize the kitchen. I was not really very hungry, I kept telling myself.

I was, though. They served up a meaty stew which smelled awfully good. I refrained from studying it or its container too closely and put it all away. Beautifully enough, they had bottled beer, with which I followed it. The help had a disconcerting habit of hurling the empties into a packing case in the corner.

When, about an hour and a half later, the driver

announced that the hour had run, I began to rise. Vera
placed her hand on my arm then and told me to wait. She
left us and approached the driver. I could not overhear
their words.

"What is happening?" Maria asked me.

I shrugged. The other passengers were filing out and
reboarding the bus.

"I don't know," I said, "though I'd imagine your guess
would be the same as mine."

"Is he here somewhere?"

"Or near here, I'd say."

The driver departed then with the rest of the passengers and Vera returned to our bench.

"You will wait here now," she said.

"For what?"

"I must carry a message."

"To Emil?"

"Perhaps."

"How long will it take?"

"I cannot say."

"Can't you give us any idea?"

"Several hours at least," she said. "You will probably
spend the night here. These people will take care of you."
Her gesture was all-inclusive. "They will provide a place
for you to sleep if you require it."

I nodded.

"Is it far from here?" Maria asked.

Vera smiled.

"I cannot say. I will hurry."

She turned then and left us.

I asked for and was given some coffee, a large tin cup
of it. It was delicious.

"Do you believe this will help to find the ones we are
looking for?" Maria asked.

"Yes."

I heard the bus' engine turn over, listened to the vehicle pull back onto the road, move off into the distance.

"I believe so, too," she said, and touched my hand. "I am sorry—again—that I grew so impatient with you."

"That's all right. Forget it."

"Are you still angry with me?"

"Some. But that's all right, too."

"I will not be that way again."

"Good."

"How did you find the woman who brought us here?"

"I didn't. She found me."

"Oh."

"Yes, old Walt's article did the trick. She identified me from the picture. Said she'd been looking in galleries and museums for several days. Following up on that bit about my being an art dealer."

"So the article did some good, after all."

"I suppose—depending on how you look at it."

"You came."

"I've paid for my ticket. I want to see the whole show."

We stared at one another for a moment and must have felt uncomfortable at the same moment, because we shifted our eyes simultaneously.

"I'd like some coffee now," she said.

I got her a cup, and we sipped them in silence a while.

I finished mine, and, "Excuse me, I've got to take a walk," I said.

She nodded, smiled faintly as I rose.

A chilly night had come upon the world, damp-smelling and punctuated by the light of kerosene lamps within the shacks. People still moved about, a few of them drunk, the rest working at small chores or talking, all of them still dressed as they were earlier and apparently oblivious to the coldness of the night. I shrugged into the cardigan I had carried all day and inquired as to the location of the nearest outhouse.

The man I had asked gave me an incredulous look, then broke into a grin. He gestured at the dense forest that surrounded the small encampment.

"Take your pick," he said.

With persistence, I did learn, however, that there was an outbuilding a few hundred yards back up the road, if anybody really wanted to use it. It was just there for the turistas and the government man who had insisted that a bus station required one. Strange. All government men and turistas were strange. I agreed with him, thanked him and left him standing there shaking his head.

Bright stars. Shiny spiderwebs. Absolutely black shadows. Incessant insect sounds.

As I was leaving the facility, I heard my name spoken somewhere off to my left. I halted and turned my head in that direction.

"Yes?" I said.

A figure advanced and paused about ten paces from me.

"There is someone who wishes to speak with you," the man said.

The voice sounded somewhat familiar, but I could not see him clearly.

"I see," I said. "Where is he?"

"Back up the road. I will take you to him."

"All right."

We began walking.

"How far is it?" I asked.

"Perhaps half a mile."

Although I slowed and drifted, hoping to fall into a position where I would be abreast of him and hopefully get a look at his features, he managed to remain somewhat to the left and the rear. I imagined he was armed.

After a time, we came upon a string of vehicles parked off to the side of the road. I could make out two automobiles and six or seven trucks. All of them were dark and muffled voices emerged from the trucks. As we drew nearer, I noted several sentries, motionless, smoking their cigarettes from cupped hands. My guide gave a password to the nearest man and escorted me around the lead car. The door on that side was open, though there was no light within the vehicle. A man, partly hidden by the door, sat sideways, observing our approach. I smelled cigarette smoke as we came up to him.

He rose to his feet.

"Good evening, Ovid," he said, partly closing the door and extending his hand.

I did not take it. Nor did I say anything.

It was Morales.

I saw then, as he moved into view, that my escort had been Dominic.

I succeeded in masking my feelings. I had actually believed that I was on my way to see Emil, that he had chosen to bring me to him, quietly and without fuss, by simply having his man wait till the overcivilized gringo went in search of the town's only crapper.

Well, the method had proven effective...

"What do you want this time?" I asked him.

He sighed.

"You are still angry with me, of course," he said. "But I hope that will not prevent you from listening to what I have to say. It is most important."

"Then say it."

"You do not trust me," he began, and I chuckled.

"...not that I ask for your trust," he continued quickly. "All that I require of you is cooperation, and I will obtain this by any means necessary. I have been waiting for this night, for you to go to Emil Bretagne. I am certain we both agree on one matter—that the man has done considerable damage to his country. Whatever your personal feelings concerning me, you must realize that I am a police officer dedicated to maintaining the security of our state. Emil Bretagne—as your superiors may have conjectured during your briefing—is also known as Saci, and he possesses the means to cause further disruption. I have been waiting for you to go to him."

He paused then, as if expecting me to say something. I lit a cigarette.

He made an impatient gesture.

"It was only a matter of time," he went on, "before this meeting, this little talk of ours. Not very much time, either. I needed only to wait, to be prepared. You know, of course, what I want. You must get it for me."

Here he raised a hand, as if to stop me from interrupting him, not realizing that I would not give him anything—not even words—unless it would contribute to his death.

"Your first reaction, of course, is to say 'no'," he stated. "I understand this perfectly. You are not anxious to do anything which would go against your agency's policies in general and your own orders in particular. Hear me out, however, and I believe you will see that what I propose should satisfy your superiors as well as my own.

"As we both know, Bretagne is an officer of a large organization, some of its interests at cross-purposes to those of the government. He manipulated some of the organization's funds in a manner which benefited the revolutionary group of which he is a part. When this activity was about to be uncovered, he fled, taking with him the records of these financial dispositions. Then, before be could be stopped, he managed to transfer sizable quantities of these assets beyond our present reach. Of course, he could not have set the operation up initially without the cooperation of some of the other individuals in various parts of the country. As a whole, however, we feel that the organization was a victim rather than a culpable party. It also represents a sufficiently significant element in the local business structure so that action against it would not be without severe repercussion. Therefore, we wish to proceed against the individuals involved, rather than their employer—and against those persons elsewhere in the country who cooperated with them. As to Bretagne himself, we do not know whether his last efforts were directed toward salvaging as much as he could for his movement or for his own personal uses. Nor is this truly material. Either way, the interests of the state and of Bassenrut are conjoined. We both want a recovery, a reorganization of the foundation's management structure and the identities of Bretagne's fellow conspirators. You may so inform your superiors and we will back you up on it. As you must be aware, their desires would coincide with our own in this matter. They wish to ensure the stability of the present political setup almost as ardently as we wish to maintain our position. Bretagne had the records we need to achieve our aims in this matter. Not trusting the officers of this state, he has elected to turn them over to your agency, achieving our embarrassment and Bassenrut's dismemberment at the cost of betraying his fellow conspirators. It is not logical that he would attempt to advance his movement's cause by destroying major figures in the movement itself. Since his actions thus far have been too shrewd to be those of a madman, the only alternative seems to be that he has thrown up his hands with the whole affair and is now attempting to create sufficient confusion and disruption to permit his flight with the funds. This, of course, will soon result in his having a third group at his heels— namely, the revolutionaries. No wonder the man is hiding out among ignorant savages! Where else in the country

has he to go? Who else would harbor him but these illiterate apes?

"Now we both want his records," he said, after a minor
throat-clearing operation which brought his voice back to
normal. "If your agency were to obtain them, what would
be the result?

"After studying them," he answered his own question,
"they would turn them over to my government, along
with unofficial recommendations concerning their use.
There would of course be a tacit element of compulsion
involved. On the other hand, were we to obtain the
records directly, rather than through a third party, we
would undertake to remedy the situation in a satisfactory
fashion. We would also be saved the embarrassment of
appearing incompetent to your government, and spared
their looking over our shoulders, getting underfoot and
in general attempting to direct the settlement of what is
really an internal problem. Surely you can understand
the situation. Your country's interests and holdings down
here are vast and its concern with our political stability
a legitimate thing. But we resent interference in our
domestic matters—and that is what would occur if Emil
Bretagne is allowed to turn his records over to your
government."

It made a certain sense, though it raised new questions concerning Emil's motives and the involvement of
his brother. I decided to seem more receptive.

"In other words," I said, "if it is indeed Emil Bretagne
that I have come here to see and he were to give me certain items he may have in his possession, you want me to
turn them over to you, despite any orders I may have to
the contrary?"

"It is good that we think alike," he said. "You are a
reasonable man, and I have explained what we would do
with them so that you would see that the effect will be

basically the same as if you turned them over to your superiors and we acted under their direction. You will allow us to save face by proceeding along our own line."

I finished my cigarette and lit another, trying to appear as agitated as I was.

"You place me in an extremely awkward position…" I began.

"I realize that and I apologize for it personally. But you can see that I have no alternative."

"Yes, I can."

I waited to see whether he had more to offer. He did.

"At no additional cost," he said, "we will provide the means for preserving your integrity in this matter."

"How so?"

"You can hardly be held liable if the records are taken from you by force—that is, the threat of violence resulting in your death."

"That seems true."

"So we are providing this threat. We know he is somewhere in this area, though we could beat the bushes for months and still possibly not turn him up. Getting out of this area undetected, however, is another matter. You are aware of our great distance from civilization, and you stand beside the only road. Once you have seen Bretagne and obtained the records, you must traverse this route, in one direction or the other. We control this road, and you may not pass unless you pay the toll."

"That does not seem to leave much in the way of alternatives."

"None, I should say."

"Supposing I were to be a real bastard and repeat everything you've just told me to Mister Bretagne?"

"Most unwise," he observed. "First, knowing the man's record for violence, I would say there is the possibility of his killing you. On the other hand, if he does not feel so inclined, he will no longer be interested in turning his records over to you. In that case, we both lose. While you would rather they go to your agency than to me, I feel your agency would agree that it is better they go to me than to no one."

"Your logic seems rather inescapable. What of Bretagne himself? Surely you want Saci as a prisoner. Or dead."

"His apprehension would be a welcome bonus. But I do not want you killing the man. He is worth much more to us alive than dead, because of the information he possesses. Right now, our main objective is to obtain his records. If he cannot be taken prisoner, he must be allowed to go free rather than be slain. But except for a minor matter, you are to leave that to us."

"Minor matter? You are going to attempt to arrest him, then?"

"Yes. When he sends for you, you will be followed—at some distance. Those savages are devilish good in the bush, though, so we cannot follow too closely and they may succeed in losing us. You can assist us with this."

He produced a small case from his side pocket, opened it and withdrew a pale object the size and approximate shape of a robin's egg.

"I want you to take this pill," he said. "It can be gulped more easily than you might think."

"What is it?"

"A small, but surprisingly effective transmitting unit," he replied. "It will make the tracking chore considerably easier."

"Why should I swallow it?"

"He is a suspicious man. He may have you searched."

"And the cyanide hit me perhaps a day from now?"

"You are also a very suspicious man."

"I'll carry it for you," I said, "but not internally. And at

first hint of search, I'll drop it and grind it into the dirt
with my heel."

"All right," he said, passing it to me.

I dropped it into my pocket and glanced at my watch.
At this, he checked his own.

"Yes, you had best be getting back now," he said. "Just
convince him that you are what you really are and get the
records. We may or may not put in an appearance. If not,
we will meet you on your way back or at the way station.
Good luck. I am glad that you are a reasonable man."

I ignored his extended hand.

"You leave me little choice."

"I am glad that you are a prudent man. Good night."

My shadow accompanied me most of the distance back,
vanishing somewhere in the vicinity of the outhouse.

Maria did not comment upon my extended absence,
but excused herself after inquiring as to the location of
the facility. I obtained another cup of coffee when she
left and considered my situation as I sipped it.

I did not give a damn about Saci, the revolutionary
movement, Bassenrut, the CIA or the government of
Brazil. Morales had been mistaken in figuring that I did
give a damn about some of these things. I was here primarily to satisfy my curiosity, since I had already seen so
much of the show. Also, now that it seemed I might soon
come into possession of something Morales wanted, it
would be pleasant to find some way of employing it that
would screw him up as much as possible. There was definitely that factor, in addition to a growing interest in Emil
Bretagne. An academic interest, of course. I didn't care
what became of him, but I was curious as to what he had
really done and why.

Maria returned before Vera did, and things were defi-

nitely on an upswing again. The woman was bad for my
peace of mind as well as my glands, but with each swing
of the pendulum I found myself getting more used to it
and, what was worse, liking those upswings more and
more. I was again the old buddy, the lover, and as we
reminisced over coffee and cigarettes I began considering
where I could put her. Half-consciously, I redesigned my
apartment. Damned insidious, it was.

Over an hour must have passed in this fashion. Save
for an old woman dozing at a corner table, Maria and I
were the only inhabitants of the rest station. The woman
had told us to help ourselves to coffee and fruit. No one
seemed curious as to why we were waiting there, but
then Vera had spoken to the woman earlier.

Maria had gotten me to talking about the Taurus, and
while I realized it was more than just a passing interest I
did not care. I was darting closer and closer to the flame
when Vera returned and Maria frowned.

She dumped four old shoes onto the table before us
and said, "Put these on. For walking."

Both pairs were too large, but if we were going to do
any real hiking they were still an improvement over our
city footgear. We stuffed wads of paper into significant
nooks and crannies. As I donned them, I channeled my
thinking back to the issue at hand. Then we followed Vera
outside.

She led us up the road away from the station, then
switched on a flashlight and located a trail that led into
the forest. We proceeded along it.

The blackness was a heavy, damp thing in under the
trees. Perspiration formed on my face and little buzzing
things orbited my head, trying to get inhaled. The trail
grew spongy, yielding with each step, occasionally surrendering a clod of soil to our boots.

"How far are we going, anyway?" I asked.

She turned quickly, raised the torch and held a finger to her lips.

"Quite a distance," she whispered. "Keep your voice low. Better not to talk at all."

Chastised, I fell into step behind her once more as she turned and continued. I thought it damned silly, and then I thought about the tiny transmitter I was carrying and the fact that someone was doubtless tracking us at that moment. I resolved to dispose of the thing before very long and to keep my mouth shut in the meantime.

We departed the trail a while later and began winding our way downhill through a heavy growth of vegetation. We followed no noticeable path. The way grew steeper, and after a time I thought I occasionally heard the sound of running water. It became more rocky, and continuing our descent, we had to hold hands in places.

We finally came upon a small stream, which we crossed by means of rocks, a log and some shallow wading. I had forced the transmitter into the crotch of a partly split stick I had picked up earlier, and it cheered me to see it depart downstream when I released it. The least it could buy us would be more time—unless they were following closely enough to actually have us in sight.

We then proceeded up a rocky incline and into the forest once more. We could not see the sky, and the only sounds were our breathing, the noises of insects and the occasional scraping of our boots on stones or sticks.

After a time, we crossed another stream, rested briefly and moved on. Perhaps twenty minutes later we came to a halt in a small clearing at the foot of a gigantic, twisted tree decorated with snake-like vines and sleeping orchids. Vera flicked her light on and off a number of times, then we waited in darkness. I lit a cigarette.

"He is to meet us here?" Maria inquired.

"No," said Vera, and she repeated the signal.

"Where, then?"

"Farther on. I do not know."

She flashed through the sequence periodically, over the next ten minutes or so.

The last time that she began it, I realized there were two men standing near us, close to the base of the tree. My peripheral vision barely caught them and I froze instantly, not wanting to stir up anyone who could approach me that silently in the brush.

Vera took note of their presence, approached them and began talking. I could not recognize the language. The men wore small loincloths, carried machetes and were very dark. They responded in what seemed to be the same language and occasionally gestured with their blades.

Vera returned to us, smiling.

"They are going to guide us to one of their camps," she said, "where he is now staying. Come."

We followed, and they led us through mazes of trees, ferns, vines and rocks, occasionally disturbing sleeping things of unknown phylum, class, order, family, genus and species, which snorted, barked or screeched, then flew, slithered, ran or climbed away. I was amazed that the men carried no lights themselves.

We received only noncommittal replies when we asked how much farther, how much longer. When we insisted, they paused somewhat grudgingly to let us rest. They did not even seem to be breathing hard.

We went on for hours. My feet grew sore and my legs began to tire. There were two more streams and a rocky ridge. We came upon something like a trail after that, and the going was somewhat easier. Then, gradually, hardly noticeable at first, a faint light made its way into the world, touching the edges of leaves, enhancing outlines, causing dewdrops to sparkle, spiderwebs to shimmer like roadmaps of celestial cities. I was drenched by then, partly from my own juices, partly from droplets from on high.

There was no surprise. It was just an insidious diffusion of light and the slow awareness that we could see where we were going once more. Then our guides called a break in a somewhat open area at the foot of a small range of hills, beside a wide, rapid stream. It was quite light by then and the sky was overcast.

We waited there for about fifteen minutes. I was very thirsty, but I did not trust the stream and none of my companions was carrying a canteen. No further information as to our destination had been volunteered, and I was not about to ask any more questions. Maria and I stood together, smoking and conjecturing. Vera and the two men paced and studied our surroundings, occasionally muttering incomprehensibles to one another.

I heard the *chunk* as the round struck the bole of the tree before I heard the weapon's report. Some buried reflex rose again and I pushed Maria to the ground and threw myself across her. Our guides remained standing, however. They were waving in the direction of the hills.

A man stood atop the middle summit. He had reslung his rifle and raised a pair of field glasses. Then, while observing us, he signaled with a handkerchief. The taller of the two men whipped off his loincloth and waved a reply, talking excitedly the while with Vera and the other.

After a final consultation, the man dropped his loincloth to the ground and took off running in the direction of the hills. He was out of sight in a matter of moments. The man on the hilltop continued to regard us, but he did not raise his rifle again.

I climbed slowly to my feet and helped Maria to hers.

"What," I asked Vera, "is going on?"

"He wishes to give us a message at this point," she said. "I do not know what it is yet."

"Who?"

"Mister Bretagne. The man on the hill."

"Oh?" said Maria. "And what is your place in all this? Both Portuguese and the native dialect seem natural to you. You seem comfortable here in the jungle, but you located Ovid in the city. What is your association with Emil?"

"My mother was native here, my father was from Rio," she said. "I have lived in many places. I am a priestess of the Church of the Spirits."

"Isn't that voodoo?"

She shrugged.

"Voodoo, Candomblé, Macumba, Xangô. All the same," she said. "I have traveled much, and it is all the same. No matter how far I travel, though, I always return here at certain times, for it is my home. As for Emil Bretagne, I have long prayed for another Rondon, and I think that perhaps he has come."

"Rondon?" Maria said. "I'm afraid that I do not understand."

Vera smiled.

"My grandmother knew Rondon," she said, "and he was an old man even then. He was a half-breed like myself, born in Matto Grosso. Long ago, when they were laying the telegraph line from Rio to Matto Grosso's capital, he was in charge of the work, going through the jungle with his men, digging holes, putting up telegraph poles. One day, they saw an Indian, and Rondon followed him. He came to a place where the tribe was massed, ready to attack his work party. They shot poisoned arrows at him and he fled. The next day he returned, bearing no weapon himself, and walked into their camp. He stood in the center of their village and did not move, waiting. The chief approached him then, with an arrow nocked and his bow drawn, but he never shot it. Instead, he was so impressed by his courage that he lowered his weapon and knelt at Rondon's feet. They were very primitive people, the Nambiquara, and though they lived on the river they did not know how to make boats. Rondon taught them to build them, and he gave them medicine for their sicknesses. They became good friends. As he moved on, placing the telegraph lines, Rondon made more and more friends among the Indians.

"When then telegraph was installed, settlers came. As in your country, there was much hostility between the settlers and the Indians. It persists to this day. There are killings on both sides, though it is now mainly the Indians who suffer. In those days it was far worse, however, so that the government came to ask Rondon to do something about it—knowing that he had many friends in the jungle. He founded the Indian Protection Service then, and he worked for peace and the betterment of the native peoples. When he died—in 1956, I think it was—he had befriended and aided over 150,000 Indians from well over 100 tribes. He had set up Indian Protection posts all over Brazil. They talked about giving him the Nobel Prize for Peace for his work.

"But despite all that Cândido Rondon did," she went on, "things are still much as they were in the Old West of your country. There are men who earn their living as professional Indian killers, for there are settlers who want their lands, rubber tappers who want their trees, miners who want their minerals. Things are better than they would have been, but still, they are far from being good. Many of the tribes are near to extinction. Civilization offers them nothing but disease, poverty and misery— and the settlers, the rubber tappers, the hunters and the miners threaten the survival of the old ways. They must be protected from Civilization. We still have the Indian Protective Service, with its parks and preserves. But this is of the government. It is not of the people. It is not enough. Another Rondon is needed."

"And you think Emil Bretagne…?" Maria began.

"Yes," Vera said. "Over the years he has helped. Not much, but always some. Then, recently, he came to the people in person. It is difficult to explain, but I was there at the time and I know it must have been like that on the day Rondon went to the chief of the Nambiquaras. There is that about the man which is powerful and honest. I knew that he was a very great man—everyone knew it. And he has already done things for my people. He is very clever. He says that he will be with us for a long while now, and I believe him. You ask my association with him? He has named me his secretary," she concluded.

The notes of dedication, ethnic pride and self-importance had been of sufficient intensity to convince me that this Bretagne brother, also, was a highly skilled con man, had there been any need for further convincing. I had nodded and smiled at all the appropriate times as she spoke, and searched my memory a bit. Yes, I had heard or read of Cândido Rondon somewhere, years ago. A positively inspired idea, taking advantage of a local legend that way. Instant loyalty. I wondered precisely how he had managed to pull it off in so short a time. My respect for the man increased further.

"…I wonder what his message could be?" Maria was saying. Our unclad guide had reached the summit and conferred with Emil and another man who had remained out of sight until his arrival. Instructions were apparently given, and our man had vanished once more.

Vera shrugged.

"I do not know."

When I looked back a few moments later, the hilltop was deserted.

From somewhere, I heard several rolls of thunder, and hoped it was raining on Morales and his crew while obliterating whatever trail we might have left. A few drags more on my cigarette, a sudden smile from Maria, a warm feeling, more thunder and a clean smell from the stream.

After a time, our guide returned. He bore with him a canteen of water, which he passed about. As we slaked our thirst, he spoke with Vera and the other man.

Then Vera turned toward us once more.

"You will come with me, and with Pomi," she said to Maria, indicating our other guide as she spoke.

"You will go with Jom," she said to me, nodding toward the man who had just returned from the hill.

"Why?" asked Maria.

"Because he wishes it so."

"But I want to meet him, too."

"Perhaps you will later. Now he wishes to speak only with Mister Wiley. Come with us, and I will see that you are comfortable."

Maria looked at me, something of uncertainty plowing her brow.

I nodded.

"Go ahead," I said. "There must be a reason. We've trusted them so far."

She nibbled her lower lip and nodded.

"Yes, that is true," she said. "Very well."

Jom came and stood beside me.

"Until later, then," I said.

"Yes. Goodbye. Take care."

The three of them moved off leftward, toward the foot of the hills. Jom led me to the right.

We passed through the brush, not following any notice-able trail for perhaps ten minutes. Then we struck a narrow, twisting pathway and remained on it. The hills were always to our left, until they passed from view. We encountered the stream again on several occasions. Finally, we remained with it, and the path widened as we moved along its bank.

Perhaps twenty-five minutes later, I caught sight of the village. Five minutes after that, we were in it.

Naked children stopped playing to stare at me, thumbs in their mouths. When I had passed them, they began to follow along behind. Naked adults kept their thumbs out of their mouths and did not follow after, but they stopped whatever they were about and stared silently. A few goats and lots of chickens ignored me for their scavenging and scratching. The huts were of rough wood and pick-your-own thatching. The stream was only a few hundred yards away, and there were canoes drawn up on the bank beside it. Some smoke drifted toward the sky's blind eye, and the aromas of unusual recipes reached my nostrils. Lightning flashed, the thunder growled once more and the dust was pocked about me. It would make a nice woodcut, I thought, glancing back over my shoulder.

As we moved along, I could see that the village was more extensive than I had first thought. It followed the curving of the stream, and when we rounded a blind of heavy brush I saw that it continued on. Jom led me that way, conducted me to one of the huts, halted before it and made motions for me to enter. I pushed back a hanging of light fabric and stepped inside.

It was deserted. There was a rude table near the center, containing stationery weighted down with a flat rock, a ballpoint pen, an empty basin with a red washcloth hung over its edge, a folded towel, a small mirror, a safety razor and a nail file. There was no writing or impressions on the paper. Two expensive-looking suitcases stood at the head of a low bed. They were locked. There was a chair at the table and a low bench beside the door. Part of a packing case in the far corner held assorted crockery and a can of tobacco. A sheathed machete hung from a peg above it. There were six small windows with rough bark ledges. They held an assortment of knickknacks, pots and tins of growing things and a red, green and yellow parrot who moved only its head, slowly, keeping an inquisitive amber eye on my every movement.

A glance out the window showed me that the parade of children had already begun to disperse, and Jom had not moved from his position beside the doorway. I took a drink of water from a small Lister bag by the window and seated myself on the bench.

Then the rain hit hard and a sudden wind lashed it through the camp. I moved to the door and held back the hanging, but Jom made noises and gestures indicating that he would not enter. I let the flap fall again. Literal-minded fellow, most likely. Been told to wait outside, and that was it.

About ten minutes later the rain let up. About five minutes after that I sprang to my feet as the hanging was pushed aside.

I recognized the Bretagne features immediately, beneath the wide, wet brim of his hat. He stamped his boots, hung the hat and rifle on a peg and extended his hand in my direction. He grinned, a disarmingly pleasant thing.

"Mr. Wiley," he said. "Sorry to have kept you waiting."

I found myself smiling back.

"That's all right," I told him, clasping his hand. "A few more minutes hardly mattered."

"I must apologize for the discomfort this roundabout way of arranging a meeting has caused you," he said. Then, "You haven't eaten since yesterday, have you?"

He did not wait for a reply—which was just as well—but stuck his head out the door and said something to Jom.

No, good my lord, I have not eaten, nor slept—and my bones remember that bus ride and my muscles this trek. Also, my eyeballs feel as if they have been scoured with steel wool and must look that way from your side, too. I could use a bath, a deodorant, a shave and some Band-Aids while you're at it.

He turned back toward me then, making a few futile attempts to brush the moisture from his khakis.

"We'll have something for you shortly," he said, moving across the room and squatting beside a small pit partly covered by a piece of perforated metal.

He soon had a fire going in the pit, produced a coffee pot from the packing case, washed it, filled it and set it to boil. He did not remove his web belt, which held a side-arm and a hunting knife.

He seated himself at his writing table, sighed and began packing his pipe. I reseated myself on the bench and lit a cigarette.

"You know why I sent for you./?" he said/asked.

"I have a pretty good idea."

"You wouldn't be here," he said, "if you didn't feel I have something you want."

"I don't deny it. *Do* you?"

He lit his pipe.

"I think so," he said. "But first I am curious as to what you know or think you know concerning my activities."

I shrugged.

"You were an office boy at the Bassenrut Foundation and you looted the petty cash box. You had always wanted to go on a camping trip…"

He chuckled.

"In a sense you are correct," he said. "It almost was petty cash to them, and I *did* always want to come here."

He puffed several aromatic clouds.

"Tell me more of the office boy's motives," he said.

"Motive for running? Because he was about to get tripped up. Motive for taking it? Political, I'd guess. He had apparently been diverting it for years, in ways that eventually got it to a revolutionary group possibly interested in seeing the State of São Paulo secede and become a separate country. He might even have been known to them as 'Saci'."

"No," he interrupted. "Saci he never was."

"Whatever," I continued, "he seemed to sour on this end of things as soon as the water got choppy. He fled, taking with him the records of his various clandestine transactions, proceeded to siphon off and sequester as much of the capital as he could in a few days' time, then went to ground and began looking for an opportunity to buy security in exchange for the knowledge of people, places and dealings he possesses which would cripple the movement and possibly result in the dismemberment of Bassenrut."

"...as well as embarrass the federal government, if you turned it over to an outside agency as powerful here as the one you represent," he finished. "That would make him a real twenty-four carat bastard, wouldn't it? Selling out his employer, government and comrades-in-arms? In return for what? Security and whatever of the money he can get away with?"

"I shall refrain from judgment," I said.

"Very Christian," he responded, chuckling. "Did you know I had a brother who was a priest?"

"Yes," I said. "I note your use of the past tense."

"Yes. He died recently. I'm sure you are aware of this."

"Yes. In Madrid."

"Lisbon."

"Pardon me."

"You feel, I take it, that I will join him soon?"

"Let me put it this way," I said. "If I were you I wouldn't start reading a long novel—or a short one. Maybe not even a short story."

He quirked an eyebrow.

"Really?" he said. "I'm quite surprised. You came a long distance, presumably to obtain something I have that you want. You must have come prepared to offer something in return for it—and you did speak of security a moment ago. Now you talk as if it is an unavailable commodity. I had expected at least an offer of safe conduct out of the country, a new identity, bodyguards, social security and Medicare, life after death. Things like that."

"Are those your terms?"

"No. I was simply speculating. But if that is not your offer, what are you prepared to give me?"

"I had nothing specific in mind," I told him. "I knew you had plenty of money, so that didn't seem a likely inducement. Offhand, I'd say some version of security seems the best bet. Life being full of vicissitudes, however, you must of course realize that it is an impossible thing to guarantee beyond certain limits. I decided it would be easiest to simply come and ask you what you want. What *do* you want?"

"Before we get into that, I feel somewhat obliged to explain some of the things I have done."

"You don't have to justify yourself to us."

"It is not justification so much as it is a belief that your agency will find the information instructive in evaluating my request."

"Which is?"

"One thing at a time. To begin with, the office boy was himself deceived. He was somewhat idealistic—still is, for that mater—and he believed that the group of people he helped to subsidize had as one of their major objectives the protection and benefaction of people such as those who surround us now. In fact, he believed that work along these lines was going on the entire while he was providing assistance. Yes, this sounds somewhat naïve. But he was that sort of person. Whatever injustices you know of as having been rendered the Indians of your continent, take these and multiply them by at least ten. The tribesmen have been suffering from a continuing unofficial policy of extermination. It would be best—for them—if they were simply left alone. This is impossible, however. The next best thing would be the provision of adequate medical and educational facilities, and some means of more adequately defending their rights. The Indian Protection Service tries, but they are understaffed, their budget is too low and their programs are insufficient. Some missionaries try, but they want their souls and their minds in return for what they give. The Church is too damn strong in this country. Private charities do not really know what to do whenever they get interested."

He stopped then, blinked, seemed to refocus his thoughts.

"Didn't mean to run on so," he said, puffing, "but I am quite moved by their position. It is not as if they are the only oppressed minority in the world. God knows, the laborers in the north spend their lives under miserable enough conditions. The government says nothing there because the large landholders are powerful, and the Church encourages their acceptance of their lot. Hell, the priests have their souls and the landowners have their asses. What's left is pretty dreary. And I won't even go into life in the *favelas*. Perhaps you're read *Child of the Dark*. The Indians are farther removed from civilization than all this. Even such supposed benefits as vitamin pills can make them violently ill, their diets are so different from those of civilized men. My point is that they must be treated almost as if they are another species if they are to survive. Since we cannot pretend they do not exist, they must be dealt with, and very carefully. This is not being done, properly, today. The office boy thought that the money he provided was helping to do it. When he learned that it was not, he grew angry. Is it difficult then to see his withdrawing this support from the movement?"

"No," I replied. "It is difficult to see why he did not become aware of this state of affairs earlier."

"Well, he was duped," he said. "It was not the first time someone had trusted the wrong people."

"True," I said. "Take the Bassenrut Foundation for an example."

"A thief has no right to the same moral indignation as an honest man, should his pocket be picked," he said.

"Oh?"

"They don't come any crookeder than Bassenrut," he stated. "Perhaps the word 'Foundation' in their corporate title brings forth visions of an organization handing out research grants, promoting the arts and engaging in generally philanthropic activities. Actually, they are a conglomerate, controlling many, many things, some of them quite legal, some of them not so. Movement is the key. You keep the funds flowing back and forth among a sufficient number of entities, and it can be made virtually impossible to tell how much is where, when, and what the precise total is. The use of various accounting methods and different fiscal years for some of them helps, too. Then you divert whenever you need it for other enterprises. You might even use that route in reverse to plow back conspicuous outside earnings."

"That office boy set up the system?"

"He discovered it on his doorstep one day, a weak, red-faced, squalling thing. He developed an affection for it, fed it on demand, educated it and brought it to responsible maturity."

"Then he undertook the task of conversion from its diversions?"

"Aptly put. Yes, this occurred when he realized that his offspring had fallen in with low companions."

"The movement? It was financed this way?" .

"Mainly, yes."

"I find it difficult to believe that the office boy was the only one involved."

"I never meant to imply that. He was the technician. He had considerable support among the directorate. Bassenrut would be the number one economic entity in the new country."

"The federal government never got suspicious?"

"We produced elegant financial reports and paid our taxes, which is more than can be said for some. Also, civil servants, like politicians, are eminently amenable to largesse. The ultimate objectives of Bassenrut were never suspect. No one ever guessed at a connection with the movement."

"Then what?"

"A big section of Matto Grasso was to have become a protectorate, and the Indians our wards. In the meantime, they were supposed to be well cared for. I learned only recently that this was not being done. Further investigation led me to the conclusion that there was no intention ever to do this. The promise was just a carrot for a single individual."

"So you decided to smash both Bassenrut and the movement?"

"Correct."

"So why not take the whole story to the federal government?"

He shook his head.

"Bassenrut is too powerful in this country. They can put pressure on a man, or possibly remove him. The only greater source of pressure I know of would be from the outside. If the United States felt its Brazilian interests were jeopardized by the movement and by Bassenrut, something would be done. That, I decided, is the best avenue of attack."

"I see," I said. "What had the Vatican to do with all this?"

He dropped his eyes quickly and was silent for a time. Then, "How much do you know?" he asked.

"I know that the amount your brother was able to authorize for shaky propositions in this country came to about three million dollars. I know they involved you on this end. I am curious how much he knew as to what was really going on."

"He was all for the underdog, too," he said, "the poor Indian. Only his motives may to a large extent have been determined by a growing dissatisfaction with the Church. The Church's record in Brazil is somewhat notorious, and since it would not be the first time it had lost money in business dealings, I believe that he felt it was a way of making reparation."

"That's an awful lot of reparation for those who are no longer around to be made whole."

He shrugged.

"The effects of the initial wrongdoings are very much present today," he said. "Since my brother, also, is no longer around, I find it equally useless to dwell upon the motives for his actions."

"But their effects, also, are very much present today."

"True," he said, smiling. "But that is now an affair between Rome and myself. I intend to see their—loan—

eventually repaid. Possibly with interest. There are oil-rich Indians in your country. This area is rich in other resources. If it must be exploited, the benefits should go to the natural owners—who are an honest sort. If the Vatican's money is dumped into yet another bucket and from there is poured out in form of development loans, they will repay it when they are able. By the way, would you be interested in becoming the U.S. representative for native artwork from this area?"

"Possibly," I said, considering it.

"It is really quite good. I must show you some before you leave. Ah—here's your breakfast."

The hanging was pushed aside, and Jom entered bearing a tray containing several fish and a variety of fruits. He placed it on the bench, nodded, smiled and left. It looked good and smelled good.

"Aren't you having any?" I asked.

"No, I've already eaten," he said. "Go ahead."

He checked the coffee, decided it was ready and poured two cups. The food *was* good, and I was quite hungry. I fell to it.

When I was finished, I sighed and pushed the tray away. He had not spoken the entire while I was eating.

"Thanks," I said, rising.

I crossed the room and helped myself to another cup of coffee. I refilled his, also.

I reseated myself then and lit another cigarette. I decided to wait and let him speak next. I wondered where Morales and his bunch were at that moment. I was engaged in a complicated internal debate as to whether or not I should warn Emil.

"Now you know why he is willing to act against his employer, his comrades and his country," he said, after a time.

"Yes," I said. "It tends to make things somewhat more clear. You indicated, however, that all of this was but preamble to your naming a price for the materials. Are you ready to go into that now?"

He nodded.

"First," he said, "I want immunity from prosecution by my own government."

"I'm afraid I'm in no position to make you such a guarantee."

"Nonsense," he replied. "Your people will be dictating all sorts of things to them on the basis of the information I provide. They can as easily add that."

"What I mean to say is that I cannot speak for my superiors in something like this. I'm not authorized to."

"Then I want your word that you will inform them that that was one of my terms for surrendering the material. There will be no compelling reason for them not to honor it, since they will have obtained what they want."

"Very well. You have my word that I will recite your request and add my personal recommendation that it be met."

"Sufficient," he said. "Second, since my government will have Bassenrut in a very uncomfortable position, I want them to use some of that leverage to persuade the organization not to make any sort of reprisal against me, legal or otherwise."

"That matter would seem to be strictly between your government and Bassenrut."

"Don't be naïve. If they can be pressured into one thing, they can be prodded into another."

"My word again, on this one? That I'll try?"

"That's the best you can give me right now. I'll have to settle for it."

"You have it, then. What about your fellow travelers?"

"Since there is nothing you can do on that count, I'll have to make my own terms with them. That's my problem."

"Agreed. Is there anything else?"

"Yes. I also want to be sure that another group leave me alone."

"Which group is that?"

"Your own agency. If they want further explanations, clarifications, explications, too bad. This is not included. I don't want to be hounded by them on matters of detail. Or any other matters."

"Are your records sufficiently clear for them to do without you?"

"Everything they will need is there. Some of it will take some digging, but enough information is provided."

"That sounds fair. Since their main interest will be in seeing the movement broken, you are also counting on this taking care of your comrades."

"Of course I am hoping this will remove all of them. Some will doubtless get by, though. As I said, that's my problem."

"This leaves you with the money you have already appropriated and a margin of safety dependent upon the adequacy of the purge and the sufficiency of your government's word to mine—should it be given."

"That is the best I can hope for. It will have to do."

"I still would not want to be in your place," I said. "Actually, it strikes me that you have little choice but to surrender the materials to my government."

"Perceptive of you," he noted.

"Which renders your bargaining position pretty much fictitious," I said.

"There are two major caveats on the other side of the globe," he said, "if you stop to think about it for a moment.

I might either enhance my position with the present regime by turning my records over to it, or perhaps suppress them and abet the revolutionaries. The new nation would be duly grateful, I am certain.

"However," he continued, "I find these alternatives distasteful and offer them only in rebuttal to your flat statement that I have no other course to follow. It is all academic now. I trust you are a man of your word. In that case, our agreement had already been concluded."

"I am, and I consider it so."

He rose then and crossed the room. From the packing case, he withdrew a hand trowel. Moving to his small cooking fire, he set the coffee pot aside, then used the tool to flip the grill away. He began shoveling out the embers, pausing to relight his pipe with one. I was apprehensive at that point and wishing he would hurry. I did not like thinking about Morales and his men skulking about in the woods, searching for this place, finding it. I had resolved to warm Emil, but not until I had the records. After all, I had given my word that I would try to see him protected, and as I saw it, the promise was already in effect. Still, I wanted the papers before I said anything. That was part of the deal, too. I was sure that enough of my jungle instinct remained so that I could find my way back to the highway unescorted, if it came to that. But that would raise more problems than it would solve. Especially Maria.

He turned his attention to his hearth once more, and I rose and began pacing slowly.

"Where is Maria—the girl who was with me?" I asked.

He began digging into soil, now he had cleared the embers.

"Nearby," he said. "I thought it best for her to rest while we talked. It was a long walk, a sleepless night, and our conversation of a tedious, technical nature. She is well taken care of and you will be reunited on the way back. I did not expect you to bring a female companion."

"Neither did I. You mean she is elsewhere in this village?"

"Nearby," he repeated, scraping something with the point of his tool as I paused near the doorway. "You say her name is Maria?"

The outline of a leather case appeared in the dirt at his feet.

"I brought her with me from Rome," I said. "She was— a friend—of your brother's."

"Oh, she is *that* Maria," he said. "Yes, he had spoken of her. What is she doing here?"

"It is a long and complicated story," I said, "but basically, she wants revenge against whoever killed Claude. She has the notion that I will eventually locate the person or persons responsible."

"Why would she believe this?"

"Because she knew me years ago and thinks I can."

"What did you do years ago?"

"I was a criminal," I replied. "Which gives rise to a question. Is there anything you can tell me concerning his death that might be of help?"

He removed the leather case from the excavation and began dusting it with a blue bandana he withdrew from his hip pocket.

"I've no solid facts," he said, "but you can have my speculations for whatever they're worth. I think he somehow got mixed up with Maria's employer."

"The Sign of the Fish? Bruno? How…?"

"Either he caught on to their operations, or they fancied that he had and might do something about them. Neither had any way of knowing that they were both serving the same master. Had I only thought of it, I could have protected him."

His face had a hard, cold look to it then, and it seemed he assailed the briefcase with an unnecessary violence.

"I'm afraid that you have lost me," I said.

"You disappoint me," he stated. "I would have thought your outfit aware of them by now. Well, perhaps they are and you are simply not privy to it. The Sign of the Fish has galleries in seventeen countries, engaged primarily in legitimate art dealings. They also enjoy an under-the-counter relationship with Bassenrut. They provide a ready avenue for the transfer of foreign funds to this country. It is done, basically, by means of converting funds from Bassenrut's undercover foreign investments into artwork in the host country, underevaluating it when shipping it here, then disposing of it for a truer price. Customs officials are hardly art critics.

"You'll find much of the story in here," he finished, slapping the side of the briefcase.

I could not but speculate for a moment as to whether this was the route taken by some of the pieces with which I had been associated. Fascinating. To consider that I might have been within a brief distance of some of them once again, all unawares. Would it not be a jest if I were to...

I shook off the daydream.

"And your brother?" I said. "How did he fit into all that?"

"It is the only thing I can see. I told you it was just a guess," he said. "But there is a connection there. The girl—Maria. If they thought, right or wrong, that he had learned of their operations from her and was planning either to blackmail them or go to the authorities, they would have acted to assure his silence."

"Maria was aware of what was going on?"

"I would imagine she knew that not all of their operations were normal. She must be an intelligent girl. My brother would not have had anything to do with her were she not."

"Why should they have assumed he was about to jeopardize their operations?"

"Because of his peculiar actions there near the end, culminating in his flight," he said. "They had no way of knowing that he was growing progressively concerned over the investigation of his accounts at the Vatican. He was exceedingly furtive and suspicious during those final weeks—I could tell that just talking to him on the telephone. This, together with his liaison with an employee over whom they kept watch—they watch them all—must have made them apprehensive enough to pursue him and destroy him when he fled."

"What did you talk about in those telephone conversations?"

"The investigation, mainly, and what he should do about it. We agreed that since it was only a matter of time until a heavy hand fell upon his shoulder, his best course of action lay in fleeing the country and coming here. I could shelter him. It is easy to obtain false papers in Portugal, and it is easy to get from Portugal to Brazil. That is why he went to Lisbon."

"At around the same time you were having second feelings about your own situation here?"

"Yes. Everything seems to happen at once, doesn't it?" he said, rising and moving to his writing table, where he deposited the briefcase.

"Here they are. All the answers you could possibly want," he announced, "and lots more."

"So you believe your brother was killed by Bruno's people?" I insisted.

"As I said, it is only a guess. But it seems to make some sense," he stated, fumbling to light his pipe once more.

I saw Martinson lying there dead in his villa, and the face of the man I had killed. I remembered lunch with Bruno, and the art leads he had furnished me, calculated to make me a tiny sum. He had seemed suspicious of something. Had this been a bribe, an attempt to satisfy me and steer me away from his business? Was it he who then had me followed to the home of our security officer, followed by men authorized to commit murder if it seemed I was betraying a fancied trust? If so, why should he have assumed I possessed inside information as to his activities? It did not make sense. And then his death. Perhaps because he had failed? Or done the wrong thing?

And what was Maria's real role in all this, then?

"Are you planning on doing anything about it?" I asked.

"There is not really anything that I can do," he said, "as I've no real information to offer the investigators. Besides, he was a religious man, who never advocated vengeance and believed *mors janua vitae*. In other words—"

"*Sod cucullus non facit monachum,*" I interrupted, "*et ignoti nulla cupido*. I understand, though. You will do nothing."

"Damn it!" he said. "I am not insensitive to my own brother's death! It is just that there is nothing that I *can* do. I doubt that his killer will ever be found. Did you come here just to bait me on that?"

"No," I said. "Sorry. It is just that I had grown very interested in the case. It was near to the point where I came in."

"I see," he said. "Don't throw any more Latin at me. I'm allergic to it. You have everything that I'm going to give you now."

He glanced out the window. The storm had turned into

a light, misty rainfall, and bits of sunlight were beginning to sneak by it.

"You are doubtless somewhat fatigued," he said, "but I would recommend your starting the return trip as quickly as possible. If you travel all day, camp out tonight and hike most of tomorrow, it will get you to a station on the highway other than the one you started from. From there you will be able to get transportation in either direction: Brasilia, or São Paulo or Rio. The tribesmen know the way. Promptness is all. The sooner those papers reach your superiors, the sooner my insurance goes into effect."

"Yes," I said. "I'm anxious to get rid of them already."

"Which way did you plan on heading, toward Disneyland or back to the south?"

"South," I said. "I know my way around a little better down there."

"Good," he said, nodding. "Tell me, do you think you could find your way back here?"

"Yes."

"I had a feeling that you might be able to," he said. "If, after delivering this bundle, you should feel inclined to make a return visit—alone or accompanied—you will find that I no longer reside here and that my whereabouts are unknown."

"Thanks for the advice."

"Just thought I'd save you a possible disappointment. I plan on moving out in a few hours, as a matter of fact."

"That, of course, leaves us with no way of advising you as to the effectuation of your requests."

"I'll find out for—"

The sound of gunfire, breaking his sentence, dictated my next move also. I had been pacing where I was pacing for a reason.

I swung his rifle down from the peg and had a shell in

the chamber before he could draw his pistol. He refrained from doing it then, because I was pointing the rifle at him. Damn Morales anyway! He must have been following closely enough to have us in sight when I ditched the transmitter. I had just lost my lead, not to mention Emil's confidence—and I had to clear out fast and take the briefcase with me. Time was burning.

"God damn you, you son of a bitch!" he said, preliminary doubtless to other remarks which I did not give him the opportunity to voice.

"Shut up and listen!" I snarled. "It's a cop named Morales whom I thought I'd shaken. I tried not to lead him here, but—"

"Morales?" he cried, his face livid—and he reached for his pistol.

I had a choice of shooting him or taking a chance.

I lunged and arced the butt of the rifle forward and up.

The blow glanced off his forearm and struck his shoulder. It was sufficient.

I knocked the gun out of his hand then and pushed him backwards as he swung an ineffectual left hook in my direction.

"Damn it! I wasn't trying to bring him here!" I said. "I tried to ditch him. I thought we had more time than we did. Listen to me. I'm on your side. We've got to get away. With Maria and the papers. Will you help?"

He was still in a half-crouch. He shook himself straight and refocused his gaze on me while rubbing his arm.

"Yes," he said softly. "Yes, damn it. How many men does he have?"

"A couple dozen, I'd guess. Pick up the gun and grab the briefcase. Take me to Maria."

The gunfire had increased, but it was still coming from the far end of the village.

I covered him while he retrieved the weapon and re-holstered it. He snatched up the briefcase with his left hand, strode to the packing case and lifted down the machete.

"This way," he said, crossing to the far wall after having glanced out the window.

With four swift chops he created an exit.

"They can see the front," he explained, stepping through.

I followed him.

He stuck the machete through the pistol belt at his left hip and drew the pistol.

He gestured toward the far end of the village.

"That way," he said.

We commenced running.

The ground was slippery and occasional drops of rain struck us as we ran. After we had gone about a hundred feet, I glanced back.

A line of khaki-clad men was moving through the village, firing at random. I saw two adults and a child on the ground. I heard screaming, and people were fleeing toward the woods and the stream.

I believe we had covered perhaps a hundred yards more when a determined yell went up and another backward glance showed me we had been discovered. Rifles were now leveled in our direction and slugs tore into trees and huts about us. A man began running toward us.

I drew abreast Emil.

"How much farther?" I shouted.

"Quite a distance," he replied. "I don't think we can make it, but she should be safe. Look!"

Ahead, I saw that the villagers were fading into the woods, mothers carrying children, young leading old, others just running like hell. It was fortunate for them that the village seemed to sprawl for well over a mile along the watercourse. It made it impossible for the few men involved in the operation to surround the place, requiring that they settle for a sweeping action instead.

I slipped once, recovered my footing, kept going. Something whistled near while I was down. The far end of the village was quickly becoming deserted. I thought I caught a glimpse of Vera leading Maria through the brush, but I could not be positive.

"She's made it!" Emil yelled back to me. "Head for cover!" and he veered and headed toward a clump of bushes to the left.

I turned also, just as he fell. At first, I thought he had slipped, and then I saw blood. It appeared on his shirt and trousers, left side. He clutched himself about the thigh and middle as I threw myself down beside him and began firing toward our pursuers. I hit one, and another fell with an arrow in his side, shot from somewhere in the jungle.

"How bad is it?" I yelled.

I missed his answer the first time around because of the noise.

"—don't think it's fatal!" I caught, as he repeated. "Take the papers and clear out!"

"Can't leave you!" I said, firing two more rounds.

"They won't kill me! Clear out! Take the machete!"

He unsnapped the pistol belt and the machete fell free. He pushed the briefcase toward me. Both bore bloodstains.

"Maria's safe! Run!" he said, making it sound like a curse.

I squeezed off the remaining rounds, dropping two more men, and let the rifle fall to the ground.

"Okay," I said, taking the blade and the case in either hand, "I will."

I scrambled to my feet and headed for the bushes, hating to leave him but having no real choice.

As I ran, there came several bursts of gunfire from close at hand. I ventured one look back before I drove into cover.

He was propped up on his elbow, covering for me with the pistol. He must have guessed wrongly about their intentions, because he slumped just then, the pistol falling from his hand.

Cursing, I crashed on through the brush.

X.

I was drenched within a matter of seconds. I had traveled only a few feet through the clinging green before the moisture had soaked through to my skin. I pressed ahead, hoping for a break, my shoulders tightened against the shot that would kill me.

The break came in a matter of a few dozen heartbeats.

A rift occurred in the foliage, angling off to my left. It was hardly a path. It was simply a lessening of resistance in that direction. I leaned into it, I moved sideways. I bent backwards to avoid low branches, and the undergrowth dragged at my ankles. I pushed myself through a tight space between two trees, thorns tearing at my clothing. The way widened slightly and I was able to sprint for perhaps twelve feet before it closed again and nooses of vine sought to entangle me.

The sounds of gunfire were muffled, grew sporadic, died down for a time. I broke through to an open area, resisted an impulse to dash across it and worked my way around. I could not hear any sounds of pursuit, but the walls of green muffled distant noises and provided sounds of their own to dampen those nearby. I seemed to be moving onto slightly higher ground.

I used the machete sparingly, not wanting to leave gross signs of my passage. After perhaps half an hour, I was gasping and bleeding lightly from numerous nicks and scrapes. This seemed to attract insects, but my constant movement and steady shedding of perspiration and rain brushed off, crushed or washed away all but the most stubborn and ingenious. The goddamn briefcase kept hooking itself onto the flora.

I was not really certain how far I had come, but I was beginning to get the feeling that I had temporarily eluded any pursuers, when I heard the sound of a helicopter. Moments later, a fat military transport-type chopper passed overhead at treetop-sweeping altitude. It was no real trick to conceal myself from it in all that foliage. I dropped low, and it shortly disappeared back in the direction from which I had come.

Further! I suddenly wanted more distance with an even greater urgency. The thought of additional hunters on my trail now caused me to swing the machete wildly, heedless of any signs that it left, to get through the dense stuff as rapidly as possible, to reach some place where I could travel more quickly. I was somewhat surprised that I had encountered none of the villagers thus far. I had half-hoped that if I made it far enough away from their settlement some of them would spot me and give me some assistance. No luck. Either they had seen me and did not want to get involved any further, or they were fleeing in another direction.

The ground took on a slight rise as I proceeded and the undergrowth let up a bit, though I still could not see for more than ten feet in any direction. After a brief while, the going got somewhat easier and I realized that I was indeed heading for higher ground. I chanced dashing across the next small clear space I came to because I realized my strength was failing and I wanted the distance. It was a gamble, but nobody shot at me and I picked up thirty or forty quick feet. The foliage was less dense on the far side.

A minute or two later I heard the sounds of distant gunfire. Perhaps some of the natives had been cornered. I wondered about Maria then, winced, pushed on. There

had been nothing I could have done to help her earlier
and there was nothing I could do now. Damn Emil and
his briefcase, anyway! He no longer had these problems.
I wondered what *mors janua vitae* meant to him, then
and now.

My feet were aching, but I had the consolation of
knowing they would soon grow numb. They always re-
signed in protest when I marched too much. Poor circu-
lation, I guess, but numbness can be a small blessing at
times.

I threw in a curse for Carl Bernini for getting dead
where he did and fetching me into this whole mess in the
first place. One of my great ambitions, if I lived, would be
to find out why. I saved my biggest and best for Collins,
though. *Anathema sit!*

The angle of the slope increased and I continued to
follow it. The forest thinned even more, and for a time I
was thankful for this. Where it was clear enough to see for
a decent distance ahead, I realized that I was climbing
into those hills from which Emil had first observed us.
From far behind me and somewhat below there still came
the sounds of shooting. I longed once more for an auto-
matic weapon and a place to curl up with it and rest.
Throw in a canteen of water while you're at it.

I did not want to be exposed on the hilltops, but if I
gained a little more height I would be able to move much
faster to the right or the left. So upward and onward then,
the briefcase growing heavier with every step.

The briefcase…I had to get rid of the thing, I decided.
Not just because of the fatigue factor. No.

If they spotted me and I did not have it, they would
not try to kill me. If they were able to take me, I would
still have a small position. Yes, the briefcase had to go.

I began searching for something in the way of a land-
mark.

About five minutes later, I could see the tops of the nearer hills. A few minutes after that I encountered a large boulder perhaps a hundred yards from a tree which reminded me of a hunchback with a cane when I moved about the stone and lined it up with the second hilltop. I excavated beside, then back under that edge of the boulder.

I deposited the briefcase there, covered it over, stamped down the earth, raked it lightly with a branch, strewed leaves, twigs and pebbles all over.

Then I moved out of the area, bearing to my left.

Within fifteen minutes I came to a brush-filled ravine which looked as if it passed through the hills. I took it. I had a strong desire to put the hills between myself and the scene of the action. I was practically sleepwalking by then, the adrenaline all used up and a soft, foggy ache in my limbs. I had to use both hands whenever I swung the machete, and it was like chopping at telephone poles. The rest of the time, I just let it trail beside me, heedless now of any marks that it left. I dropped it several times, almost losing it once. I had to go back twenty-two paces to retrieve it.

On the other side of the hills the sun was shining and the land sloped downward, heading into heavy green once more. It helped that the way was downhill.

I trudged off in search of a place to rest.

Half an hour later, maybe, in a damp hollow beside a rotten log, I covered myself with branches, and heedless of the insects about me or the orchids above me, clutched my machete like a teddy bear and went to a far, far better place.

It was well into the afternoon when I was awakened. The thing that caused it was the sound of gunfire. How long it had been going on, I could not say. The reports slowly filtered down to that central sensory clearing house that handles matters such as this. The place hummed and buzzed a while, then began jolting me back toward wakefulness.

I lay there wishing I weren't. I was thirsty and drenched with perspiration. I ached all over. I did not move. I just lay there and listened.

There was silence for a time, then another burst of gunfire, then silence. There had been a few shouts during the shooting, but I had been unable to distinguish any of the words. It had all sounded to be on my side of the hills.

All of my senses finally came alive. Which was somewhat unfortunate, for I dared not move. I had given up on the notion of comfort a long while before, however. I cultivated stoicism and wondered what was going on.

It did not make particular sense for them to be hunting down the natives and slaughtering them. To indulge in such brutality was also to lose time during which a reprisal might be readied. An altogether stupid act, considering the villagers' knowledge of the area. They must have had more in mind than that, I decided. Perhaps they were under the impression that one of the natives had the records.

I shifted my position only slightly, trying to relax as much as possible. I waited.

After an hour, I was still waiting. I had heard nothing more than the normal sounds of the forest.

It was well into the second hour before anything changed.

The birds grew silent. I had listened to them for so long that they had become a thing ignored, but when their sounds ceased abruptly it was more startling than any noise.

I was afraid even to turn my head at that point. There was no way of telling how near the intruder was until he betrayed himself. I began tensing and relaxing my muscles, tensing them and relaxing them, to make certain all systems were set for "go" and to let them know I was still in the driver's seat.

It was another long while before I heard them.

The sounds of their movements through the brush reached me, halted, continued, halted again, continued. Occasionally, I heard a voice, though I could not distinguish words. I could not tell how distant they were, but I was beginning to get an idea as to their direction.

They were moving quite slowly, passing me widely and heading toward what seemed to be the northeast. Gradually, the sounds of their passage diminished.

It was then that I moved.

Slowly, painfully, I drew my knees to my chest and rolled onto my side.

Then over onto all fours, machete extended...

Then forward, clearing the way before me with my hand before I moved my knee to it...

Gently, slowly, quietly...

Then the other...

I began to gain on them. Finally, I obtained a position to the left and in the rear of the party. I paced them, straining my ears, ready to drop or dash in an instant.

When they halted, I did the same. When they moved, I moved...

Finally, they were still for an unusually long while, and I ventured to draw nearer.

There were three of them and they were talking. I still could not distinguish the words, but I recognized Morales' voice.

Lying flat on my belly, I peered at them through a dense green wall. They were over forty feet away, resting in a narrow glade—two of them standing, one seated on the ground—and my vision was a partial thing, shifting with their movements and currents of air that eddied among the branches.

Gradually, I came to realize that the other two men were Victor and Dominic. Victor was the one seated with his back against a tree trunk. He was breathing heavily. He moaned once. Dominic and Morales were standing apart, apparently conversing softly. This went on for a long while, with considerable gesturing on both sides.

Finally, Dominic went over to Victor and helped him drink some water from a canteen. I licked my lips and lusted after the liquid. Dominic lit a cigarette then and held it for him. Morales remained apart.

After a few moments, Dominic's right hand moved quickly, and it took me a few moments to realize what had occurred. He had drawn a knife from a sheath at his hip and with one rapid movement cut the other man's throat.

He moved methodically then, grinding out the cigarette butt and removing the other's pistol belt, which contained a canteen, knife and handgun. This he slung over his shoulder. Then he went through the man's pockets, appropriating items that I could not see from where I lay. After that, he stretched him out and folded his arms across his chest. Morales called him a fool, loudly enough for me to hear, but ignoring this Dominic proceeded to cut fronds and lay them across the body. Then he stood beside it for a few moments with his head bowed, crossed himself and picked up the other's rifle.

Morales, who had moved to his side by then, muttered something and the two of them turned and continued on in the direction they had been heading, moving more quickly now.

I lay where I was for a long while, considering what had happened.

You do not normally kill your wounded when you are being pursued unless they can tell the enemy something damaging. What could Victor have told to a group of illiterate natives that would be detrimental to Morales? Little, if anything, I decided. Therefore, considering the fact that there had been gunfire and Morales was obviously on the run, I could only conclude that he was being pursued by someone other than the locals. Who?

While I could not even venture a guess, I was cautioned thereby. Apparently the woods were full of fleeing Indians, Morales' men and nameless pursuers of the latter. Whatever the grand total of everything involved might come to, it all seemed to go back to one basic thing: the Bretagne papers. As the only person who knew where they were, I felt as conspicuous as a good painting in the John and Mable Ringling Museum of Art. I would have to be wary behind as well as before, not to mention right, left and above.

These thoughts in mind, I advanced slowly.

From a distance of only a few yards, I surveyed the clearing. I could see nothing to be gained by entering it, so I skirted the thing and took off after Morales and Dominic.

There were no traps and I could detect no pursuit. Within an hour, I had closed the distance and was dogging them once again, from behind and far to the right.

It was perhaps two hours before they paused to rest, and I was thankful for the break myself. I lay on my belly once again and watched them, seated on a fallen tree, smoking, rifles at ready. I ventured nearer this time, as it was beginning to grow dark.

Morales, Morales… To have you so close without a rifle in my hands was indeed a pity.

But right then we seemed alone, the only two rafts on a great, green ocean and you not aware of mine yet, as we

drifted closer and closer together. Patience? Not only did
I possess it, I could enjoy its exercise because of that
thing known as anticipation. If you and Dominic were to
separate, but for even a small while, it would make things
so much easier. If not…The night would be long and very
dark.

They moved again, one more time, however, before
the final curtain fell on day. I followed quietly, of course,
and found myself a shrub-shrouded spot for lurking when
they halted.

They cut fronds for bedding and cursed the jungle frequently, though softly. They did not build a fire. They
smoked and drank from their canteens and discussed the
possibility of shooting something to eat on the morrow.

I thought back to our incarceration and questioning,
to my promise…

No, there would be no hunting for you tomorrow,
Morales. As a matter of principle, I would be against your
being tried and executed for anything, Morales. But my
principles allow for your death by violence, at my hand. I
do not believe in capital punishment, for I do not believe
the state has the right to deprive a man of his life. However, I am not against murder. I was never party to any
social contract and I am, by inclination and belief, an
anarchist. Not being responsible for the way the world is
set up, I do not feel bound by its rules. As a victim of
society, I am willing to coexist with evils greater than
myself unless they push me beyond the point of beara-
bility. When this occurs, I either run or hit back, often
anonymously, with the weapons I possess rather than the
ones I have been assigned. I am happy, of course, that
everyone does not feel this way, or I could not exist as I
do, somewhere midway between civilization and its dis-
contents—for the former situation might be absent and
my *aurea mediocritas* thrown way out of whack. The pos-

sibility of this occurring is still sufficiently remote, however, to keep a pragmatist like myself in decent spirit. *Mediocrita firma*, Morales. I do not fight to win, but to maintain a balance. There is no victory, but your death will contribute to my continuing stalemate with existence. Rest a while now. I am. You might as well. There will be no hunting for you tomorrow.

They sat and talked for a long while, then stretched out as if to sleep. But they continued to talk. It was quite frustrating. Whenever I thought they had finally drowsed off, one of them would mutter something and they would start in again. Insomnia? Jitters? Probably. I was beginning to grow sleepy myself, though.

It had grown quite dark, with only a bit of starlight to help outline things, when the helicopter passed. It was some distance away, but the sound was unmistakable. I thought I had heard it several times earlier, but was not certain except for the one previous occasion.

Its passage, of course, woke up the camp and set off another bout of conversation. After a time, they lit fresh cigarettes. I was tempted to move closer and see whether I could pick up what was being said. I decided against this. It did not matter that much to me.

Finally, their voices rose and I heard several references to "times," accompanied by a waving of left hands, then a synchronization of their wristwatches.

With a sigh, Dominic rose, walked away, paced a bit, poked at several nearby bushes, then seated himself on a rock with his rifle across his knees. Morales resumed his recumbent position.

How excellent! I had been afraid all along that they might neglect guard duty. It made things easier to have them separated that way.

I rubbed fresh dirt on my hands and face, just in case

the old was flaking off. It smelled good, that damp mixture of compost and soil. Then I backed carefully away from my position and scouted to the rear and the flanks. I moved about the camp three times in widening circles, to be certain someone was not doing unto me as I was to my prey. If they were, I decided after a long while, then they were so good that any speculation concerning them belonged in the realms of metaphysics.

I closed upon the camp once more, drawing much nearer than I had previously. Dominic was up and making his rounds again. I watched him for perhaps fifteen minutes as he paced and poked his way around, as he peered into the shadows. My eyes had by then adapted, of course, as far as Purkinje permitted, and the halo of a smothered moon assisted me slightly from on high.

He returned to his rock, and I advanced a few feet after he had seated himself. If I were to charge him right then, I felt that I could take him with the machete. But I was equally certain that he would get off a few yells and possibly fire a couple rounds also, before I dispatched him. Morales would be awake in an instant and I would be dead in an instant and a half. I had to take Dominic in complete silence.

I wormed my way nearer, breathing open-mouthed.

He stood again and looked all around him. I froze.

Then he moved off to his left and halted. This brought him slightly closer to me and twenty to twenty-five feet away from Morales. Though he still wore the pistol, he had left his rifle behind, leaning against the stone. I was at a loss to understand his actions.

…until he tore a handful of leaves from the nearest branch, unfastened his pistol belt and placed it on the ground, then unbuckled his trousers and pushed them down, along with his shorts.

I was moving before he had fully squatted.

I crept up silently behind him.

It is a hell of a way to die, I'll admit, but I was not going to look this gift horse in the mouth.

He had to die, of course. I could not take a chance at a knockout attempt. If the first blow was off, I could not deal with him and Morales both.

I raised the blade.

He had both hands resting on the ground for balance and his head was far forward.

I rose to my knees, then moved my left leg forward. I pushed the blade high up over my head, then stood.

To err is so human. Pity.

Some damn vine caught at the blade as I began to swing.

He heard it, let out a croak, threw up his arm and toppled, falling onto his left side.

I heard the bone in his arm crunch as I missed my target, his neck. He cried out again then, but Morales was already astir.

I released the handle of the machete and clawed after the pistol belt with my right hand. With my left, I hooked him around the neck and dragged him in front of me.

I saw the flash and heard it just as my fingers found and unsnapped the holster. Two more came my way before I could get the pistol out and return the fire. With each shot, Dominic jerked slightly. Morales emptied his pistol as I fired twice, then he dropped it and slumped.

Dominic had gone limp in my arms and I could hear Morales cursing. I released my grip on my shield and let him fall to the ground. As I did, my left hand brushed my side and felt something wet and sticky. Whether it was his blood or mine, I could not tell.

I stepped around Dominic and moved slowly in the direction from which he had come. When I reached the rock he had occupied, I sat on it and watched Morales.

He raised his head and looked back at me. I could not distinguish his features.

"I am wounded," he said, after a time.

"I never would have guessed."

There was a long silence, then, "Wiley? Ovid Wiley?" he asked. "That is you?"

"Whatever is left of me," I said.

"I should never have trusted you."

"Perceptive of you."

A stray beam of moonlight showed me then that his rifle lay fairly close to him.

I rose and went to him, keeping him covered. I kicked his empty pistol into the brush and moved the rifle far out of reach.

Then I returned and rolled him over onto his back. He permitted this without making a sound. There was blood on his shirt and trousers.

I stuck the pistol behind my belt and carefully removed his shirt. I struck a match then and regarded him.

"How bad is it?" he asked, our eyes meeting.

"You have holes in your shoulder and belly," I told him, shaking out the light. "Do you hurt anywhere else?"

"I don't think so," he said, with a heavy exhalation. "I don't know. It's the one in my stomach that's getting to me."

I located his canteen, took a drink, propped him up and gave him one, took another myself. I used his shirt to wipe off his shoulder, then wadded it and soaked it, pressed it against the wound in his abdomen. I placed his good hand upon it, then propped him in a sitting position, his back against the bole of the nearest tree. I took another drink of water, then lit a cigarette and gave it to him.

"Thanks," he said.

I returned to the rock, taking the canteen with me.

"You carried it off neatly," he said. "I never expected to run into that."

I grunted, thinking he was talking about what had just occurred. He went on, however:

"How did you get them to the village that quickly? Was the timing accidental, or do you deserve full credit?"

"There was some luck involved," I said, not willing to let him know that I did not understand.

He coughed then and let out a brief groan.

"Well?" he asked, his voice sounding strained. "Did you get what you were after?"

"Yes."

"Are you certain?"

"What do you mean?"

He chuckled weakly.

"Just so. Just so," he said. "I meant only that a man can never be too certain, can he?"

I decided not to grant him the Pyrrhic victory of being bothered by his suggestion. After all, what was it to me whether there was something wrong with the papers?

Yet it did bother me. After what we had been through, to have them turn out worthless would be a hell of an epilogue. There could be no such thing, in a moral sense, as seeing the right thing done with the papers. But Emil's notion struck me as being the least disagreeable, and I was willing to help effectuate it. It seemed most likely that Morales was just bowing out ungracefully, and I decided not to pursue the matter with him.

I went and fetched Dominic's canteen. I did not feel up to touching him, let alone covering him over at the moment.

I took Morales a drink and listened approvingly as his breath came faster and faster.

"How long have you known about me?" he said.

"That you have been acting in your capacity as a Tupamara—or whatever the hell you want to call yourself—rather than a cop? That you may indeed be Saci?" I asked. "I don't know. I got to thinking about it sometime after you released us."

He snorted.

"Was your job to get the papers or to get me?"

I could not avoid a small feeling of triumph, since I had been wandering blindfolded with the donkey's tail tickling my forearms.

"The papers, of course," I said. "You are not considered especially important."

He snarled and spat.

"I will be a *cause célèbre*! A rallying cry for the movement! Diplomats will be kidnapped and exchanged for my freedom. You have grasped more than you can hold, Ovid. By taking me, you further the cause!"

Here he broke into another coughing spell, seized his stomach and bit back a moan.

"How much longer until they arrive?" he asked.

"Who?"

"Your co-workers, your fellow officious intermeddlers. Whatever the hell you call the other pigs. You have had your moment of glory now. When do they close in?"

"Is it getting bad?" I asked him.

He cursed.

Then, "You could have carried some morphine, for emergencies!" he snarled.

"You seem to be laboring under a misapprehension," I said, returning to the stone and taking another drink of water. "It does not matter to me one way or another whether you are or are not Saci. The only thing that matters is that you are Morales, and that I have promised to kill you."

"You are lying!" he said. "Dead, I would be a martyr. I am too big for you to touch, dead or alive."

Then, "Who did you promise?" he asked.

"I promised myself," I told him, "because of the way you treated Maria, and me. But don't flatter yourself you'll be a martyr. Che Guevara you are not. You'll sink without a ripple. How many people know who Saci really is?"

"I do not believe you," he said. "If you are not lying, why don't you use another bullet and be done with it?"

I lit my first cigarette of the century.

"Because I want to watch you die," I said.

After his next, longest bout of coughing and cursing, he steadied his voice and said softly, "I can hurt you yet."

I continued smoking. Let him talk. It was all he could do now. And what did he think he could tell me that would hurt me?

"The man who gave you the papers," Morales said, with vicious pleasure in his voice. "I don't know who he is—but he is not Emil Bretagne."

So. I kept my own voice neutral, except for a note of fatigue it was not hard for me to inject.

"I don't care," I said.

He had more to say, but I didn't give him the satisfaction of appearing to pay attention. Bit by bit, he wound down, his final sally a failure. Eventually he sank into silence. I waited for the night to pass.

I insisted on speaking with him in private. I clammed up on everything else and kept repeating my request until they finally got the idea that I meant what I was saying.

They chased Maria out of the hut and left me alone with him. I doubted they had had time to bug the place, but we spoke in whispers.

"Claude?" I said. "How do you feel?"

He was lying on a cot, regarding the roof, several fresh

dressings on his upper body. He smiled faintly, then said, "I'll recover."

He turned his head then and met my eyes.

"How did you find out?" he asked.

"Morales told me you were not Emil. He thought I would find it distressing. He was wrong."

"Where is Morales now?"

"Dead."

"How?"

"I killed him."

"Were you alone with him when he told you?"

"Except for a corpse."

"Have you told anyone else?"

"No. Nor do I intend to."

"That is good of you. It gives me some time. What made you decide I was Claude when you learned I was not Emil?"

"Actually, I had suspected you of being Claude earlier. Emil disappeared prior to your apparent death. It seemed doubtful to me that he could have learned of it so quickly, while flitting about the country rechanneling money. And why would it be necessary for him to break into his own safe to get the records? And his disappearance, your apparent death and his reappearance with a whole new set of objectives seemed a bit strange. But it was your avoidance of Maria yesterday that told me who you really were. Even Morales was not certain as to your true identity, though. It puzzled him that a man trained in finance, with full knowledge of the enterprise and a strong physical resemblance should suddenly appear on the scene and cause a stir. He speculated that you were a Soviet agent engaged in an elaborate scheme to embarrass the CIA. He was somewhat hurt that his organization had not been taken into confidence on this, because they would have assisted, he said. He did not get to question you for very long, did he?"

"No. It was only a matter of minutes before the counterattack came."

His eyes wandered toward the roof once more.

"You have guessed what became of my brother then," he said.

"When you ran into difficulties in Rome, I assume you discussed with him the matter of coming to Brazil in a hurry. He was quite concerned over this because he was in with Morales' crowd—which is the reason Morales spotted you as an impostor immediately—and he was not living up to his end of the bargain with you, as to the disbursement of the funds you were diverting. He persuaded you to meet with him in Lisbon, where he tried to explain what he had done and swing you over to his way of thinking before you came to Brazil, saw it for yourself and caused him trouble. I choose to believe that he had the gun, and when a fight followed the inevitable argument it was discharged accidentally, killing him—a facial wound at that, enough to fool even Maria as to who it was, for the brief look she had. The thought occurred to you also, and you decided to assume his identity and undo as much as you could of what he had done."

"Thank you," he said. "That is essentially correct. Only the three of us know it—for now."

The three of us. He, I—and Maria. Or to put it in the proper order, he and Maria. And I.

"Tell me, would you have access to the funds you succeeded in sequestering if you were someone other than Emil Bretagne?"

"Yes," he said, turning his head toward me once more, eyes narrowing, "I set it up that way. Some are even in a thumbprint account. My thumb, naturally. Why?"

"If you were to die again, then both Bretagnes would be completely out of the picture and you would be free to direct the expenditures you had in mind for this area personally."

"I do not understand."

"The doctor they brought, the one who patched you up, said that you would live."

"Yes."

"Then it is really quite simple. He was mistaken in his prognosis. He will come in and spend some time with you, then step outside and let it be known that you suffered a relapse with massive internal hemorrhaging and ultimate cardiac arrest, then sign a death certificate stating that Emil Bretagne died here today. Then we will all depart, leaving you to recuperate and go about your business. Oh, yes. Your deathbed request was that your remains be interred here by the natives you had come to love so dearly for their simple kindness, etcetera."

"How would you manage this? And why would you do it?"

"Do you get the newspaper every day?"

"Yes. Usually it's a day or two late, though. The bus drivers drop off a few at the stations. One of the tribesmen gets me one."

"Thank you. That clears up something. You sent Vera hunting for me because of that write-up in the paper, correct?"

"Yes. That made you the only CIA agent I knew of. I read her the article and told her I had to talk with you. She said that she would locate you and bring you here. She is a very strange, resourceful woman."

"I daresay. Still, he couldn't have known all that. He must really have been down to his last card for this round."

"Who are you talking about?"

"I've known the CIA man who is in charge of this operation for a long while. I was not aware that he was an agency man until he led the rescue party to me in the jungle this morning. I've known him for years as a second-rate art critic. It was very good cover. It gave him a reason for running all over Europe and having free time on his hands. It must have been in this role—perhaps even the reason for his assuming it—that he backed into this thing by way of his investigation of Sign of the Fish operations. It will hardly be a great distortion that I will be asking him to have confirmed—that Emil Bretagne died here, today, rather than a few weeks ago in Lisbon."

"He is so good a friend that he would do this thing if you ask him?"

"Hell, no. But you are no longer important to him. It's those records that he wants. And since I'm the only person who knows where they are I am certain that we can reach an understanding."

He lay there a while, apparently thinking it over, then said, "I don't know how to thank you."

I hauled out my filthy wallet and fetched forth a soiled card.

"Here," I said. "Keep me in mind when there's some native artwork that needs marketing."

He accepted it and nodded. He smiled.

"*Requiescat in pace*," I said. "*Mors janua vitae.*"

Later, I was to see small, cryptic reports in the back pages of the *Times* concerning Bassenrut, minor governmental shakeups and a continuing crackdown on revolutionaries. The usual stuff. Maria had seen me off at the airport, and she had brought Vera along. Vera had given me a *figa*—a thumb-through-fist good luck charm—which I had dropped into my pocket, and Maria had given me a luke-warm goodbye kiss which I could not gracefully decline.

She was remaining, of course, to do some sort of work with the tribes of the Matto Grasso. They both saw me off again, several hours later, after my plane blew three tires on its left side, flopped about a bit and had its fuel catch fire. I do not know whether it was the figa or Berwick's good luck hypothesis catching up with me, but there were two deaths and I was the only passenger who was not injured in some way. My second departure worked all right, though it is an awkward thing to say goodbye twice in the same morning.

The rest of the journey was without significant outward scent. I spent a lot of time alternating between thinking about what life with Maria would have been like and thinking about an *autoból* match we had seen in Rio the day before leaving for the airport. There is a growing enthusiasm for *autoból* these days, a sport which started out modestly enough as an outgrowth of the traffic situation. A wide, blocked-off street serves as a playing field where two teams, consisting of five drivers and their autos, play soccer with a tough, four-foot diameter ball. Usually, old junkers are employed, and demolished, in the game. The one we saw, however, involved late-model cars and drew an enormous crowd. As I watched them tear into one another, gradually transforming their sleek, colorful lines of power into the uncertain outlines of premature decrepitude and collapse, I thought about Maria— who, along with Vera, stood at my side then, cheering wildly at the mayhem—and I felt an uncomfortable sympathy for the ball, which, like myself, had initially occupied a classical, middle-of-the-road position. Yes, the gaping pit was closed and I realized that someone like Claude, who might, in his way, be an incipient saint and possessed of spiritual stamina, would be the better mate for a minor Fury. It was not without a certain regret, though, that I sniffed the last of the brimstone along with the exhaust fumes. But I had a philosophical bent of mind with which to console myself and a handy metaphor to objectify the moral. I also ate, drank and slept on the flight home.

Walt had taken things graciously enough, after discovering that appeals to my patriotism and my cupidity were equally fruitless, and that there really was only one thing that I would settle for.

"All right, you son of a bitch," he had said, lighting a cigar.

"All right, you son of a bitch," he had repeated, waving it in my direction like a branding iron. "Now Emil is dead, too. A pox on both of them! I'll even mail you a copy of the death certificate. I suppose you want to approve my report before I submit it, too?"

"That won't be necessary," I said. "Having read your articles over the years, I am certain that you will be able to obscure the issue sufficiently without much extra effort."

"All right, you son of a bitch," he had said. "Now take me to those papers."

I had led him off into the jungle then, toward the hills, to the place where the large boulder faces the tree that reminded me of a hunchback with a cane.

We had shaken hands on the deal, and later in Rio he had taken me to dinner at an excellent place of his own choosing, to show me that there were no hard feelings. Mine vanished as I ate of the magnificent spread he had ordered, even up to and including the resentment that had remained over his talking Maria into carrying the transmitter—not unlike the one Morales had tried to get me to swallow—which had allowed him to follow the entire parade with his superior force; as well as any remaining feelings over his having had my every move watched, from the time he located us after our release up until the rendezvous. He had not tried to make me party to his plan because he had guessed—correctly—that I would have refused. He was able to get to Maria because of her feeling that I was doing nothing to further her objective, with a promise that this would help. Yes, he had known all about Claude and Maria. He kept tabs on everybody connected with the Sign of the Fish. Would he keep his promise to me? I thought that he might, because even if he did not, there would be little reason to resurrect Claude Bretagne to help remedy the situation in Brazil. In fact, such an action could even produce an impediment. Better to let Rover keep snoring.

Upon my return, Bill Mailer welcomed me. He had let himself into the Taurus after my departure and remained there, "to keep a finger in the hole" as he put it, during my absence. Because of this, the place was in even better shape than I had left it. He had done some painting, washed the windows and shampooed the carpeting. On learning that I was off the hook with the law, he embraced me with tears in his eyes, then dashed off, rounded up people and reestablished his commune in the rear rooms. I gave a party that night to celebrate my return, and the smell of incense and innocence is with me once again, as well as music, laughter and things that go bump in the night.

It was several months later that I received an approval shipment of native artwork, mostly carved wood, from a new outfit in Brazil. Much of it was quite good. I put it on display and it has been doing well enough. However, there was one particularly ugly specimen: a hollow-bellied individual with prominent genitalia, an awful expression on his face and a small dog biting his left leg. This, I purchased myself and sent to my brother and sister-in-law for an anniversary present, to let them know my peeves were cooling. I hope it is a fertility deity. Serve them right.

The stuff set me to thinking, though. Prematurely. For

it is not yet time to think along those lines. But during that brief cloudburst, my mind rushed along the curb toward the inevitable. I relived that journey once more, to jail, Virginia, Rome, Brazil and home again, seeing all the bodies, violence and bad business it had contained, along with a few cherishable moments that had somehow slipped in, and I recalled what Maria had told me on that final day—probably because she felt she owed me the explanation, possibly because she had to tell someone and Claude was the one person she could not.

She and Carl Bernini had hit upon a rather naïve scheme to reverse their fortunes. In earlier days, before his brain had become tinctured in alcohol, I do not believe he would have gone along with it. But he was apparently getting desperate. You have to be, to consider blackmailing an organization with a built-in defense against just such a thing. He and Maria faked their quarrel and breakup to defend against any suspicion of collusion on their part. She even took up with the first presentable man available—who just happened to be Claude—to let it be known that Carl was definitely a thing of the past, never guessing how she would come to feel about this strange man. Then Carl, after lying low for several months, communicated with her a final time. During some of his more lucid moments, he had been having second thoughts on the matter. He decided that for safety's sake and for added brainpower, he wanted a third party in on the thing—a lucky, successful criminal type, whom he had worked with before and thought he could trust—namely, me. So he made his way to New York to look me up. Later, when I telephoned her in Rome, she thought that it meant I had agreed and that we were both back in town. She was torn at that time between her original notion of blackmailing the Sign of the Fish because of its smuggling activities and her concern over her new love, then in Lisbon. I resolved everything a few sentences later, however, by telling her that Carl was dead. Freed of her commitment to Carl, she went immediately to Lisbon, only to discover that Claude was apparently dead, too. She returned home and got drunk, burning with remorse and anger.

That was her story, and the only additional information I was able to obtain concerning my former partner.

But, as in all matters of import, speculation is born at the point where the facts cease.

I see only two alternatives. The first possibility is that the Fish people got wind of the plan. Perhaps Carl's tongue loosened when he drank. They let him get as far as my place and killed him on the premises—or else took him there and did it—leaving him as an object lesson to me, in case there had been any prior communication on the subject and I should consider trying it alone. This thought did tend to make me somewhat leery of my Piscean competitors, so much so that I never did attempt to contact any of the artists on the list Bruno had given me. But perhaps I wrong them. For there is another, even more unsavory possibility that comes to mind.

If he had wanted me, just me—because Maria knew me and trusted me, and through her I could reach Claude, and through Claude reach into that tangled mess in Brazil, whether in the manner in which things actually worked out or in accordance with some other plan that folded—would Collins have possessed the willingness to sacrifice a friendless, down and out, alcoholic criminal who was possibly even in this country illegally, and do this thing in a fashion calculated both to incriminate me and to arouse my curiosity, so that he could not only dragoon me into running his errand but have me at least partly desirous of seeing it carried to a successful conclusion? I wondered.

The anonymous telephone call to the police, poking a hole in my story and strengthening the circumstantial case against me, was a thing that troubled me all along. And then there was the matter of the alleged fingerprints on the weapon.

But I do not really care which guess is the correct one, whether he seized an opportunity or created it. Collins had used me with, if anything, greater callousness than Morales had, and he made the same mistake that Morales did. He assumed that once it was all over, if I lived, I would shift my mental gears and learn to live with what had occurred, I would accept it because there was nothing that I could do about it. In this, he would be correct, if I were to play by his rules. Collins and Morales represent a segment of society which, if attacked with the weapons society sanctions, one finds buffered by innumerable layers of law, bureaucracy, lies, evasions. They rest secure within their palaces, confident that they possess defenses against all possible attacks within the rules of the game, yet willing to violate those rules themselves.

It is not yet time to think about it, for I still have a long, innocuous while in which to fade from memory into oblivion, but that shipment of wood, shaped into life by the loving hands of the pathetically stepped-upon tribes-men whose brothers Morales shot down as one beheads a daisy with a stick, reminded me of another, silent promise that I made, contingent upon my surviving a final en-counter with that man, and it sent me off upon this reverie. That is all.

Collins, master of small destinies, maker of decisions that can kill, maim, half a world or half a block away, sometimes to a good end, sometimes uselessly, we are related, we are brothers, you and I. For beyond victory, a loss, a stalemate, we both understand the fourth way in which a game of chess can be concluded. We both know that although it is not listed in the rules, a player can end the game by kicking over the board and throttling his opponent.

It is early, though the hour is late, and you still have time for some hunting—of men, secrets, power—living, in your genteel way, per Aristotle's dictum, feeling that the best place, really, for violence, is offstage where you cannot see it.

Rest. Rest a while now. I am. You might as well.

THE DEAD MAN'S BROTHER
An Afterword by Trent Zelazny

I'm pleased to have the chance to acknowledge both my father and my admiration for his work. Though known for his tales of fantasy and science fiction, Roger Zelazny's interests ran amuck throughout all worlds, both real and imagined. He was a voracious reader, on average reading about eight or nine books at a time, some fiction, some not. Many of my childhood recollections involve hobbies of his such as lock picking, collecting knives and decks of playing cards, and (my personal favorite) having one of his children time how long it took for him to escape from a straitjacket (his best time was about three minutes). It was a surprise when Kirby McCauley, his agent, called to say he had discovered this manuscript.

A surprise, but in no way a shock.

Dean Koontz said of my father, "Roger Zelazny is a science fiction writer, but he clearly could have written anything he chose to write." Mr. Koontz is dead on with this. My father once told me that his true passion was poetry followed next by science fiction. He also told me to read at least a little in every genre and on as many subjects as possible, as you never know what's waiting for you on the next page.

To quote Shunryu Suzuki: "In the beginner's mind

there are many possibilities, but in the expert's mind there are few." The truly great writers know this. They sift through their mental garbage, overwhelmed by all the possibilities that are no longer possible, until they come upon one of those rare few. They consider the possibility, analyze it. A plot, a character, a paragraph, or even a sentence with vague familiarity is, as a general rule, expunged. They draw upon everything, yet do their best to mimic none. The great writers find a style or genre—or lack of—which best suits their needs for telling the stories they have inside them.

But Roger Zelazny could no more stick exclusively to science fiction than James Cagney could stick to gangster films. Nobody can stick to one kind of thing 24 hours a day, no matter how much they love it. Cagney will always be remembered best for *The Public Enemy* and *White Heat*, but thinking a little further, we will then remember *Yankee Doodle Dandy*.

To my knowledge, nobody knows exactly when this book was written. The earliest and probably most accurate estimate is around 1970 or 1971, still a handful of years before I entered the world. Some think it was his attempt to break into the mainstream. Maybe partially true, but I don't believe this was his priority. I believe that an idea came to him, and though it fell into a different genre from his norm, he acted on it nonetheless.

Great writers will never hold back due to genre. They will tell the story they want—or must—in spite of the limiting labels designed by publishers. They don't think of themselves as science fiction writers or mystery writers or western writers. They think of themselves simply as writers, period.

And so, rather than writing about gods, people who become gods, struggles between worlds of magic and technology or sentient space-exploration robots, this time my father wrote an international intrigue thriller. If the aforementioned date is correct, it speaks to the fact that my father was indeed interested in crime and mystery fiction at the time. Also around the time he penned *Today We Choose Faces*, a story about a mobster who wakes up from a cryogenic sleep for one last job, and the three novelettes that constitute *My Name is Legion*, about a nameless man who destroys his personal data before it's entered into a global computer network and becomes a multiple-identity private investigator; so it's clear that mysteries and crime were running through his head. Whether it troubled him that *The Dead Man's Brother* was leaving out the science fiction aspect or not, I don't know.

A part of me is tempted to go more deeply into the storyline of the book you're currently holding, but there doesn't seem much point in that, as you've either just read it or are about to (I also tend to shy away from academic approaches). I will say that *The Dead Man's Brother*, despite being over 35 years old, holds its own in the sophisticated contemporary world of mystery. It's a smart book, entertaining as hell, very well thought out, and, of course, well written.

I hope you are half as fond of it as I am. I'm thrilled that Hard Case Crime is the publisher bringing it to you. They are the perfect folks for this one, and I know my father would be very pleased. Somewhere, I imagine he's smiling a bit, hands clasped behind his head, saying something to the effect of, "Thanks."

As I said earlier, a part of me was surprised when told about the manuscript, but in no way was I shocked. Now, I won't even be surprised if another turns up down the road. Thrilled beyond imagining, yes, but not surprised,

as writers usually have material that has never been published, or has been lost in the mists of time.

The man clearly could have written anything he chose
to write. He will likely always be remembered best for
Lord of Light and *The Chronicles of Amber*, but thinking
a little further, we will then remember *The Dead Man's
Brother*, and what a wonderful tale it is.